ALSO BY SCOTT HENRY

SEVEN: The Prime Quartet, Volume III

THREE

THE PRIME QUARTET

Volume II

Scott Henry

CHERRY GROVE   FIRE ISLAND

Published in the United States by Scott Henry,
Eleven Enterprises,
Cherry Grove, Fire Island.

LIBRARY OF CONGRESS CONTROL NUMBER: 2021904990

PUBLISHER'S CATALOGING-IN-PUBLICATION DATA
Names: Henry, Scott, 1948- author.
Title: Three / Scott Henry.
Description: Cherry Grove, Fire Island, [New York] :
Scott Henry, Eleven Enterprises, [2021] |
Series: The prime quartet ; volume 2 |
Story presented in both prose and a three-act play.
Identifiers: ISBN 9781734675511 (paperback) |
ISBN 9781734675528 (ebook)
Subjects: LCSH: Henry, Scott, 1948---Fiction. |
Dysfunctional families--United States--Fiction. |
Occult--Fiction. | Delusions--Fiction. |
Sexual orientation--Fiction. | Gay men--Fiction. |
Dysfunctional families--United States--Drama. |
Occult--Drama. | Delusions--Drama. |
LCGFT: Nonfiction novels. | Biographical fiction. |
Historical fiction.
Classification: LCC PS3608.E5798 T47 2021 (print) | LCC
PS3608.E5798 (ebook) | DDC 813/.6--dc23

Printed in the United States of America

COVER DESIGN: Scott Henry

Book design by Scott Henry

TO LOUISE EDDY

The Immaculate Conception is commonly confused with the Virgin Birth of Jesus. The birth of Jesus is covered by the Doctrine of Incarnation, which defines the Son as both "truly God and truly man." The Immaculate Conception refers to the Virgin Mary, who was "free from all sin, original or personal."

—SCOTT HENRY

If it's not one thing, it's your mother.

—JULIA SWEENEY

CONTENTS

SATURDAY || SEPTEMBER 21, 1968

SUNDAY || SEPTEMBER 22, 1968

MONDAY || SEPTEMBER 23, 1968

THREE || A Play in Three Acts

SATURDAY

SEPTEMBER 21, 1968

9:00 AM

Everything was happening at breakneck speed—velocity pushing forward, momentum pressing back, air becoming heavy, noise becoming white—but then, slipping free of gravity's embrace, the vibration eased off as the 727 lifted away from the ground. Never having flown before, Scott kept his face toward the window, as much to watch the passing scenery as to conceal his apparent delight.

When two stewards (surprising personnel for a first-time flyer) began the flight's beverage service, Scott was pleased to learn an unexpected benefit of sitting in the rear of the cabin: One of the stewards pushed his cart to the end of the aisle before offering passengers in the last row a choice of refreshments. From window to aisle, one side after the other, the pleasant young man fulfilled beverage requests with deft conservation of movement: cup-ice-pour-napkin-place, peanuts?

When the cart came to a stop at Scott's row, he did not register the flirtatious pause as the steward looked across the aisle seat and asked, "What's your pleasure?" Scott did, however, note the look of recognition in the man's eyes, as if they'd met on a previous occasion, which, for all intents and purposes, was unthinkable.

"7 Up," Scott replied. "And,"—a playful grimace—"is it possible to have more than one bag of peanuts?"

The man smiled at Scott as he scooped ice into a cup. "We're allowed to give two bags when requested." The steward removed the cap from a bottle of 7 Up, filled the cup, placed a napkin on

Scott's tray, placed the cup on the napkin, the open bottle beside the cup—a consideration, as far as Scott could tell, which had not been extended to anyone else—as well as three bags of peanuts beside the bottle.

"Wow," said Scott, raising his brow. "My cup runneth over."

"Is that a fact?" the man replied, nodding slowly. "I'm Robert, by the way." Robert smiled impishly, pointing to his nametag. "If there's anything else you'd like, don't hesitate to ask."

Scott smiled uncertainly. "Okay. Well, you know, thanks for the peanuts."

Robert held his eyes on Scott for a moment, then pushed his cart a few feet forward and inquired of the passenger sitting next to the window, "Something to drink?"

Entrancing as the cloud cover was when viewed from above, Scott pulled his weekender from beneath his seat and removed the paperback edition of *Siddhartha* he needed to read for an upcoming discussion of Hermann Hesse in his Modern and Contemporary Literature class. Flipping through the first few pages, Scott was pleasantly surprised by the writing's rhythm and flow, a prose-poem quality that reminded him of Kahlil Gibran.

As if in conversation with himself, which he typically was, Scott tilted his head in a show of appreciation. He flipped back to the beginning of the book and started reading as he normally would.

By the end of the fifth page, Scott shifted his focus from Govinda, who "loved everything that Siddhartha did and said," to identifying with Siddhartha himself, who "had begun to feel the seeds of discontent within him." The irony escaped Scott that he was reading about the quest for inner stillness while streaking through the sky at six hundred miles an hour.

A short time later, Scott sensed the shift from upward to downward as the plane began its approach to the San Francisco airport. Not only was this Scott's first time flying, but also his first visit to Northern California, where his sister, mother, and stepfather had recently moved. As much as Scott would have enjoyed sightseeing in San Francisco, his mother had told him they'd be driving straight back to Santa Rosa, sixty miles north of the Golden Gate Bridge, after they collected him from the airport.

Disembarking ten minutes after applause for a safe landing subsided was the least enjoyable aspect of Scott's flying experience. Following the lead of a few passengers who knew the ins and outs of air travel, Scott sat down in an empty seat and waited for the shuffling herd to exit the plane.

When he finally entered the gate area, a curious choreography ensued as Scott, six-foot-two, suntanned skin and sun-bleached hair, greeted his family for the first time in over a year: His five-foot-two mother, bubbling with enthusiasm, stepped forward with outstretched arms; his rail-thin stepfather, unsmiling and beady-eyed, crossed his arms and remained where he was; his fifteen-year-old sister, a prettier version of himself, stepped aside and watched her mother inflict excessive affection on her prodigal son.

"Gee whiz, Scott," Louise complained. "Can't you give your poor old mother a kiss?"

"Mom," said Scott, shifting free of her embrace. "I need to find a restroom."

"All right, honey." Louise put her arm through Scott's. "We'll find you a restroom, sweetheart, and then we'll hit the road. We have many wonderful things planned for your first day home with the family."

"Hi, sis," said Scott, stepping off in the direction of the walkway.

"Hi," said Kathy, with a look that telegraphed, *I know.*

Scott and Allison, his stepfather—or, more appropriately, his mother's second husband—took advantage of Louise's exuberance to ignore one another's presence as they made their way through the airport.

In the parking lot, Scott was nonplussed when the group came to a stop beside a two-tone green Volkswagen Bus.

"How do you like our new car?" said Louise.

"Now, Louise, we've discussed this several times," said Allison. "This is not a car, sweetheart. It's a bus."

Louise smiled at Allison. "Yes, dear." Then to Scott, she said, "How do you like our new bus, Scott?"

"Very interesting." Scott glanced at Kathy, then back to Louise. "Do you still have the Cadillac?"

"No, honey," Louise replied, opening the passenger door. "We sold that in Long Beach before we moved up here. Don't you think the bus is fun?"

Scott considered the question as he opened the rear door. He shot a look at Kathy before she climbed in and slid across the back seat. To Louise, Scott said, "At least the Cadillac had two rear doors."

"Well, yes, *Scott*, but look at all the room." Louise turned partway around. "And we get twenty miles per gallon on the highway. That's almost twice as much as the Cadillac, honey, not to mention the overall savings with maintenance and upkeep."

"Okay, Mom," said Scott. "Thanks for the sales pitch."

Allison started the engine, and Scott envisioned rats on running wheels attached to outsize rubber bands.

"I don't think I've ever mentioned this," said Allison, pulling to a stop behind two vehicles waiting to pay their parking lot fees. "The day I met your father, Scott, we discussed the first shipment of Porsches delivered to the United States. Jerry was quite the enthusiast, having driven one of those first models. I'm not sure how that came to pass, in that he was no more than"—looking at

Louise—"how old was Jerry when he brought us home to meet you?"

"Well," said Louise, tilting her head from side to side as she did the math. "I was eight months pregnant with Scott, so Jerry would have been twenty-two. Both of us were twenty-two, as a matter of fact."

"Yikes," said Scott. "The two of you were twenty when you got married, right?"

"Yes, honey."

"Hard to believe." Scott exhaled. "That was a different universe. I'm going to be twenty in three months, and I don't know what I want for dinner, let alone who I want to spend the rest of my life with. Not that 'wanting' has anything to do with how things work out."

Louise turned her head and said, "Didn't you tell me Brooke was living down the street from you, honey? Have the two of you been getting together once in a while?"

"Yes and no," said Scott, curling his lip. "Brooke does live a block away from me, which is a bizarre coincidence, but we definitely do not get together once in a while."

Scott pondered how completely opposite the direction his relationship with Brooke had taken from his mother's hopeful expectation. So opposite in fact that Brooke had threatened a restraining order the next time she returned home to find him lurking near her driveway.

"Who's she living with?" said Kathy, genuinely interested after witnessing the ups and downs of her brother's high school romance.

"A friend of her aunt's. An older woman who'd been living alone in a big house on First Street since her husband passed away ten years ago."

"I thought she was living in South Gate." Kathy frowned.

7

"She was, but now she's living a stone's throw from my apartment. Literally."

Scott focused his attention on South San Francisco as thoughts of unsuccessful attempts at reconciliation with Brooke crowded their way to the surface of his mind.

BROOKE

A year or so earlier, on a Saturday afternoon, Scott had run into Brooke's half-sister, Debbie, as he was walking back to work after lunch.

Spotting each other at the same time, Scott and Debbie's reactions mirrored the nature of their connection, in that each of them regarded the other as an inconsequential aspect of their relationship with Brooke. Scott slowed down as he considered what line to take when they met. Debbie, on the other hand, interacted with her friends as if she'd not seen a familiar face.

"Hey," said Scott, stopping a few feet short of the girls. He met Debbie's eyes. "How's it going?"

"Okay," Debbie replied with a schoolgirl shrug.

Scott smiled. "You cut your hair."

Debbie kept her eyes on Scott as she cracked her gum.

"It looks good."

"Thanks."

"So, listen, I don't know if you're sworn to secrecy"—looking at once hopeful and dismayed—"but I really need to talk to Brooke. Do you know where she's staying?"

Debbie frowned. "She'd kill me if she found out I told you."

Scott interpreted Debbie's reluctance as an arm waiting to be twisted. He decided the best approach was to take a step back.

"I was going to talk to her at graduation, but she didn't show up." Scott raised his hands in a gesture of helplessness?

"Yeah, well, you're the reason she didn't show up."

"Oh, boy." Scott exhaled. "Really, Debs, this silent treatment is killing me. And, as far as I can tell, it's not working so well for Brooke either. Don't you think it'd be better all-around if we hashed things out? I mean, come on, both of us left home on our eighteenth birthday in the middle of our senior year of high school. That pretty much blew everyone's mind."

"Yeah," said Debbie, rolling her eyes. "My parents are never going to get over it."

"Jesus Christ," Scott exclaimed. "That's why we left, our so-called parents, who think everything's about them. Bonnie and Louise should stand trial for subjecting their children to the abuses perpetrated by their socio-pathetic second husbands."

"Okay, okay." Debbie staggered playfully against the on-slaught of Scott's tirade.

"Sorry. It's not your fault your father's a piece of shit."

"I could say the same for you."

"Allison's not my father."

"Oops, right, sorry. Anyway,"—squinting for emphasis—"I don't think giving you Brooke's address is a good idea."

"Cross my heart and hope to die. She'll never know how I found out."

Debbie kept her eyes on Scott as she considered the consequences.

Scott brought his hands together in prayer.

Debbie sighed, then shook her head. "She's staying with her cousin in South Gate. He's in the phone book—James Buchanan."

"Like the president?"

"The president of what?"

Scott smiled. "These here United States."

"Not this James Buchanan. He's a plumber."

"Okay, well, thanks. I owe you one."

"Oh, no, you don't. As far as this goes, you haven't seen me since the last time we were all at church together, which is what? A year ago?"

"At least." Scott nodded, thinking, *Tempus fug it.*

"I've gotta go," said Debbie, stepping away.

There was a flurry of chatter as Debbie rejoined her friends. Scott and the gaggle of girls continued in opposite directions: Scott, traveling south, relieved that the girls were not coming to Leeds to try on shoes; the girls, heading north, discussing who among them would be the first to go all the way with Justin Briggs.

That night, after polishing off an open-faced chili burger and a family-size bag of potato chips, Scott turned on the radio and settled himself in the apartment's only chair with a pad of blue-lined paper, a ballpoint pen, and Kahlil Gibran's *The Prophet*. The book fell open where its spine was broken, and Scott, undistracted by the Top Forty Hits on KRLA, began to copy the words he'd read so often:

> Then said Almitra, Speak to us of Love.
>
> And he raised his head and looked upon the people, and there fell a silence upon them. And with a great voice he said:
>
> When love beckons to you, follow him,
> Though his ways are hard and steep.
> And when his wings enfold you yield to him,
> Though the sword hidden among his pinions may wound you.
> And when he speaks to you believe in him,
> Thought his voice may shatter your dreams as the north wind lays waste the garden.

For even as love crowns you so shall he crucify you. Even as he is for your growth so is he for your pruning.

Even as he ascends to your height and caresses your tenderest branches that quiver in the sun,

So shall he descend to your roots and shake them in their clinging to the earth.

Like sheaves of corn he gathers you unto himself.

He threshes you to make you naked.

He sifts you to free you from your husks.

He grinds you to whiteness.

He kneads you until you are pliant;

And then he assigns you to his sacred fire, that you may become sacred bread for God's sacred feast.

All these things shall love do unto you that you may know the secrets of your heart, and in that knowledge become a fragment of Life's heart.

But if in your fear you would seek only love's peace and love's pleasure,

Then it is better for you that you cover your nakedness and pass out of love's threshing-floor,

Into the seasonless world where you shall laugh, but not all of your laughter, and weep, but not all of your tears.

Love gives naught but itself and takes naught but from itself.
Love possesses not nor would it be possessed;
For love is sufficient unto love.

When you love you should not say, "God is in my heart," but rather, "I am in the heart of God."
And think not you can direct the course of love, for love, if it finds you worthy, directs your course.

Love has no other desire but to fulfil itself.
But if you love and must needs have desires, let these be your desires:
To melt and be like a running brook that sings its melody to the night.
To know the pain of too much tenderness.
To be wounded by your own understanding of love;
And to bleed willingly and joyfully.
To wake at dawn with a winged heart and give thanks for another day of loving;
To rest at the noon hour and meditate love's ecstasy;
To return home at eventide with gratitude;

And then to sleep with a prayer for the
beloved in your heart and a song of praise
upon your lips.

Scott checked what he'd written for appearance and mistakes. Satisfied with his efforts, Scott folded the sheets of paper by thirds and slid them into an envelope on which he simply wrote the letter *B*. Scott reached over to the table beside the chair and brought the telephone onto his lap. He lifted the handset and dialed 1-555-1212. After two rings, the line was answered:

"What city, please?"

"South Gate."

"The party's name?"

"James Buchanan."

"Like the president?"

"Thank you," Scott replied. "And, yes."

"One moment, please. . . . I have a James Buchanan on McKinley Avenue."

"James doesn't have his own avenue?" Scott printed *M-c-K-i-n-l-e-y*.

"Apparently not. Would you like the number?"

"Yes, please, and the address." Scott grimaced, knowing the last request could go either way.

There was a pause as the operator decided whether she'd convey the non-essential information.

"There's been a death in the family, and I'd like to send flowers," said Scott, hoping to tip the scales.

"Oh my, well, let's see here. That's James Buchanan, 6042 McKinley Avenue, 561-6201. Will there be anything else?

"No, thank you." Scott scribbled two sets of numbers.

"All right, then. Goodbye."

"Goodbye."

Scott placed the telephone back on the table. Considering the best way to get from Long Beach to South Gate, Scott decided he'd invite himself to dinner with his grandparents the following evening so he could check out his grandfather's collection of street maps.

Monday morning, shaved, showered, and dressed by eight o'clock, Scott made a half-hearted attempt at cleaning the apartment, which ended with him staring at the ceiling from the center of his unmade bed. He planned to set off for Brooke's current address at nine o'clock, thinking anyone else who lived there would have gone to school or work by the time he arrived.

At five to nine, Scott sat up, slipped on a pair of shoes, grabbed the envelope, and left the apartment. The previous evening, on his way to dinner, Scott had filled the tank of his 1964 Porsche, a graduation gift from his stepmother in honor of his deceased father. Scott had also added a quart of oil to the reservoir, which he had to do every couple of weeks after the car's engine case cracked when he'd driven through an uneven intersection at breakneck speed. Now, after waiting for the engine to warm up, Scott shifted into first, drove to the end of the alley, and coasted around the corner onto Junipero Avenue.

Half an hour later, Scott pulled to the curb in front of 6042 McKinley Avenue, where he sat for a minute collecting his thoughts. As prepared as he thought possible, considering the circumstances, Scott climbed out of the car, strode up the front walk, and rang the doorbell. After a moment, the door swung open to reveal Brooke in a short-sleeved jumpsuit, shaking her head.

"I'm going to kill Debbie," she said, then stepped aside so Scott could enter the house.

"What would that accomplish?" Scott replied, noting the living room's suite of Early American furniture and earth-tone rag rug.

"She needs to learn what it means when someone says 'cross my heart and hope to die.' "

"So you're going to teach her the literal consequence of a playground promise."

"For a start. Then we'll move on to what it means when you ask someone if you can *borrow* their sweater."

"Didn't she buy you a new sweater?"

"I didn't want a new sweater. I wanted my old sweater. Enough already." Brooke rolled her eyes. "Why are you here?"

"*Jeez.*" Scott adopted a hangdog look.

"Don't 'jeez' me. Answer the question."

"I thought we could go somewhere and talk."

"About what?"

"About us."

"There is no 'us.' You've made that perfectly clear."

"That's not fair."

"Are you out of your mind? You seriously think you can show up after ignoring me for half a year and tell me what's fair? Give me a break."

"Maybe we could go somewhere and have breakfast."

"I've already had breakfast."

"Brunch then."

Brooke chuckled despite herself. "I'm not hungry."

"Not even for blueberry pancakes?"

"No."

"Would you sit with me while I have blueberry pancakes?"

"No."

"That's not very friendly."

Brooke narrowed her eyes.

"At least come and see my car."

Brooke paused as she considered the alternative. Finally, she exhaled and said, "I'll come see your car. Then you have to leave."

Scott paid more attention to Brooke's pause than her words. "Whatever you say."

Scott stepped toward the front door as Brooke opened it. Brooke followed Scott outside, closed the door behind her, then continued down the walk to the curb, where Scott slowed to a stop beside his shiny new toy.

"Wow," murmured Brooke, shaking her head.

"I know," replied Scott, brimming with pride.

"That's not what I meant." Brooke looked impatient. "But it doesn't matter. Okay, I've seen your car, now—"

"Hold on, hold on." Scott opened the passenger door, and Brooke saw the envelope with her initial on it lying on the seat. "It took me a while to write that," said Scott. "The least you could do is sit in the car with me and read it before I go."

"You could've mailed it. You've got the address, obviously."

"I couldn't take the chance of it getting lost or falling into the wrong hands."

"*The wrong hands.*"

"I wouldn't say it's top secret, but it is for your eyes only."

"Oh, brother." Brooke's tone was losing its edge.

Scott reached down and picked up the envelope. He extended his other hand toward the bucket seat and said, "*Mademoiselle.*"

Brooke inhaled. She looked at Scott without expression, then lowered herself into the passenger seat. Scott closed the door, walked around to the other side of the car, and climbed into the driver's seat. The envelope was now in Brook's lap, on top of which rested her clasped hands. Brooke kept her eyes on the parked car in front of Scott's until Scott broke the silence.

"Would you rather I read it to you?"

Brooke looked toward the sidewalk, shaking her head slowly, not so much in answer to Scott's question as to express her feelings about the entire situation. She was about to speak when Scott said: "They're not my words if that's what you're worried about."

Brooke turned to Scott. "It doesn't matter whose words they are. Nothing's going to change the way I feel."

Scott shrugged. "Okay, but I'm not going to leave until you've read them. If nothing else, they express a beautiful thought."

"I'm sure that's true, but the lack of beautiful thoughts has never been a problem for you."

"Fair enough, but here's the thing. If we can't learn from our mistakes, what's the point of making an effort? I mean,"—shrugging for effect—"doesn't everyone deserve a second chance?"

"You're way beyond second chances, buster. You're in double-digit chances—high double-digit chances. Let me answer your question with another question—"

"Because you know how much I like that."

Brooke narrowed her eyes. "What's the point of giving someone any number of second chances if they don't learn from their mistakes?"

" '*Any number of second chances*'?"

Brooke reached for the door handle.

"Okay, okay, okay." Scott inhaled. "Let me think about that while you read what's in the envelope."

Brooke turned her eyes to the sidewalk again, then to the envelope in her lap. With a sigh of resignation, Brooke pulled out the sheets of paper and unfolded them. Scott looked over and read the opening lines at the same time Brooke began reading, sensing a connection as they saw the same words, in the same place, at the same time.

Scott twisted around and adjusted something behind Brooke's seat. Brooke glanced in Scott's direction, then returned her attention to the poetry. Scott checked the back window for approaching cars and saw there were none.

In a smooth progression of movements, Scott pressed the

clutch to the floor, pushed the stick into first gear, turned the ignition key, revved the engine, spun the steering wheel, and shot away from the curb.

"What are you doing?" cried Brooke, craning her neck.

"I'm taking us somewhere else, so we can talk." Scott shifted into second gear and raced across Hoover Avenue without slowing down.

"I don't want to be taken anywhere else, and I don't want to talk. Stop the car and let me out." Brooke shouted, "Now! Stop the car and let me out, now!"

Scott careened around the corner onto Paramount Boulevard. He shifted into third gear and sped along six short blocks to Somerset Ranch Road, where he turned right without checking for traffic. Scott glanced in Brooke's direction as she fumbled for the door handle.

"Really?" said Scott. He checked the rearview mirror, shifted into third gear, and zigzagged through slow-moving traffic as they approached the entrance to the Long Beach Freeway.

Brooke gripped the door handle, ready to jump out at the first opportunity.

Aware of Brooke's intention, Scott sped through an amber light as it changed to red. He pushed the Porsche's rack-and-pinion steering to its limit on the tight curve of the freeway onramp.

The color drained from Brooke's face as she kept her eyes glued to the road. She breathed slowly, striving to slow her racing heart. She closed her eyes for a moment and felt the chill of perspiration descending her ribcage. Her eyes opened with a start when Scott shifted into fourth gear and maneuvered across two lanes of slow-moving traffic into the fast lane. For lack of something more emphatic, Brooke started ripping a page of poetry into tiny pieces.

Scott was miffed at first by Brooke's disregard for his time and effort but then alarmed when she rolled down her window and tossed the makeshift confetti into the wind.

"What are you doing?" Scott exclaimed, checking the rearview mirror for Highway Patrol cars.

"If you don't turn around and take me back now, I'll keep throwing stuff out the window until the police pull you over for littering. What do you think they'll do when I tell them you're trying to kidnap me."

"I'm not trying to *kidnap* you. I just want to go someplace quiet where we can talk."

"Potato, potahto. We'll let the police decide who's telling the truth—the teenage boy with a red sports car or the teenage girl in tears. Now, take me home, or the rest of this paper goes out the window."

Scott looked at Brooke, then over his shoulder as he veered into the exit lane for Artesia Boulevard.

Waiting for the light to change when they reached the street, Scott turned his head and said, "You're sure about the blueberry pancakes?"

Brooke did not respond.

After a beat, Scott said, "No, then."

The light turned green, and Scott turned left onto Artesia Boulevard. He stayed in second gear for a hundred feet, then turned onto the northbound ramp for the Long Beach Freeway.

The erstwhile sweethearts remained silent for the rest of the drive back to McKinley Avenue. Before Scott came to a complete stop at the curb, Brooke opened the passenger door. As soon as she had both feet on the sidewalk, she slammed the door shut. Without so much as a glance in Scott's direction, Brooke strode up the walk and disappeared inside the house.

So much for Plan A, thought Scott, pulling away from the curb. *As for Plan B—I've got nothin'.*

Four days later, Friday evening around seven o'clock, Brooke walked into the shoe store with a weekender strap over her shoulder, a standard-size pillow under one arm, a teddy bear under the other. She walked to the back of the sales floor, where Scott was standing near the passageway to the stockroom.

As if nothing out of the ordinary, Brooke said, "Is it okay if I stay with you tonight?"

Scott repeated Brooke's words to himself to make sure he'd heard correctly, then said, "Yeah, sure, of course."

"Can I leave my stuff here until you get off work?"

Scott said, "Yes," glancing in the store manager's direction. As casually as possible, considering Mr. Gary's watchful eye, Scott switched everything from Brooke's shoulder and arms to his own.

"What time should I come back?" Brooke looked into a nearby mirror, then back at Scott.

"Meet me out front at nine fifteen."

Brooke nodded, then said, "Have you had dinner?"

"Yes."

"Okay. I'll get something to eat." Brooke smiled briefly, then left the store.

Scott stepped into the stockroom and placed Brooke's belongings on an empty shelf. He returned to the sales floor and stood as far as possible from the front of the store and the amused expression on Mr. Gary's face.

Half an hour later, Scott walked a customer to the front of the store and placed two shoeboxes and a handbag on the counter.

Mr. Gary looked at Scott with a twinkle in his eye.

Scott shrugged.

Mr. Gary chuckled, then turned his attention to the merchandise on the counter.

Scott thanked his customer and wished her, "Bon voyage. I'm sure you'll enjoy Hawaii. Thanks again. Good night."

There was a flurry of business around eight thirty. Scott and Mr. Gary strode to and from the stockroom with selections to be tried on by last-minute shoppers. When the last two customers were at the front counter paying for their purchases, Scott reorganized shoes into boxes and boxes into the stockroom. In the stockroom, Scott collected Brooke's belongings, then stepped through the curtains into the passageway. He scanned the sales floor as he walked toward the front door, pushing shoe-fitting stools closer to chairs and a handbag back in place along the way.

Mr. Gary was locking the front door behind the last customer when Scott skidded to a stop on the entryway floor.

"Everything's in order?" Mr. Gary asked, more as a tease than a question.

"As much as it's going to be." Scott suffered his boss's lingering stare for about ten seconds. "Yes, yes, yes. I'll see you tomorrow morning at eight thirty. Now, please let me out."

"If you're not here by eight thirty-five, I'm sending Andy to get you. No way we're making it through tomorrow morning one man short."

"Not to worry. I'll be here with bells on."

"Suit and tie will be sufficient. Be careful, kid, all right?"

"Absolutely," Scott replied, tilting his head toward the door.

"And get some sleep. I mean it about tomorrow. It's going to be a zoo around here."

"And that's different how?"

"Get out of here." Mr. Gary smiled to himself as he relocked the door.

Scott and Brooke were silent on the drive to Scott's apartment. Scott kept his eyes on the road, while Brooke paid attention to the passing scenery. When Scott pulled to a stop in front of his garage, he turned to Brooke and said, "You have to get out before I pull in. The garage is too narrow for both doors to open if I park in the middle, so I park closer to the passenger-side wall." Scott got out and unlocked the garage door.

Brooke climbed out of the car. She pulled her things from the back seat, stepped aside, and waited for Scott to emerge from the garage. After he locked the doors, Scott placed the strap of Brooke's weekender on his shoulder and gestured toward the gate a few feet down the alley.

"Be it ever so humble," said Scott, pushing the gate open.

Brooke peered into the darkness but then looked at Scott.

"Straight ahead to the tree," said Scott. "I'll be right behind you. After that, you can follow me the rest of the way. A couple of steps, a flight of stairs, and it's windows on the world."

"If I don't get to a bathroom in the next five seconds, it's going to be more like Wreck of the Hesperus."

"That's oblique, but I get your point. Okay, follow me. I'll have you there in no time."

A few minutes later, Scott was standing near the kitchen doorway when Brooke opened the bathroom door and stepped into the main room.

"Would you like something to drink? I've got milk, orange juice, or ice water."

"I'm okay." Brooke sat down on the corner of the full-size mattress sitting on the floor in the middle of the room.

Scott stepped around the mattress to the apartment's overstuffed chair and perched himself on the arm closest to Brooke.

"You want to watch TV?" Scott tilted his head toward the television set on the chest of drawers between the bathroom and kitchen doorways.

"Not really." Brooke noticed the alarm clock sitting beside the TV. "I have to get up early, so I should get ready for bed."

"How early?"

"I need to leave by seven o'clock."

"Why the hell by seven o'clock?"

"Because I do. If that's a problem, I can take a cab to a friend's house."

"It's not a problem. I'm just wondering why you need to leave so early?"

"It doesn't matter why. I just do. So, should I stay, or should I go?"

"You should stay."

"If I stay, you need to set the alarm for six thirty."

"Okay."

"I need to see you set the alarm for six thirty."

"Jesus Christ." Scott crossed the room to the chest of drawers.

Brooke picked up her weekender and walked to the bureau to see the clock for herself. When Scott was done fiddling, she said, "That light means the alarm's on?"

"Yes."

"Thank you." Brooke walked into the bathroom and closed the door.

Scott stepped out of his loafers, toe against heel, one after the other. He shrugged off his sport coat, grabbed a hanger from the clothes rack, and hung it up. He removed his shirt and tie, organized them on a hanger, slipped off his trousers, and placed them on another. He pulled off his socks, considering whether he'd wear them one more time, then threw them in the laundry basket. He slid off his underpants and tossed them in the basket as well.

Scott turned off the floor lamp near the front door. He made sure the door was locked, then crawled under the white cotton top sheet, the extent of his bedding for that time of year. Scott stretched out with his head propped on his hand.

Light fell into the room when Brooke, wearing a sleeveless nightgown, opened the bathroom door. She paused to get her bearings, then switched off the light and stepped to the bed. Brooke slipped under the top sheet and stretched out on her back with her arms at her sides. When Scott leaned toward her, Brooke closed her eyes. Scott leaned closer and kissed one of her eyelids, then the other. He continued kissing her gently, her eyelids, her nose, her ear, sucking her earlobe until she gasped, and then her mouth. Scott edged himself closer but drew back his head. When he brought his mouth back to hers, their lips parted, and their tongues rose to the occasion with a tender exchange of parries and thrusts.

Scott slid his hand from one of Brooke's breasts to the other, dividing his attention between them, kissing them through the lightweight cotton until her nipples pressed their shape into the wet fabric. Scott returned his mouth to Brooke's and kissed her more urgently, keeping her focus away from his hand as he inched the hem of her nightgown higher.

Brooke did not object when Scott pulled her nightgown over her shoulders, did not resist when he rolled on top of her and pressed his erection between her legs. Scott centered his attention on Brooke's ears, stuck his tongue in one after the other, sucked on her earlobes, made her twist and turn. Brooke tilted her hips and pressed her pelvis forward and backward, pubic hair chaffing Scott's erection from above and beneath.

Now, Scott tilted his hips. He pushed his pelvis forward and backward, forward and backward, adjusting his position until his glans lodged in the opening of Brooke's vagina.

Brooke gasped, then said, "No." She arched her back and secured Scott's erection between her thighs. Scott rolled onto his side, bringing Brooke onto her side as well. Wrapping his arms around her shoulders, Scott rolled onto his back with Brooke lying on top of him.

"Someday, it'll be 'yes,' " said Scott, fingering Brooke's vagina from behind. He pressed his erection against her clitoris.

"And it'll be 'yes' for the first time for both of us."

Scott sensed the shift in Brooke's posture, the increase of weight, the lack of movement, the absence of warmth as she rolled off his body to lie on her back.

"What just happened?" Scott turned toward Brooke.

Brooke inhaled. She studied the ceiling for a moment, then said, "It won't be the first time for both of us."

Scott heard the words but did not understand. He narrowed his eyes and tilted his head.

Having seen this response on numerous occasions, Brooke knew what it meant. All the same, she chose not to clarify her statement unless Scott pressed further, which Scott then did.

"What's that mean?"

Brooke closed her eyes. After a moment, her eyes still closed, she said, "It means I have a boyfriend."

"You have a boyfriend," Scott said slowly, more for himself than for Brooke.

Brooke remained silent.

"If you have a boyfriend, why are you here?"

"I'm here because I felt bad about how things ended up on Monday."

"*And* this is your way of making up for that?"

"It's the best I could do, or so I thought. Do you want me to leave?"

"No, I don't want you to leave—it's almost midnight. Where would you go?" Scott rolled onto his back.

"I'm not sure, but I'd figure something out."

"Do you want to leave?"

"If I didn't want to be here, I wouldn't have come in the first place."

"Wow." Scott turned his head toward Brooke. "Who are you, and what have you done with my girlfriend?"

"That's the thing," Brooke replied, "I'm not your girlfriend. I'd say 'anymore,' but I've never really been your 'girlfriend,' not when you come down to it. I mean, Friday nights, once or twice a month, making out on my living-room couch, *if* my parents were out for the evening, and your parents thought they were in. That's pretty much the extent of our boyfriend-girlfriend relationship for the two years it lasted."

"What about the night we spent together in LA? That wasn't making out on your living-room couch."

"No." Brooke sighed, "it wasn't. But after the night we spent together in LA, you didn't speak to me for six months."

"Yeah, well, a couple of days later, I moved out of my house. You had already moved out of your house. I was camping at David Whitcomb's—a guy I hardly knew. You were staying with your aunt and uncle in a two-bedroom apartment. We were in the middle of our senior year of high school. Everything was crazy— Hieronymus Bosch crazy. So, you know, the significance of spending the night with you was more than I could come to terms with at the time."

" 'Come to terms with,' " Brooke repeated, shaking her head. "I apologize for the inconvenience."

"That's not what I meant."

"Whatever you meant . . ." Brooke inhaled. "It doesn't really matter. I didn't come here to work things out. If this is too weird for you, I can leave."

"You're not going to leave, not on my account anyway. At this point, the most we can hope for is a couple of hours of sleep. Can you fall asleep?"

"I can if you stop talking."

By way of response, Scott rolled onto his side, facing away from Brooke. He closed his eyes and concentrated on his plans for a couple of partition walls in the apartment.

At six twenty-nine, Scott turned the alarm clock off before it buzzed. He shaved, showered, and dressed for work. When he stepped out of the bathroom, Brooke was dressed and ready to go. They acknowledged each other without speaking. Brooke preceded Scott out of the apartment and continued down the stairs as he locked the door. In the car, Scott broke the silence.

"Where to?"

"The Greyhound Bus Terminal."

"On Long Beach Boulevard?"

"Yes."

Fifteen minutes later, Scott waited at the curb until Brooke stepped inside the terminal. After a minute or two, thinking she might have a change of heart, Scott pulled into slow-moving traffic and followed Long Beach Boulevard to Fourth Street, where he rounded the corner as the traffic light turned red. Keeping an eye out for a parking space, Scott proceeded along Fourth Street to Pine Avenue. Halfway through the intersection of Fourth and Pine, Scott checked his rearview mirror for approaching vehicles, downshifted into second gear, and made a tight U-turn that ended with him in one of his preferred parking spaces—visible through the shoe store's windows—on the south side of the street.

"That's one of the benefits of being the first one in on Saturday morning," said Mr. Gary, opening the glass door for Scott.

"What's that?" replied Scott, standing by as Mr. Gary locked the door.

"You get the best parking space."

Scott nodded, then said, "What's the other benefit?"

"You get to be first up when the early birds flock in."

"The parking space, I like," said Scott, heading toward the storeroom. "The 'early bird' thing, not so much. Don't you think Andy should *benefit* every other week?"

"Fine by me, but you do the asking."

Scott frowned. "Why me? You're the boss."

"Yes, and as the boss, I see no problem with the current arrangement."

"Aargh," said Scott, raising a fist.

"All right, matey," said Mr. Gary in his best impersonation of Long John Silver. "If this place isn't shipshape by nine o'clock, it'll be the gangplank for ye at nine-o-five."

"Shiver me timbers," said Scott. "And that's the extent of my pirate-speak. If you need me, I'll be in my office." Scott walked from the sales floor into the storeroom.

A few days after Brooke's sleepover, Scott asked his grandfather to help him get the building materials for a project he had in mind.

Gus replied, "Make a list of everything you need—all the lumber, with exact measurements, nails, screws, brackets, and bolts. Then we'll talk."

Scott returned the following afternoon.

Gus looked over the list, smiled at Scott, and said, "Okay, Scotty-Boy, let's go get you some wood."

The two of them walked from the garage to the street, climbed into Gus's pickup truck, and drove off. A few minutes later, they walked into the cutting room of a small lumber yard, where the owner's eyes lit up when he saw Gus.

"Brother Horn, what a nice surprise." The man shook hands with Gus, then looked at Scott with warm expectation. "And who do we have here?"

"My pipsqueak grandson." Gus, five-foot-nothing, patted Scott, six-foot-two, on the back. "Scotty-Boy, this is my good friend, Mr. Peterson." Gus looked at Mr. Peterson and said, "Brother Peterson, this is my second-youngest grandson, Scott. He's also my favorite, but don't tell him that."

"Pleased to meet you," said Scott, shaking Mr. Peterson's hand.

"The pleasure's mine." Mr. Peterson smiled. "What have they been feeding you, son? Jack's magic beans or some such thing?"

"I'm not picky, sir. I'll eat whatever I'm served, except raw fish—or squid, no matter how it's cooked."

"Okay, Brother Peterson," said Gus, getting down to business, "Scott has a construction project in mind, and we were hoping you'd help us out by cutting everything to size."

"Absolutely. Do you have everything written down?"

"Yes, sir." Gus pulled the list from his back pocket.

Gus and Mr. Peterson discussed the list of materials on one side of the paper, then pointed out a couple of questions as they reviewed Scott's diagram on the other side.

"Young man," said Mr. Peterson, turning to Scott. "You have all of your plywood standing on end. Your walls will be twice as strong if you stagger the plywood lengthwise. Here, let me show you." Mr. Peterson removed a rectangular pencil from behind his ear. He made a quick drawing that showed the sheets of plywood on their sides like horizontal brickwork.

"Okay." Scott adjusted the picture in his mind. "That makes sense to me. The walls will still be eight feet high, though, right?"

"Yes, indeed," said Mr. Peterson, nodding for emphasis. "Let me make a couple of adjustments to your diagram, so you can put the puzzle together when you get home. What's the cutout for?"

"I'm going to put my television set behind the wall with a piece of framed artwork on a hinge in front of the opening. When you want to watch a program, you swing the artwork open, and there's the TV."

"Very clever," said Mr. Peterson, looking at Gus. "I see why he's your favorite."

"He's my favorite because he still helps with the yard work."

30

Mr. Peterson smiled. "All right, then, let me get started on this. Did you want to wait or come back in an hour?"

Gus looked at Scott.

"Can we help?" said Scott.

"You bet." Mr. Peterson pointed his finger. "Grab that trolley, and we'll go out and pull your lumber."

An hour later, Gus and Scott were on their way to drop off the building materials at Scott's apartment. It didn't take long once they were parked in front of Scott's garage.

"Shouldn't I help you get the plywood upstairs?" said Gus.

"In the garage is fine. My friend Andy will help me get it upstairs. You've already done more than enough. And, scout's honor, I didn't ask for your help so you'd pay for the lumber."

"Think of it as your Christmas present, six months early. After we get this stuff squared away, we'll go back to the house and get your hardware. I'll throw in a hammer and a couple of screwdrivers, wish you happy birthday and send you on your way. This little project of yours is working out pretty good for everybody. I'm saving your grandmother time and money on shopping and wrapping paper."

Scott chuckled in response to his grandfather's grin.

Along with an assortment of nails, screws, and corner braces for securing the partition wall to the existing wall, Gus placed a new hammer and two reversible screwdrivers, slot head and Phillips, in a cardboard box.

"Where'd those come from?" said Scott, eyeing the tools.

"I paid a visit to our friendly neighborhood hardware store yesterday afternoon and picked them up for you. I thought they might come in handy."

"Okay, but that's it. For Christmas *and* my birthday present."

Scott's grandmother entered the garage through the side door. "Would you like a sandwich before you leave, dear?"

"No." Scott kissed Marguerite on the cheek. "I want to get started on my apartment. Thanks for all of my gifts. Everything's perfect."

Gus winked at Marguerite. "We gave him lumber for Christmas and tools for his birthday."

"Oh well," said Marguerite, turning to Scott. "Mrs. Claus may have something to say about that when the holidays roll around. Are you sure you don't want a sandwich, sweetheart? Maybe you'd like to take one with you?"

"No, ma'am." Scott stepped off toward the driveway. "I've got cows to milk and fields to plow."

"That's the spirit," said Gus. "Call us if you need anything."

"Okey-dokey." Scott waved a hand as he continued down the driveway, adding over his shoulder, "I'll drop by tomorrow afternoon with a progress report."

By the time Scott stopped for grilled cheese sandwiches, he'd nailed together the framing studs for both walls; he'd raised the short section and attached it to the wall right beside the kitchen doorway; he'd raised the long section and attached it to the short section. Scott's "Yahoo!" had caused a ripple of concern among the sunbathers in the backyard of the sorority house in front of his apartment. The adjustment of bathing suit straps had gone unnoticed by Scott as he danced around his newly defined living room to Marvin Gaye's version of "I Heard It Through the Grapevine."

Andy arrived while Scott was finishing his second sandwich.

"Want something to eat?" said Scott, talking with a full mouth.

Andy shook his head as he surveyed the new layout. "I had lunch at Jack in the Box."

"Shoot," said Scott, "why didn't you come and get me?"

32

"Because you were doing this, and I was doing Charlene."

"Yeah, well, hell. I could've put a couple of tacos and an order of onion rings to good use."

"This looks awesome. Where's the plywood? In the garage?"

"Yep."

"Okay, let's get a move on. I have to leave in an hour."

"Are you kidding me? You're going back for more?"

"I assume you're not referring to Jack in the Box."

"Your assumption would be correct."

"No, I have to meet a man about a thing."

"Is the man's name Bond, James Bond?"

"No, it's Mike, Mike Wilson, and I'm trying to find a part for my car. Chop-chop. I think you're going to need help with more than getting the plywood up here."

"To say the least—ba dum tss."

"Yeah, all right, come on." Andy stepped out to the landing, where he noticed the coeds sunning themselves in the yard below. He stuck his head back through the doorway and whisper-shouted, "Holy crap! Have you seen what's going on in your front yard?"

"Keep your voice down," Scott hissed, crossing the room. "Yeah, of course I've seen them, and it's not my front yard. If they make a complaint, I'm out on the street. So shut up and tread lightly. I mean it, or I'll be camping at your house again, which works for me as I very much prefer your mother's cooking to mine."

Andy returned his focus to the spectacle of baby-oiled flesh. Scott gave him a push and continued applying pressure to his shoulders as they descended the stairs. In the garage, Andy assured Scott they could manage two sheets of plywood at the same time, which they did as far as the bottom of the staircase.

"I don't think these stairs will support you and me and a hundred pounds of wood," said Scott, somewhat short of breath.

"Don't be ridiculous." Andy stepped closer to the shrubbery and stood on tiptoes, hoping to see across the fence.

Scott secured a grip on one sheet of plywood and lifted his end onto the first step. "Would you please act your age?"

"I am acting my age." Andy hefted his end of the plywood. "It's you we need to worry about."

"Let's concentrate on the plywood," said Scott, "before delving into my shortcomings."

On their third trip, the boys maneuvered two six-foot sheets at one time up to the apartment. Scott slid one of the six-foot sheets in place against the framework facing the front door.

"I'll nail this in place," said Scott, "while you get the two cutoff pieces and lock the garage, okay?"

"You're the boss, boss." Andy paused on the landing for another look at the coeds.

When Andy returned, he and Scott lifted the second six-foot sheet and held it in place above the first one while Scott drove home half a dozen nails.

"I can finish all the nailing after you leave," said Scott, stepping around to the living room side of the structure. "Okay, a full sheet comes all the way to the corner on the bottom, the one with the cutout for the TV."

"Far out," said Andy, sliding the eight-foot sheet into place.

Scott secured the plywood with a few nails. He then positioned a two-foot cutoff beside the length already in place and nailed it into the stud Mr. Peterson had drawn for securing the junction. Scott placed the second cutoff above the full sheet at the other end of the wall and nailed it in place.

"Okay, then, one piece to go," said Scott, as the boys lifted the second eight-foot length into place. Scott hammered in half a dozen nails, stepped back, and pronounced, "*Et voila.*"

"Totally *et voila*," said Andy, walking around the room.

"I couldn't have done it without you."

"Yeah, right. . . . Okay, I have to go. You need anything else?"

"A couple of tacos would hit the spot."

"Tomorrow, bro. I'll swing by around noon."

"I'll be ready and waiting. And, seriously, Drew, thanks for your help."

"Hey, no problemo. Not to mention, I'm moving in as soon as you get this place the way you want it." Andy crossed the room to the front door. "Okay, bud, I'm already late. I'll see you tomorrow." Andy descended the stairs without pausing, which suggested the sunbathers had repaired to the inner sanctum of Gamma Phi Beta.

Scott sank down on the bed and studied the room's transformation. Pleased with his efforts, for the most part, Scott found a hundred square feet of unfinished plywood somewhat disconcerting, especially since he'd spent the previous day painting the surrounding walls "Super White." With a flash of inspiration, Scott rose to his feet and walked to the kitchen. He removed the wrapper from a one-inch brush and brought the remaining can of paint into the "foyer." The lid came off the can rather too easily, but the dregs appeared suitable to the task Scott had in mind. He swirled the can a couple of times, dipped the brush, then stood in front of the newly installed six-foot wall and began to print something he remembered from a friend's collection of favorite quotes.

Half an hour later, Scott stepped back and reviewed his work. As usual, he was less than pleased with his handwriting, although applying flat paint to unfinished plywood had to account for some degree of its slapdash appearance.

Oh, well, he mused, *it's the thought that counts.* Scott returned the can to the kitchen, rinsed the brush, grabbed his car keys, and left the apartment.

Scott drove to a nearby hardware store, where he purchased a gallon of floor adhesive, a flooring trowel, two boxes of white, and two boxes of black one-foot-square vinyl tiles. When he asked the salesman for installation advice, the old-timer had two rules of thumb: one, apply the adhesive as evenly as possible; and two, place the first tile in the most visible corner and work from there in both directions.

"Okay," said Scott, visualizing the process. "Yes, I see what you mean. Thank you. I may need more tiles. Are you low on stock?"

Scott was assured they were not, as long as he returned within the next couple of weeks.

Scott laughed. "If you don't see me in the next couple of hours, I'll be here when you unlock the doors tomorrow morning," which, as it turned out, was the case.

The next morning, when the salesman turned the "CLOSED" sign around to read "OPEN," Scott entered the store with a jaunty salute. "Two more boxes of each should do the trick," he said, holding up a black tile to jog the fellow's memory. "Shall I get them off the shelf, or would you rather bring them out from the stockroom?"

From the stockroom it was.

By the time Andy arrived at the apartment, a few minutes before noon, Scott was laying tiles behind the partition wall in the "walk-in closet." Andy stepped through the front door and slowed to a stop. The newly defined L-shaped floor, "foyer" into "living room," was an immaculate checkerboard of black and white tiles. Staring at the floor until his eyes went out of focus, Andy blinked, then noticed the wall directly in front of him. He tilted his head and read what Scott had written the previous afternoon:

IT IS BETTER TO FACE CHAOS COURAGEOUSLY

THAN TO CHERISH THE DREAM OF RETURNING
TO AN OUTWORN SYNTHESIS.

LEWIS MUMFORD

"Who's Lewis Mumford?" said Andy, reading the quote a second time.

Scott stuck his head through the cutout for the television set. "Beats me."

"Yeah, okay, so where'd this come from?"

"One of Faith Ann's books. You know, one of the books she made, full of handwritten quotes and pictures of artwork. I showed them to you when I took you to meet her, right?"

"That's not what I remember about meeting Faith Ann."

"*Come on.*" Scott frowned. "She's happily married and seven months pregnant."

"Seven months pregnant and eight on the Richter scale—a lollapalooza."

"That's not a real word," said Scott and then, "*ouch*" as his head disappeared from view

"What happened?"

"I got a splinter in my neck."

"That'll teach ya."

Scott walked into the living room. "So, what do you think?"

"About the quote?"

Scott rolled his eyes.

"The quote will make people stop and think."

"Then my work here is done. No, dimwit, the floor."

"What about the floor?" Andy looked around. "Am I missing something?"

"Yeah, the part of your spinal cord that connects to your brain."

"It's awesome, man. Totally awesome. We should get some really big chess pieces."

"Actually," Scott mused, "I like that idea."

"Yeah, well, I wouldn't know where to get something like that. I do know where to get tacos and onion rings, though."

"Excellent. You're driving."

Driving was never the short straw for Andy, in that his 1958 Turquoise Corvette was an extension of everything he liked about himself. The only person allowed to drive Andy's pride and joy, other than himself, was Scott. And this for no other reason than trading cars every so often provided Andy with the added prestige of tooling around town in Scott's Ruby Red Porsche.

On the way to Jack in the Box, Andy grilled Scott about his plans for the apartment: "No" was the response to painting the ply-wood; the partition walls would be covered in black burlap. "Where do you get that?" and "How's it go on?" were answered respectively, "The Fabric Barn" and "Some kind of glue." "What about the inside of the partition?" was met with inconclusive si-lence, while "What are we going to sleep on?" received a lengthy explanation involving split-level twin mattresses placed along two walls at a 90-degree angle that would also serve as daytime seating.

Andy pulled to a stop at the drive-thru intercom.

"Welcome to Jack in the Box" was garbled remotely. "May I take your order" was a barely intelligible burst of static, after which Andy tilted his head toward the machine and waited to see if it was his turn to talk.

When the silence was certain, Andy raised his voice, as if vol-ume would temper technology, and said, "We'd like six tacos, four orders of onion rings, and two large Dr Peppers."

Another burst of static confirmed their order or possibly not.

Andy cocked his head. After a moment, he pulled forward to the pickup window, handed the cashier a five-dollar bill, turned to Scott, and said, "Lunch is on me."

Scott narrowed his eyes. "What's the catch?"

"No catch, bud, it's the least I can do."

"Now that you mention it—"

"Hey, man, don't stick your dick in a gift horse mouth."

Scott winced. "Does that even qualify as a mixed metaphor?"

"You want ketchup?"

"Is Martin Luther a Lutheran?"

Over the next several months, Scott continued working on the apartment at a progressively slower pace for financial reasons, as well as his inclination to lose interest before a project's completion. Whether decorating his apartment or clipping his nails, Scott's focus shifted to something new as soon as he visualized the outcome of his endeavor. That, and also, aspects of a project deemed "not worth the effort"—bathroom and kitchen, as cases in point—were abandoned early on if any attention had been given at all.

On September 9, the fall semester at Long Beach City College commenced. While Scott arrived as a freshman and Andy returned as a sophomore, they both impressed their teachers as mediocre students. Andy, riding high on testosterone, was preoccupied with the latest crop of campus coeds. Whereas Scott, withdrawn and depressed, could not stop thinking about Brooke.

THREE

BAILEY

Scott's state of mind dropped a notch lower when Andy delayed moving into the apartment because of "unforeseen financial obligations," otherwise known as new chrome wheels. In addition to everything else in play—Brooke's ambivalence, Andy's vacillation, adjusting to college—was the unforeseen circumstance of Scott having moved into one of the city's busiest cruising areas. At any hour of the day, a slow procession of late-model vehicles— sometimes one or two, sometimes one after another—could be seen traveling in either direction on First Street, from Bixby Park to Temple Avenue.

When vehicles approached from opposite directions, the speed at which they passed was adjusted for a variety of reasons: time of day, darkness requiring deceleration; make, model, and year of the car, a courtship display in and of itself; a driver's apparent age, which tipped the scales more often than not; appearance and grooming, an exercise in eye-foot coordination; chemistry, if words were exchanged; compatibility, if conversation progressed to particulars. The proximity of this phenomenon, literally at his doorstep, went unnoticed by Scott until a Mercedes-Benz pulled to the side of the street one night as he was walking from Brooke's house to his apartment.

A short time after nine o'clock, Scott had given up waiting for Brooke's Volkswagen to appear, having no idea where she was or when she'd return. Not that where or when mattered, in that Brooke had no idea Scott was waiting and would have conducted herself as though he weren't there if she'd arrived to find him lean-ing against the palm tree in front of her house. Scott had spent the better part of an hour focusing his attention on the intersection of First Street and Kennebec Avenue, hoping to see Brooke's powder-blue Beetle approaching from the west. He'd been so in-tent upon Brooke's arrival that he hadn't given a second thought to the slow-moving Mercedes-Benz the third time it passed by.

Scott had pushed away from the palm tree and stood on the sidewalk a minute longer, thinking Brooke's car would appear the moment he stopped looking, but that little irony could not prove itself true as long as he kept his eyes on the street. Hormones surg-ing and nowhere to go, Scott had shoved his hands in his pockets and headed for home. As he'd crossed Kennebec Avenue, the Mercedes-Benz pulled to the curb just beyond the intersection.

When Scott stepped onto the sidewalk, the driver leaned over and said something through the passenger door window.

"What's that?" said Scott, slowing to a stop. At first glance, Scott sensed the driver's intentions were not above board.

Scott tamped down memories of the talkative man who'd fol-lowed him to the front door of his apartment on a hot afternoon four months earlier.

◆   ◆   ◆

Thinking the man's request not unreasonable, Scott allowed him to come into the apartment for a glass of water. At a loss for words when the fellow's glass was empty, Scott made a comment about the late-day heat, which the man interpreted as an invitation to un-dress.

Yielding to an attraction Scott did not understand, he acqui-esced to the fellow's advances until he climaxed, which triggered the residual effect of his first sexual experience with a man, his stepmother's friend Lieutenant Colonel Gaylord Hall, who'd introduced ten-year-old Scotty to the shock and awe of adult-male ejaculation. When Gaylord had begun ejaculating into the bathroom sink, he'd coaxed Scotty to stroke his blue-veined erection as several more splashes coated the porcelain. Scotty, overwhelmed and horrified, had barely contained his nausea, had tasted the bile rising in his throat, and thus the bitter imprint that soured sexual interaction for him the rest of his life.

Rising to his feet, Scott threatened to call the police if the man did not leave his apartment at once. The fellow got dressed and left but returned the next afternoon, knocking on Scott's front door until the landlord told him to leave the premises. The fellow returned later that day, banging on Scott's back door until the landlord threatened to call the police.

Andy stopped by on his way home from work to see why Scott hadn't shown up for his shift. After knocking at the front door several times, Andy got the landlord to let him in. When it became clear Scott was not going to answer his questions, Andy brought him to his parents' house, where Scott stayed for the next several days under the watchful eye of Andy's mother.

A consequence of the incident was Scott's eviction from his apartment with the loss of his deposit and half a month's rent. The silver lining was Scott's finding his present apartment, which, apart from being located at the center of a cruising area, surpassed his previous apartment in every other respect.

◆ ◆ ◆

The driver of the Mercedes-Benz smiled as he turned down the radio and said, "I was wondering if you live in this neighborhood, mate?"

Scott tilted his head as he considered the question. After a moment, he said, "Yes," then focused his eyes, wondering if a context was forthcoming. Scott noticed the wedding ring on the driver's manicured hand—a doctor, or a lawyer perhaps, although he looked relatively young.

The man leaned toward the open window. His white teeth and blue eyes were arresting against his suntanned skin. He was not handsome, nor was he unattractive, definitely athletic by the way he handled himself, a clean-shaven professional with sharp features and red hair. Scott liked his casual attire, his light-brown V-neck sweater, his white crew-neck T-shirt, his wash-worn jeans.

"I'm new to the city," the man continued. "This area seems like it'd be a nice place to live. As a resident, would you agree or disagree?" The fellow looked at Scott with friendly expectation.

Despite the innocent pretext, Scott sensed an ulterior motive. Whatever it was, potentially dangerous or utterly harmless, he had no frame of reference for how to proceed. All the same, he did not want to be rude.

Scott pointed toward the west. "You've got Bixby Park one block in that direction,"—pointed toward the south—"the Pacific Ocean one block in that direction. What's not to like?"

The man responded with a lighthearted laugh. "Yes, of course, thank you for stating the obvious. If I had more time, I'd like to hear anything else you have to say. But I'm running a little late." He shrugged, then raised his brow. "If I gave you a lift, I could ask a couple of questions on the way. How's that sound?"

Scott lowered his brow. "I'm just around the corner at the end of the block, so—"

"No problem." The man pushed the passenger door open. "I bet I can get two questions answered by the time we get there, maybe three."

Scott considered the situation as reason and sensibility reared their heads, but then an unfamiliar stillness settled his nerves. Scott stepped to the car, climbed inside, and closed the door. Without thinking, his hand went from the armrest to the crank and rolled up the window. Aware of his racing heart, Scott exhaled, then took a breath. He felt the flow of air from the heater, breathed in the smell of warm beer and English Leather.

"My name's Bailey," the man said, extending his hand.

"Scott," replied Scott, shaking hands awkwardly. "Bailey's your first name?"

"Bailey's my last name. But that's what everybody calls me, so 'Bailey' it is."

Scott laughed nervously. "Scott's my middle name, but that's what everybody calls me."

"So 'Scott' it is." Bailey pulled away from the curb. "You said 'just around the corner at the end of the block,' right?"

"Yes." Scott kept his eyes on the road.

"Do you live with your parents?"

"No," Scott replied somewhat brusquely.

"Okay." Bailey chuckled to himself. "I didn't mean to hit a nerve."

"You didn't hit a nerve."

Bailey looked at Scott and smiled. "Whatever you say, mate. It's just that you look too young to have your own place. How old are you?"

"Eighteen."

"Eighteen, and you're living on your own?"

"Yes."

"For how long?"

"Depends."

"Depends?"

"On how you look at it. Okay, I can get out here."

"Come on now, that's not fair. Just when the conversation's getting interesting." Bailey edged the car into the intersection of First and Junipero. "Should I turn right or left?"

Scott blinked slowly, then said, "Right."

"You live across from the park?" Bailey kept his foot off the accelerator as the car inched along the street.

"Not exactly."

" '*Not exactly.*' " Bailey nodded slowly. "This gets more and more interesting. '*Depends on how you look at it.*' '*Not exactly.*' It all sounds very mysterious. Are you an undercover cop?"

"Not quite. Okay, really, this is fine. I can get out here."

"That's where you live?" Bailey leaned forward to get a better look at the rundown property on the south side of Dodge Way, a ten-block alley that allowed owners of stately homes on First Street access to their garages without allocating prime real estate for unsightly driveways.

"That's not where I live, but I can walk from here." Scott reached for the door handle.

"Hold on a minute." Bailey turned into the alley. "Is it one of these garage apartments?"

"Yes," replied Scott. "So please stop the car."

Bailey pulled to the side of the alley, directly in front of Scott's garage.

"Okay." Scott opened the passenger door. "Thanks for the lift." He glanced at Bailey, then leaned toward the door.

"Hey, one more thing." Bailey placed his hand on Scott's knee long enough to stop his movement.

Scott looked over his shoulder.

"My teeth are floating, mate, and I have a long drive ahead of me." Bailey grimaced. "A pit stop would be much appreciated."

"You want to use my bathroom?"

"That'd be great." Bailey turned off the engine and stepped out of the car. He locked his door, walked around, and locked the passenger door. Telegraphing a sense of urgency, Bailey strode to where Scott was standing in front of his open gate.

"This is rustic," said Bailey, following Scott to the bottom of his stairs. "Rustic and rather charming, when you consider where it's tucked away—one block from Bixby Park and one block from the Pacific Ocean. What's not to like?"

"Those relationships no longer apply, but close enough." Scott unlocked his front door. He stepped inside and turned on the floor lamp at the foot of the double mattress.

"Well," said Bailey, stepping inside and looking around. "We're not in Kansas anymore." He turned to Scott. "You did all this?"

Scott raised his brow and nodded. He then sat down—feet apart, elbows on knees, hands clasped—on the double mattress of the L-shaped seating arrangement.

Bailey tilted his head toward the end of the partition wall. "Men's room?"

Scott nodded again, although this time, it was barely perceptible.

Bailey walked through the passageway and switched on the bathroom light. A moment later, Scott heard urine streaming into the toilet through the open door. The noise continued long enough for Scott to widen his eyes, duly impressed, despite the circumstances. Scott shrugged off his jacket and tossed it to the far end of the mattress.

After a final spurt, Bailey called out, "I well and truly needed that."

Scott turned his head and started counting the number of black floor tiles in one row after another. He was focused on a section at the end of the partition wall when Bailey's bare feet stepped into view. Scott's first reaction was to assure himself that the man had entered the apartment wearing shoes and socks. Yes, of course, Scott remembered suede loafers and white socks. Curiously, the suntanned feet were the same shade of brown as the absent shoes.

The appearance of Bailey's feet was so unexpected that Scott studied them without reservation or self-reproach. Of greatest interest, having spent hours poring over books on Renaissance sculpture, Bailey's curved nail beds and square-cut toenails were the feet Michelangelo had in mind when he created his David. After perusing close-up photographs of the seventeen-foot-tall hero, Scott had trimmed his toenails in the same fashion as David's. When the result fell short of his expectation, it wasn't until further review of David's left foot that Scott realized his nail beds were flat and his toenails would have to be round instead of square, as he and the sixteenth-century arbiter of masculine perfection preferred. One aspect on which Scott and the sculptor in question were not in accord was the preference for a long second toe: Michelangelo was in favor of a second toe longer than the big toe, as evidenced by David's colossal feet, whereas Scott was partial to a shorter second toe, as was the case with the suntanned pair now on display.

"Pardon my feet," said Bailey, "but I've always wanted to know what one of these felt like." He stepped onto the rug that squared the seating arrangement and scuffed around like a child in a puddle. "This feels great. It's some kind of sheepskin, right?"

"No skin, just wool."

"What's it called? A 'flotaki'?"

"Flokati."

"Right, right." Bailey stepped off the rug, raised his arms, and exhaled through pursed lips. "Why's it so warm in here, mate? I think there's actual steam on your windows." He collapsed on the orange velvet chair, arms and legs akimbo.

"I just watered my plants, and I haven't figured out the heater yet. This is my first cold night in the apartment." Scott paused for a moment, then added, "I left the heater on high because I thought my girlfriend was coming back with me."

"I guess that didn't work out the way you hoped."

"Yeah, well, at my age, that's the lay of the land."

"So to speak."

Scott laughed. "Not a problem for you, though. How long have you been married?"

Bailey held up his left hand. "You mean this?"

Scott nodded.

"I'm not married, mate. I wear this to keep the sheilas away."

" 'The sheilas' ?"

"Young ladies with white picket fences and baby carriages on their minds. I may be older than you, but I'm not ready to settle down."

"How old are you?"

"Twenty-seven last week and fit as a fiddle." Bailey stood up and struck a strongman pose. He then wiped his brow. "Man, oh, man," he sighed dramatically. "It might be the middle of November outside, but it's the fourth of July in here." Bailey took hold of his sweater and pulled it off over his head. The sweater brought Bailey's T-shirt up along with it. Before the T-shirt slid back in place, Scott noticed the top two buttons of Bailey's fly were undone, that his 501s were riding low on his hips. Scott saw no evidence of underpants or a tan-line, which, everything else notwithstanding, struck him as odd. Scott also saw, before he looked away, the trail of red hair below Bailey's navel.

Bailey draped his sweater over the pillows along the wall at the end of the single mattress. He sat back in the chair, hands behind his head, and said, "A glass of water would hit the spot."

Scott took a slow breath. He then stood up and walked to the kitchen.

"Thanks, mate. Bloody hell, it's like a sauna in here."

Scott returned with a glass of water to see Bailey had removed his T-shirt as well. Scott slowed his step but continued across the room as if nothing was out of place. He handed Bailey the glass of

48

water and saw the faint sheen of perspiration on the man's forehead and neck. Scott took in the damp ringlets of Bailey's underarm hair, the muscled contours of his belly and chest, his large areolas and erect nipples, his flawless skin.

Scott walked to the other side of the room and sat down.

"You don't mind if I cool off a bit, do you, mate?" Bailey sat forward and stretched his neck.

"Yeah," said Scott. "I mean, no. You know, whatever."

"That's the spirit." Bailey took a long drink of water. He then made a show of studying the art on the partition wall. After a moment, he said, "You covered that wall with black burlap?"

"Yes," said Scott, eyeing the tattoo on Bailey's arm.

"How'd you make it stick?"

"Wallpaper glue."

"Well done."

"Thanks." Scott paused, then said, "Can I ask you a question?"

"Absolutely."

"Does your tattoo have a specific meaning?"

Bailey shifted his left arm forward. He flexed the biceps and said, "This is a small section of a traditional Maori tattoo. I tried to honor my heritage, but I didn't have what it takes to do the whole thing."

Scott tilted his head.

"My father was from New Zealand, and my mother was from Australia," Bailey explained, "which makes me half Kiwi and half Aussie."

Scott laughed through his nose. "Which side is which?"

"Sorry?"

"Which side is the Kiwi half? The side with the Maori tattoo?"

"No, mate, you've got it wrong." Bailey gestured toward his belly. "I'm Kiwi from the waist up, which includes the tattoo, and Aussie from the waist down, for reasons that remain to be seen."

Scott narrowed his eyes as he considered Bailey's words, then looked away.

"No cause for concern, mate. Just something Australian's like to boast about."

"Which is?"

"I'm not one to brag, but *healthy* is the word that comes to mind." Bailey raised both arms and flexed his biceps.

"Red hair doesn't make me think of Australia."

"It's not that unusual, laddie boy. Mum descended from good Scottish stock, and Grandpa Bailey was born in Dublin. What about you? From which distant lands do your people hail? Must have been cold weather climes, from the look of you, so cool and collected, sitting there in that flannel shirt."

"I'm all right."

"You've got a T-shirt on as well. You must have ice water in your veins."

"Actually, the flannel shirt is a little uncomfortable."

"Actually, the flannel shirt is making me uncomfortable." Bailey finished his water, then held the glass up as a visual aid. "Mind if I help myself?"

Scott gestured toward the kitchen.

When Bailey stood up, his Levi's slipped lower on his hips, emphasizing his narrow waist and the trail of hair beneath his navel. He walked across the room as if strolling down a sidewalk, not a trace of self-consciousness, prideful or modest. Bailey's unabashed poise diminished Scott's wariness. Scott unbuttoned his flannel shirt, slipped it off, and tossed it on top of his jacket.

"That's more like it," said Bailey, crossing the room. He remained standing as he emptied his glass in one long swallow. "All this water's great for the body."

"You're ahead of the game in that respect." Scott clenched his teeth when he realized he'd spoken before considering his words.

"Thank you, mate. It doesn't come easy." Bailey shifted his stance for a better view of his torso. "Hey, listen, do you have any beer? I know you're only eighteen, but I was drinking a six-pack every Saturday night when I was your age."

"I'm not much of a beer drinker." Scott paused for a beat, then said, "A friend of mine is, though. He keeps a few bottles in my refrigerator for when he stops by."

"Will he be stopping by tonight?"

"No."

"How about I leave a dollar for your friend, and we break into his stash?"

"I don't want a beer," Scott replied. "But"—he inhaled—"I guess it's okay if you have one."

"Should I get it myself?"

Scott stood up as Bailey stepped over and handed him his empty glass. A minute later, Scott gave Bailey a bottle of beer. Bailey took a long swig as Scott returned to the double mattress and sat down.

Bailey placed the half-empty bottle on the table beside the chair, looked at Scott, then shook his head. "It's too bloody hot in here, mate. Are you sure you turned the heat off?" Bailey raised his hands above his head to display the damp coils of hair in his armpits. He looked down for a moment, then at Scott. "Why the hell not? We're men among men, right?"

Scott wasn't sure what he meant.

"Right," said Bailey, answering the question himself. He undid the next two buttons of his fly and slid his Levi's down until he stepped out of the legs, one after the other. As Scott suspected, Bailey was not wearing underpants. He tossed his jeans on the chair, pulled his foreskin down, gave his scrotum a tug, grabbed his bottle of beer, stepped over to the single mattress, and stretched out on his side, legs crossed at the ankles, head propped on his arm. "This is much better, mate. It's like a day at the beach—Sunday afternoon at Karekare." Bailey took a swig of beer.

Scott's curiosity was aroused by Bailey's suntanned belly and thighs. As if from a distance, he heard himself say, "You don't wear a bathing suit at the beach?"

"Not so easy at the beach, mate, unless I'm in the South of France. But there's a pool where I'm staying, so in the buff's my usual routine." With a sweep of his hand, Bailey directed Scott's attention to his body, from his navel to his knees. "Looks good, though, right?"

"I've never seen someone without a tan line. Not that I've seen so many tan lines. Well, you know, except at school—in the showers after PE. Okay, I'll shut up."

"Not a problem, mate." Bailey clasped his hands behind his head, flexed the muscles of his chest and belly, and said, "Take a good look. I'm not shy."

At the risk of seeming unsophisticated, Scott studied Bailey's body as he would a work of art. He moved his eyes from one area to another, the well-developed shoulders and arms, the hairless chest, the inverted navel, the dense patch of pubic hair, the swelling at the base of his penis. Scott turned his head toward the kitchen as if remembering something important.

"Safe to say you have a tan line."

Scott looked in Bailey's direction and saw his glans had extended beyond the foreskin. He shifted his focus to Bailey's face. "Not so much now."

"How's that?" Bailey brushed his hand down the front of his chest, gave his belly a casual scratch, pulled his foreskin away from the glans, adjusted his hips until his penis curved away from his body.

Scott could not help but notice Bailey's glans was becoming darker than the foreskin, changing from rose to violet as it continued swelling. Scott tilted his head from side to side to relieve the tension in his neck. Looking into the middle distance, he said, "I read this article in *The New York Times* about most of the people who live in Manhattan have never been to the Empire State Building or the Statue of Liberty. That's surprising, wouldn't you say?" Scott looked to Bailey for agreement.

Bailey nodded slowly. "Yes, I would." To keep Scott's eyes on him, Bailey added, "And this applies how?"

"Okay, well, it kind of applies to me. I've been living a block from the beach for the last four months, but I haven't been down there once."

"That's not healthy, mate. Your skin needs to breathe." Bailey swung his feet to the floor and sat up with his erection flat against his belly. He finished his beer in one last gulp, set the bottle on the table, then looked at Scott. "Believe it or not, I've got to pee."

"Wow," said Scott, at once dubious and impressed. "I'd say you have a small bladder, but it doesn't sound like it."

Bailey stood up and patted his belly, the back of his hand tapping his erection. "My bladder's fine, mate. It's the six-pack I had before I left home." Bailey sauntered toward the bathroom.

As soon as Bailey was out of sight, Scott adjusted his erection, which had been caught in the leg of his underpants for the last twenty minutes. Scott's breath caught when he moved his penis to the crease at the top of his thigh. Bailey walked back into the room as Scott was adjusting his T-shirt.

Scott kept his eyes on Bailey's face as he picked up the empty bottle from the table and walked toward the kitchen, his semi-erect penis bobbing this way and that as he crossed the room. Bailey returned with a full bottle of beer. He placed the bottle on the floor beside the single mattress and continued toward the bathroom. From the passageway, Bailey called out, "There was a temporary delay due to technical difficulties. I think we're good to go now."

"Right," said Scott, thinking a response was required.

A moment later, the splash of Bailey's urine made Scott blink in wonder. The noise continued longer than Scott thought possible, then stopped without tapering off or a final spurt. There was a moment of silence before Bailey reappeared, his penis once again fully erect. Bailey slowed his step when he saw Scott's eyes fixed on his groin. At the edge of the single mattress, Bailey stopped with his arms outstretched and his feet apart. As if working out a kink, he arched his back and twisted from side to side.

Bailey sighed. Scott raised his eyes from Bailey's midsection to his face. Bailey gave Scott a sly smile. "Now that I'm getting used to the heat in here, I'm starting to feel a little homesick."

Scott looked puzzled. "I'm not sure what that means."

"It's going to be summer soon in New Zealand, my favorite time of year." Bailey took a swig of beer, lowered himself to the mattress, and stretched out in the same position as before. "In the summer, I live at the beach. That's why I told you this reminds me of Karekare." Bailey gestured at the sitting area with a slow sweep of the beer bottle, which completed its trajectory at his lips. Bailey took a sip, then placed the bottle on the windowsill. He rubbed the condensation from the palm of one hand on the fake-fur bed cover as he began stroking his penis absentmindedly with the other.

Scott was intrigued by the changing color of Bailey's glans, once again turning violet. Bailey pulled his foreskin all the way back, then held his penis away from his body. He flexed his glans until the corona was almost purple. After a moment, he released the foreskin, and it slid back in place. Bailey reached for his beer, finished it in one long gulp, then returned the bottle to the windowsill.

Scott appeared to be staring at Bailey's genitals, while in truth, he was a million miles away.

Bailey flexed his penis, then said, "Have you traveled much?"

Scott blinked slowly. "Sorry?"

"I asked if you've traveled much?"

"Not at all."

"Okay. So, you've never been to New Zealand?"

Scott chuckled. "Stands to reason. But my father has. He spent some time with Edmund Hillary in New Zealand."

"No shit."

"Yes shit."

"Did he go to Karekare?"

"I couldn't say. Why? Is that somewhere special?"

"It is if you ask me."

"I just did."

"Right you are. Okay, well, Karekare is this beach in New Zealand that has black sand." Bailey pushed himself up to sitting with his legs straight out. "These beds are like the black sand at Karekare, and the Flokati is like the white foam of breaking waves." Bailey swiveled around and stretched out on the rug, making backstroke motions with his arms and legs. As a result of his exertions, Bailey's foreskin had receded, and his glans was halfway exposed. Taking his devil-may-care behavior to the next level, Bailey flexed his penis, smiled at Scott, and said, "Come on in, mate, the water's fine."

"Yeah, I don't think so." Scott looked down.

"At least dangle your feet." Bailey stood up with athletic ease. His erection swung from side to side as he stepped over to Scott. Scott sat up straight to avoid contact, but Bailey reached out and gave his shoulder a push. "Lean back and relax, mate. It's only your shoes and socks."

Scott fell back to rest on his elbows with his head up and his eyes on Bailey. Bailey squatted down, knees wide, penis bobbing. It looked to Scott like Bailey kept moving his hips to keep his penis in motion. Scott took advantage of Bailey's focus to take a closer look at his penis. More than the impressive length and girth, the absolute rigidity when fully aroused, the color of the glans, it was the foreskin that fascinated Scott. Bailey's foreskin was as thin and transparent as parchment. So thin, in fact, you could see the precise shape of the glans inside it. Of greater interest was the foreskin extending slightly short of the mark, straining beyond the corona, but not much farther, presenting, as it were, the condition and color of the swollen glans. As if reading Scott's mind, Bailey pulled his foreskin back until the glans was fully exposed. Scott steeled himself for what came next, but Bailey stood up, turned around, and walked toward the bathroom.

"That beer's gone straight through me, mate. I'll drop your shoes in the closet on my way to the loo. You could make a trip to the fridge if it's not too much trouble." There was a soft thud as shoes hit the closet floor. A moment later, Scott heard the splash of Bailey relieving himself.

Scott stood up. He took the empty bottle from the windowsill and walked into the kitchen. He returned with a full bottle just as the toilet flushed. Scott hurried across the room, set the bottle on the table, and returned to sit where he'd been since their arrival.

The bathroom light went out.

"How long have you lived here?" said Bailey.

The question drew Scott's eyes to the passageway as Bailey entered the room, stroking his erect penis. Scott swallowed hard but continued looking at Bailey when he said, "Four months."

Bailey picked up the bottle of beer and drank half the contents in a single swig. He remained where he was with his feet apart, one arm at his side, one leg bent at the knee, his upward-curved penis pulsing in time with his heartbeat. Bailey drank the rest of the beer, then held out the bottle as if considering another.

"This is weird." Scott looked down but still saw Bailey.

"What's that?" Bailey set the bottle on the table, brushed his hand across his belly, ran his fingers through his pubic hair, took hold of his penis, and drew back the foreskin.

Scott inhaled, then said, "You remind me of Michelangelo."

"The artist?"

"As opposed to?"

Bailey chuckled. "Well, thank you, mate. I'll take that as a compliment." He attempted a theatrical bow: one foot forward, a hand at the waist, an arm outstretched, a tilt of the torso. Bailey righted himself with a bit of a flourish, which brought forth a strand of clear fluid from the tip of his penis.

"Whoops, sorry about that." Bailey caught the strand with a forefinger and placed it in his mouth. Checking his penis for more of the same, Bailey removed his finger from his mouth and said, "There we go, no muss, no fuss. Now, why do I remind you of Michelangelo? No. Wait a minute, wait a minute. Before you answer the question, I think it's only fair that we exchange roles, just for a minute, on behalf of leveling the playing field."

Scott furrowed his brow.

"Yes, yes, yes," said Bailey. "It makes perfect sense. I'll go to the kitchen and get you a glass of water, and you'll take off your T-shirt, so I don't feel so underdressed."

"That's okay. If I want a glass of water, I'll get it myself."

"Good enough." Bailey stepped forward, his penis swaying from side to side. "You be in charge of the water. I'll be in charge of the shirt." Bailey pulled Scott's T-shirt up as far as his arms. "Now, don't be difficult." Bailey raised one of Scott's arms, lowered it through a sleeve, and repeated the process on the other side. Bailey pulled the shirt over Scott's head, then tousled his hair. "There now, slap me on the ass if that doesn't feel better."

Scott kept his eyes on Bailey's face.

Bailey winked and said, "I'll take that as a 'yes.' " Bailey turned around and walked toward the passageway. "This goes in the laundry basket, I presume." He stepped behind the partition for a moment. "I'm such a good sport," he called out, "I'll even get you the glass of water."

Once again, Bailey's voice had drawn Scott's eyes to the passageway before he emerged. Scott blinked slowly when Bailey walked out, his penis more erect than before, his foreskin pulled all the way back, his glans glistening wet as he crossed the room.

Bailey glanced at Scott. "Where are the glasses, mate?"

"Take one from the dish rack. They're all clean."

"I'm sure they are. All righty, then." Water from the kitchen tap splattered in the sink. "One glass of water coming right up."

Before Bailey walked into view, Scott saw his penis out of the corner of his eye. He turned toward Bailey to preempt any funny business, which, by the smile on his face, may have been forthcoming. Bailey handed Scott the glass of water and proceeded to the single mattress, where he assumed his previous position of groin and legs on the bed, torso and arms on the floor.

"I have to get one of these rugs," said Bailey, moving his hands like he was treading water.

"There's a furniture store on Pacific Coast Highway," said Scott, "a block west of Redondo."

"Thanks, mate. I'll check it out." Bailey scratched his chest just below his left nipple. "I don't mean to be impolite,"—his hand brushed across the muscles of his belly and his pubic hair—"but what's the ballpark for one of these babies?" His hand slid to the base of his penis and pushed it back until it was standing straight up.

Scott opened his mouth to answer, but something caught in his throat. Bailey started stroking his penis as Scott picked up his glass of water and drank half of it. Scott set the glass down and began to answer the question but then looked in Bailey's direction and saw clear fluid oozing from his urethra. Scott was transfixed.

"More than twenty dollars?" said Bailey, turning his head toward Scott.

Scott showed no expression. He could feel his heart racing, but he had years of experience at hiding his emotions. This was feeling like a test of who could sustain their nonchalance the longest—the exhibitionist or the voyeur?

Scott met Bailey's eyes. "This one cost twenty-four dollars and ninety-nine cents. That always pisses me off, the ninety-nine cents part. If you want twenty-five dollars for something, put twenty-five dollars on the price tag."

"I'm with you on that." Bailey winced, then sighed. His breathing became shallow as he began stroking himself faster. He looked at Scott with half-open eyes. "Don't mind me, mate. I just need to relieve the pressure a little before we go on talking." Bailey held Scott's gaze as his abdominal muscles contracted and a stream of semen splashed across his chest.

Scott was stunned.

Bailey's head tilted back as streams of semen landed on his belly and chest. He continued stroking himself as white fluid coated his hand and pubic hair. His hand finally slowed to a stop at the base of his penis while semen still oozed from his glans. When his body relaxed, Bailey took a slow breath, turned his head toward Scott, and said, "See what I mean?"

Scott inhaled.

"About relieving the pressure a little. That was crazy, right?"

Scott tilted his head. "That was a little?"

"I'd say about average." Bailey raised himself on one elbow and surveyed his torso. When he lifted his hand from his penis, strands of semen stretched and sagged until they pooled on his belly. "For the first go-round."

"What?" said Scott, making a face.

Bailey looked at Scott, then back to his belly. "This is pretty much my typical load,"—nodding slowly—"for the first go-round."

"What's that mean? 'The first go-round'?"

"Well, you know, mate. The first time I came today."

"Uh . . ." Scott blinked slowly.

"What? You're eighteen, and you don't cum more than once a day?"

"I . . . uh—"

"Okay, we'll discuss that in a minute. Right now, I need a washcloth or a towel before I drip on the bed. I'd stand up and go to the kitchen, but I'd leave a trail from here to there." He swiped his hand on the side of his chest before a dribble slid to the rug. "Would you mind bringing me something?"

"Uh, right." Scott stood up and walked toward the kitchen. "Is a paper towel okay?"

"Better make it two."

Scott returned with three sheets of paper towel. He laid them on the rug beside Bailey, returned to his seat, and watched Bailey clean himself up. As Bailey wiped semen from his chest and belly, Scott wondered why he wadded the towels so quickly.

Bailey crumpled the three towels together and extended his hand toward Scott. "Here you go, mate. I'm going to need a couple more. I'd get them myself, but I'm still afraid I might drip. I guess it was a bit more than average for a first go-round. That's what I get for waiting this late in the day. Actually, a couple of wet towels would be just the ticket."

Despite his calm exterior, Scott did not comprehend what was happening at the moment, did not have a clue about what would happen next. He did not know what to say; he did not know what to think. The situation was so far beyond Scott's range of experience, he felt adrift in the flow of Bailey's erotic scenario. Scott stood up and took the wadded towels from Bailey's hand. He glanced at the semen on Bailey's chest, walked to the kitchen, and turned on the tap.

"Since you've got the water running," called Bailey, "would you mind filling my glass and bringing that as well?"

Wet paper towels in one hand, a glass of water in the other, Scott returned to the living room to find Bailey sitting at the edge of the single mattress, legs bent at the knees, feet flat on the floor. As Scott stepped closer, he saw Bailey's penis curving away from his body, its length and girth all the more striking against the black fabric. Bailey swiveled toward Scott and extended his legs on either side of him. Scott saw the snarls of semen in Bailey's pubic hair.

"What are you doing." Scott held an arm out to keep the water from spilling.

"Lending a helping hand." Bailey unbuttoned Scott's jeans.

"Hold on a minute." Scott tried to back away without spilling the water, but Bailey pulled him closer by the waistline of his pants. In one deft movement, Bailey pulled Scott's zipper down and lowered his pants to the floor. Bailey paid no attention to the horizontal bulge in Scott's cotton briefs; all the same, his glans protruded from his foreskin, and his penis began to rise.

"Relax, amigo," Bailey teased. "You get to leave your undies on. We'll think of them as your bathers, but these jeans have got to go. Now, please step out of them before I wrestle them off, and that glass of water goes through the window."

Scott looked from the glass to the window, then back to Bailey. Bailey lifted one of Scott's ankles out of his pants. He repeated the process with Scott's other ankle, then tossed the pants on the chair.

"There you go, mate. You're one step closer to what God had in mind."

"According to who?"

"According to me. The gospel according to Bailey."

Scott's expression did not change. "Where do you want the water?"

Bailey took the glass from Scott, reached around, and placed it on the windowsill. Scott looked down to see clear fluid oozing from Bailey's urethra. Bailey turned back and smiled, noting the focus of Scott's gaze. He looked down and saw the pre-ejaculate.

"Not to worry, mate. It won't hit your rug." Bailey wiped an index finger across his glans, licked it clean, then reached out for the wet paper towels. Scott laid the towels on Bailey's open palm, stepped over to the double mattress, and sat down. Bailey dabbed the semen from his pubic hair, holding his penis to one side after the other, sliding his foreskin a fraction of an inch with each adjustment. "That'll do it," he said, rising to his feet. He took a step closer to Scott, bringing his semi-erect penis within a foot of Scott's face. Scott raised his eyes to see Bailey's expression. Bailey raised his eyebrows and nodded. "Clean as a whistle, right?"

"I'll take your word for it." Scott sat up straight without moving his hands.

"Good enough." Bailey smiled, then walked to the kitchen.

Scott took advantage of Bailey's momentary absence. He stood up and crossed the room, calling out, "I need to pee."

"Take your time," Bailey replied. "It looks like you might have technical difficulties of your own."

Scott closed the bathroom door as far as the jamb thinking the sound of closing it completely would make him seem overly self-conscious. In his present condition, it would be impossible to pee standing up. Scott lowered the toilet seat soundlessly. He pushed his underpants to his ankles, sat down with his knees wide apart, and angled his erection toward the bowl. He'd been waiting so long, it took a moment for everything to engage, but then a short spurt followed by a steady stream splashed the water.

As if on cue, Bailey entered the bathroom. There was nothing

Scott could do but keep his erection angled toward the bowl until his bladder was empty. Bailey squatted down, removed Scott's underpants from his ankles, stood up, and walked into the passageway.

"Now your skin can breathe," said Bailey, over his shoulder. "Not to mention providing your guest with a pleasant diversion."

"What?" said Scott, leaning sideways to hear a response.

Bailey did not respond.

Scott remained sitting longer than necessary, hoping his erection would subside. He stood up and faced himself in the mirror, noticing more clearly than he'd expected the faint signs of a suntan line across his belly and thighs. Scott pushed his erection down, but it swung back to its upward curve. *What the hell*, he thought, *when in Rome*. Scott took a slow breath, relaxed his shoulders, and walked into the living room as unselfconsciously as he could manage.

Bailey was sitting at the edge of the single mattress with his knees drawn up, his feet flat on the floor, his erect penis flat against his belly. As Scott crossed the room, he saw Bailey's foreskin was pulled all the way back, the purplish glans, shiny with slick. Bailey extended his arm in front of Scott's thighs, which slowed him to a stop. Bailey turned Scott toward him and studied his penis.

"Good for you," he finally said. "Not as thick as mine but the same length, if not a hair longer, and hard as calculus." Bailey looked up. "You don't get pre-cum?"

Scott shook his head.

"That's hardly fair, no pun intended." Bailey looked at his own penis. He stroked it a couple of times, drew back the foreskin, and a dribble of clear liquid oozed from the urethra. Bailey collected the discharge with two fingers, then smeared it on Scott's glans until it was as shiny as his own. Bailey slapped Scott on the thigh and said, "That should do you for a minute or two. Now, don't waste it." He took hold of Scott's erection and brushed his thumb back and forth across the glans. "How about another beer?"

Scott blinked slowly, turned around, and walked to the kitchen. When he returned, Bailey was standing in the middle of the rug, stroking his penis with his right hand. Bailey reached his left hand out and took the bottle from Scott. He removed his right hand from his penis and clapped Scott on the shoulder.

"Thanks, mate, you're the best." He took a swig of beer, set the bottle on the floor, and began stroking himself again. "So, what classes are you taking this semester?"

Scott wasn't sure if Bailey was serious. By the look on his face, however, he was expecting an answer.

"Uh, you know, reading, writing, and arithmetic."

"Well, it looks like you've got a firm grip on calculus." Bailey's hand sped up as he lowered his eyelids. He let go of his penis, and a drop of clear liquid swung away from his glans on a shiny thread. Bailey looked from his penis to Scott. "Do you want to get that, or should I?"

Scott was at a loss for words.

"It's not going to hurt you, mate. It's totally natural." Bailey shifted his hips in Scott's direction, and the thread stretched an inch lower.

Scott frowned. "I don't want it to fall on the rug."

"Okay, then, it's now or never."

"What am I supposed to do?"

"Just hold out your hand, mate."

Scott considered the implications.

"You've got two seconds before bombs away."

Scott extended his right hand, palm up. Bailey stepped closer and bent his knees. He slowly pushed his penis in the direction of Scott's hand until the ooze coated his palm. At the last moment,

Bailey pushed his glans lower, tapped the puddle a couple of times, then smeared the slick down the length of his penis.

"Thank you very much." Bailey took a step backward. "You did that like a pro. The rest is for you. Waste not, want not." Bailey began stroking his penis more forcefully.

Scott sat perfectly still.

"Come on now," Bailey coaxed. "It's good for your skin." He paused for a moment, then said, "If you don't do it, I'll come over there and do it for you."

Scott took a breath, then rubbed his palm across the top of his penis.

"No wonder you don't cum more than once a day. You're going about it all wrong." Bailey's head tilted slightly backward; he stuck a foot out behind him to steady himself, then stepped forward to recover his balance. "If you don't want this to go on the rug, you might want to get some paper towels."

Scott slid sideways before he stood up. He hurried to the kitchen and returned with a handful of paper towels.

"Where should I put them?" Scott stood at the edge of the rug.

"Hold on to them for a minute. Go ahead and sit down. This is going to take a little longer than the first time."

Scott sat down and slid back in front of Bailey.

"You might want to knock one out before I get too far ahead of you."

"What's that mean?"

"Shoot your wad, mate. I'm going to be two loads ahead of you in about one minute. Take it from me . . . it's the best form of therapy." That said, Bailey gasped; he gripped the base of his penis, stood utterly still for a moment, then began stroking faster.

"Okay, mate, you hold the towels for me, so we don't get anything on the rug." Bailey took a step closer, spread his feet, bent his knees, and pushed his hips toward Scott. Scott looked from

Bailey's groin to his face to see his features soften as if in a swoon. Bailey's breath caught. He groaned. He inhaled slowly, then said, "There it goes." Bailey took another step closer, bringing his penis within an inch of Scott's outstretched hand. The first jet of semen shot across the towel and splashed onto Scott's forearm, surprising him for its volume and warmth. Bailey groaned, and the second stream splashed across Scott's chest, and then another, and another. Scott was dazed. He could not process the turn of events at the speed they were unfolding. He dabbed a paper towel at his belly as warm liquid trickled down his chest. Another stream splashed across the back of his hand. Scott draped a paper towel over Bailey's glans and held it in place.

"What the hell?" said Scott, wiping his chest. "I thought this time there'd be less."

"That's usually the case." Bailey shrugged, arms at his sides. "What can I say? My cup runneth over."

Scott groaned, then said, "We need more paper towels."

"Allow me." Bailey stepped back, applied pressure to the paper towel at the end of his penis, then removed it and wadded it up. He stepped back farther, squatted down, and took a swig of beer.

"You're dripping," said Scott, looking at Bailey's penis.

Bailey lifted his penis with one hand and caught a short strand of semen in the crumpled paper towel. Bailey stood up and walked to the kitchen, his tumescent penis bobbing and swaying. He returned with a wad of wet paper towels, squatted down in front of Scott, and pulled a single sheet from the soggy mass.

"What are you doing?" Scott reached for the paper towel.

Bailey jerked his hand out of reach. "I'm going to return the favor, mate. Just relax." He brought the towel to Scott's chest and began to wipe away streaks of semen. Scott kept his hands in his lap, thinking they provided some degree of cover.

"You think I can't see your hard-on?" Bailey moved Scott's

arms to his sides, and his erection sprang up against his belly. Bailey continued wiping and dabbing the towel at Scott's chest, now and then moving lower, which brought his forearm in contact with Scott's erection. Scott breathed slowly, his eyes out of focus.

"That should do it." Bailey made one last swipe across Scott's belly and stood up. He presented his semi-erect penis within a foot of Scott's face and asked, "Does this look clean enough to you? Can I sit on the velvet chair?"

"No," said Scott, his faculties reinstated.

"Okey-dokey." Bailey winked at Scott. "I didn't want to sit way over there, anyway." He picked up his beer and sat down on the single mattress with one leg bent at the knee. He raised the bottle in Scott's direction, then finished the contents in three large gulps. He looked at the empty bottle, then at Scott. "Are there any more of these?"

"Yes." Scott's tone was more resigned than hospitable.

"No, please." Bailey stood up. "I'll get it myself."

Bailey returned from the kitchen, holding a bottle by its neck. "I don't mean to drink you out of house and home, but I need to replenish my liquids if we keep going like this."

Scott wanted to respond but fumbled for something appropriate. Finally, for lack of anything better, he said, "I have an early class in the morning."

Bailey stopped midway across the room. He turned to Scott and said, "Does that mean we should go to bed?"

"No." Scott returned his hands to his lap. "It means I can't stay up all night. I have a full day tomorrow, and that ain't easy under the best of circumstances, as in a full night's sleep and all of my reading completed."

"If you need to do some homework, I can entertain myself."

"That goes without saying."

"You're just jealous."

Scott inhaled.

"I can finish my beer, though, right?"

Scott did not respond.

Bailey took a swig.

"Actually," said Scott, standing up, "I will have a beer. It'll help me get to sleep." Scott walked into the kitchen.

Bailey raised his voice. "So, we are going to bed."

Scott walked back into the room and slowed to a stop facing Bailey. "No, we are not going to bed." He sat down and took a swig of beer.

"It's good to see you strutting your stuff." Bailey swiveled his hips for emphasis. He caught his penis mid-swing, then eased the foreskin back to reveal a drop of pre-ejaculate. He looked from his penis to Scott. "Being self-conscious about one's sexuality is for the birds. Well, not really"—finger quotes—"for the birds. The birds are perfectly fine with their sexuality. We're the only animals who shriek at the thought. Whoops. Did I say '*shriek* at the thought'? I meant to say '*shrink* at the thought.' Either way, now that I think about it. Okay, okay, don't get me started." Bailey lowered himself to sit cross-legged within reach of Scott's bare feet.

Scott took a swig of beer. Bailey took a sip from his bottle, then placed it on a black tile. He reached out and lifted Scott's feet onto his calves, causing Scott's legs to fall open in the shape of a square, one point where his bare feet rested sole-to-sole on Bailey's legs, another at the base of his erection.

"You have handsome feet, " said Bailey, tilting his head for a better view.

"So do you." Scott smiled tipsily.

Bailey looked up. "Are you drunk?"

"No." Scott exhaled. "I don't know . . . maybe a little."

"That's adorable." Bailey slid his hands along Scott's shins to his knees and then a bit higher. "A little drunk on half a beer."

Scott held his bottle up to the light. "I drank more than half. It's almost empty." Scott raised the bottle to his lips and finished it off. "There, you see?" He held the bottle out for Bailey. Bailey took the bottle, held it to the light, then placed it beside his bottle on the floor. He brought his half-full bottle to his lips and took a sip as his other hand advanced onto Scott's thigh to keep himself from falling backward. Bailey offered his bottle to Scott, but Scott shook his head. Bailey returned the bottle to the floor, then placed his hand midway along Scott's other thigh. At this point, Scott's erection was pulsing in time with his heartbeat, and Bailey's head was nodding ever so slightly in response.

"Now I know how a snake charmer feels." Bailey raised his hands and played an imaginary flute. He held Scott's gaze as he returned his hands to Scott's body, stroking his penis with one, caressing his testes with the other. Scott's eyelids lowered slowly, then raised halfway.

"Have you ever had a 'beer-job'?" Bailey continued stroking Scott's penis with the same detachment he'd exercised with himself throughout the evening.

Scott lowered his brow. "I'm not sure I understand the question." He leaned slightly backward, supporting himself on straight arms. "You mean work in a bar?"

Bailey picked up his bottle and took a sip. He then rolled onto his knees and slid the glans of Scott's penis into his mouth.

Scott gasped at the shock of cold liquid and warm lips. Bailey worked his mouth slowly up and down just beyond the corona of Scott's swollen glans. When the beer started to trickle from the corner of his mouth, Bailey swallowed the liquid and pushed his mouth halfway down the length of Scott's erection. Scott sat up, which brought him closer to the edge of the mattress. Bailey placed his hands on Scott's buttocks and dragged him forward until he was on his feet. Scott stood up while Bailey continued sliding his mouth up and down his penis. After a moment, Bailey pulled away, wiping tears from his eyes.

"I'm not sure I'm man enough," said Bailey, taking a breath. "But I'll never forgive myself if I don't give it the old college try." He placed his hands at Scott's waist and moved him around to the single mattress. "You need to lie down with your legs and ass on the mattress and your head and chest on the rug like I was a little while ago." Bailey adjusted Scott with his hands until he was lying down, halfway on the mattress, halfway on the rug.

Scott folded his hands behind his head and closed his eyes. Bailey placed Scott's erection in his mouth and lowered his head until he pressed his nose into pubic hair. Scott groaned and lifted his hips, pushing his penis farther still. Bailey held himself in place for a moment, then pulled his head back, gasping for air, strands of saliva stretching from his mouth to Scott's glans. As if in a trance, Bailey lowered his head and slid his mouth up and down Scott's erection, changing his tempo from slow glide to eager piston, farther and farther until his lips were pressing against pubic bone.

Scott was overwhelmed by mixed emotions. As much as he dreaded ejaculation with its attendant nausea, guilt, and self-recrimination, he could not resist the warm-wet friction of Bailey's mouth. After an hour of visual foreplay, the rush of Scott's climax came as much of a surprise to him as it did to Bailey. Scott's pelvis lifted in response to Bailey's hand cupping his testes; his breath caught, and everything stopped . . . everything but the excruciating tension, suspended between fulfillment and devastation, tilting toward one with certainty of the other, and then he bucked; he bucked and writhed; his penis, contracting with each pulse of semen; Bailey groaning, stroking, swallowing, matching Scott's movements as if born to the sport.

No sooner had Scott taken a slow breath than he pulled Bailey's head away from his groin. Bailey looked up, features slack, eyes out of focus. He mumbled, "Oh my God," then opened his mouth and lowered his head toward Scott's penis.

"You need to leave." Scott slid sideways, stood up, and walked around to the closet. He reached out and steadied himself as half a dozen chemicals coursed through his veins. Scott took a deep breath, then pulled on his jeans. He yanked a shirt from a hanger, pushed one arm after the other through the sleeves, slipped his feet into a pair of deck shoes. Scott was buttoning the front of his shirt as he walked into the living room and said, "You need to leave."

"Are you serious?" Bailey was sitting on the rug with his back against the double mattress.

"Don't talk. You need to get dressed and leave. I mean it. Get up and get out of here, or I'm going to call the police."

Bailey shook his head. "Seriously, mate, tell me what's wrong."

"I'm telling you—don't talk. I'm telling you— get out of here." Scott clenched his fists. "If you don't get out of here *now*, I'll throw your clothes outside and call the police."

"Jesus Christ." Bailey rose to his feet. "I thought we were having a good time."

"What don't you understand about not talking? If you say one more word, I'm going downstairs to get your license plate number. Get dressed and get out of here *now*."

Scott stood where he was until Bailey left the apartment. As soon as Scott heard the gate close, he stepped to the door, turned the lock, and switched off the porch light. Scott switched off the floor lamp, and the room was transformed from tropical rain forest to pale-blue moonscape, eerily quiet, calm, and cool. Scott walked into the bathroom and looked out the window to see the swirl of exhaust from Bailey's Mercedes-Benz as it pulled into the alley and disappeared from view.

Scott returned to the living room with a standard pillow under his arm. He tossed the throw pillows from the single mattress onto the double mattress, pulled back the faux-fur cover, the top sheet, and blanket. Scott threw off his clothes, crawled into bed, and closed his eyes.

11:00 AM

"What's that?" Scott craned his neck for a better view of a sky-scraper under construction.

"The Bank of America Building," said Allison, slowing down for a red light.

"Holy cow." Scott rolled down his window. "How tall is it?"

"Fifty-two stories. It's the tallest building west of the Missis-sippi. Another geographic reference would be the architecture of the top floors, which some say are meant to suggest the High Sierras." Allison laughed to himself. "Others say they look like the coin dispenser on a conductor's belt."

"I vote for the last one," said Scott. "That's hilarious."

"Either way," Allison replied, "it sticks out like a sore thumb."

"Everyone's a critic." Scott rolled up his window as they turned onto Lombard Street.

"Actually, Scott," said Allison, looking in the rearview mirror, "that's the consensus of opinion."

Scott paused before he replied, "Which is why I said 'every-one.' "

Allison held his eyes on Scott for a beat before returning them to the road.

"Daddy," said Louise, "since we're only a couple of blocks away, wouldn't it be nice to drive by the Palace of Fine Arts?"

Allison looked at his watch. "I don't know, Mother. It's already eleven fifteen."

"We don't have to stop," Louise replied, her voice buoyant and bright. "It's such a beautiful day, darling. I love seeing the lake when the sun's reflecting off the water. We could drive by, turn around, and come right back. That way, we'd see it coming and going, and we'd be back where we started in no time." Louise turned to Kathy. "Wouldn't you like to see the Palace of Fine Arts on this beautiful morning, Kathy Sue?"

Kathy offered a perfunctory smile, then said, "Yes."

In support of her request, Louise started describing the landmark to Scott. "The Palace of Fine Arts is this really pretty building. Well, I don't know if you'd call it a *building*, really"—looking at Allison—"would you, Daddy?"

"I'd say more of an open-air structure," Allison replied as he turned onto Baker Street.

Louise giggled, then said, "Oh, thank you, sweetheart." She reached over and caressed Allison's shoulder. "Well, Scott, you're going to see it for yourself in about two shakes of a lamb's tail."

Kathy inhaled. Scott rolled his eyes for Kathy's benefit, which prompted a ripple of laughter. Allison cleared his throat as a warning shot across the bow. Louise looked out the window, anticipating the scene as it came into view.

"Oh look, Scott," cried Louise. "There it is, honey. Isn't that *beautiful*?"

"As a matter of fact," said Scott, leaning toward Kathy's window, "that is very beautiful." Scott scooted closer. "Gosh, when I grow up, I want to live there. Is that it? Not that anything's lacking. But is there a building attached that's, you know, weatherproof? Is there a garage?"

"Well, yes, honey," said Louise. "There's a building behind what you can see from the street, but I'm not sure about a garage."

"That's okay."

A family of swans, snow white and stately, glided through passing reflections of the clouds overhead. Late morning sunlight illuminated the rotunda, the curved pergolas, the shimmering foliage of the surrounding trees.

"Which are the most dangerous," said Kathy, leaning away from Scott, "swans or geese?"

Scott looked at Kathy. He narrowed his eyes and said, "Is this a trick question?"

"Nope," said Kathy, meeting his gaze. "The answer is swans."

"Swans?" Louise looked at Kathy.

"Yep," Kathy replied, curiously smug. "Swans are so territorial when they're nesting that geese never make a home in the same location. All the same, geese should not be considered friendly fowl."

Scott laughed through his nose.

"That's very interesting, Kathy." Louise smiled, then added, "But I'm pretty sure 'dangerous' is too strong a word."

"No," said Scott, "Kathy's right. When it comes to swans and geese, white makes right."

Kathy nodded, then asked, "Do you know the difference between monkeys and apes."

"Are you serious?" Scott made a face. "Or is this a joke? Like what's the difference between ignorance and apathy?"

"Not a joke," Kathy replied. "Do you know the difference between monkeys and apes?"

"Monkeys have tails," said Scott, "and we don't."

"A-plus for remembering your high school biology." Kathy furrowed her brow. "What about that other one? The difference between—"

"Ignorance and apathy?"

Kathy nodded.

"I don't know," said Scott, shrugging his shoulders, "and I don't care."

It took Kathy a moment, but then her laughter bubbled over.

"Scott," said Louise, turning partway around. "Did you have breakfast, honey?"

"No, I left my apartment at seven o'clock. But I'm not much of a breakfast person unless it's waffles with bacon and eggs, which I have for dinner every so often."

"That sounds good," said Kathy. "We should have waffles for dinner once in a while."

"Well, Kathy Sue," said Louise, "you know where the waffle iron is. Whenever it strikes your fancy, you're more than welcome to—"

"Wow," said Scott, "that's the Golden Gate Bridge." He leaned forward as they followed Doyle Drive toward the bridge. Cables curving from tower to tower were a testament to man's ingenuity. The towers themselves held Scott's attention; for several breaths, he considered their function, their relationship, their asymmetry. "I knew it was red, which has always confused me, but, *holy cow*, that's one heck of a structure."

"That's a common misconception," said Allison, more than happy to point one out. " 'The Golden Gate' is the mile-wide strait that connects the San Francisco Bay with the Pacific Ocean. Therefore the bridge is named for the body of water it spans, not the precious metal."

"Good to know," said Scott. "That's one less thing for me to fret about. Actually—I just learned this—I should've said 'one *fewer* thing for me to fret about' because the things I fret about can be counted—unless 'infinite' throws a wrench in the works—or, recalling our earlier topic, throws a *monkey wrench* in the works. Anyway, the word 'less' is used when you refer to something that cannot be counted, like—I have *less* money than I need. Although, now that I think about it, 'one less thing to fret about' is probably a colloquialism and sounds familiar to the ear. Be that as it may, 'one fewer thing to fret about' has nice consonance, if you care one way or another about that sort of thing. What do you think, Kathy Sue?"

"Mom," said Kathy, ignoring Scott altogether. "I have to wash my gym clothes before Monday."

"Well," said Louise, tilting her head from side to side, "I'm sure that can be arranged."

"That's surprising," said Scott, leaning toward his window. "I didn't know people could walk across the bridge." Scott turned his attention from the sidewalk on the east side of the bridge to the sidewalk on the west side. "Oh wow, people are riding bikes across over there. This is fantastic."

Seagulls, riding easterly currents, dipped and soared in the cloud-swept sky.

"We're coming into Marin County, Scott." Louise turned her head. "After we pass through the tunnel there, you'll be able to see Sausalito. It's really pretty, with restaurants and shops right on the water and a marina full of artistic houseboats. You'd really like it.

"If we had more time, honey, we could stop for lunch and stroll around a bit. . . . Maybe on your next visit."

12:00 PM

A few minutes past noon, Allison pulled off the road in front of a wrought-iron gate attached by hinges to a pair of brick columns. The column on the right featured a black metal plaque with the word "OAKCREST" in bold relief.

"Wow," said Scott, leaning forward as Allison unlocked the padlock and pushed the gate open.

"You ain't seen nothin' yet," said Louise, sliding over to the driver's side of the seat. She shifted into first gear and drove far enough down the driveway for Allison to close the gate behind them. Louise slid back to the passenger's side of the seat as Allison climbed inside the bus.

Proceeding down the driveway, Scott looked from window to window, taking in the sun-dappled woods along both sides of the road. A hundred yards farther, Scott leaned to the left to get a better view of an unpainted clapboard house as the bus crunched to a stop on raked gravel. Scott hopped out of the car and walked toward the single-story building, noting the paned windows with open shutters, the stonework chimney, the bent-willow chairs on the shaded porch, the rough-hewn front door.

Scott continued walking like he knew where he was going. He followed the stone path around the side of the house, drawn in that direction by the sound of rushing water. When he rounded the corner, he slowed to a stop and drank in the beauty of the cabin's "backyard." Three separate decks of varied shape and size were connected by wooden stairs that descended a steep slope to the lowest deck, a cantilevered rectangle above a boulder-strewn riverbed.

Scott strode across the first deck, observing the round table with umbrella and chairs, the chaise lounges with small tables between them. He ran down the first set of stairs and jogged across the middle deck. Scott descended the second set of stairs at the same pace but then slowed his step as he crossed the lower deck, where he came to a stop with his waist against the railing. Scott could not remember air so fragrant. He felt the moisture on his lips and eyelashes, tasted pine needles and riverbed algae with every breath. The slopes of the ravine, studded with rocks and alpine greenery, magnified the sounds of the river below, the low hum of deep currents, the high notes of white water splashing over rocks. A trio of barn swallows, streaks of brown and green following the river's path, winged past the deck.

"Yahoo," shouted Scott, cheering them on as they disappeared from view.

From the middle deck, Louise called out, "What's happening down there?"

Scott turned around and called back, "Some feathered friends on their way to something very important downstream." Scott retraced his steps to the stairs.

"In their case," said Louise, "it really is the journey, not the destination. They're eating mosquitos right out of the air."

"God bless them." Scott climbed the stairs to join Louise. "I never understood the point of mosquitos until I learned they were bird food."

"Speaking of food,"—Louise put her arm through Scott's—"we'll be having lunch on the upper deck."

"Sounds like we're on an ocean liner—but I'd rather be here. This place is amazing."

"Yes, Scott, it is." Louise pulled herself closer. "Oakcrest is why we moved to Santa Rosa, honey. We weren't planning to move here. But you know how it goes. Sometimes, an opportunity presents itself when you least expect it. We were driving through these mountains a year ago, just for the scenery, when we saw the 'FOR SALE' sign. We put down a deposit that afternoon."

"Let me just say, if you put my name next to 'Oakcrest' in your will, I'd be much obliged."

"Well," said Louise, shaking her head, "I'll keep that in mind." She tugged Scott closer. "First things first, honey. While I organize our lunch in the kitchen, you can help your sister bring everything to the table. We're having ham and cheese sandwiches on rye bread, homemade coleslaw, potato chips, and iced tea. How's that sound?"

"Do you have any milk?"

"Yes, Scott, we do." Louise paused for a beat, then said, "Would you prefer a glass of milk, honey?"

"Yes, Louise, I would." Scott gave his mother a sidelong glance.

"All right, sweetheart." Louise smiled uncertainly.

By way of changing the subject, Scott asked if there was indoor plumbing?

"Yes, sweetheart. Do you need to use the little boys' room?"

"That will have to do if there isn't a men's facility."

"Whatever you want to call it, Scott, we do have indoor plumbing."

After lunch, Kathy offered to clear the table and do the dishes. "There's not that much to do," she said, loading a tray with plates and glasses.

"Thank you, sweetheart." Louise stood up from the table. "Scott, you and I can go down to the middle deck and have a nice chat. Daddy,"—turning to Allison—"would you like to join us?"

"I believe I'll take advantage of the weather and clear the brambles from behind the woodshed," said Allison.

"All right, darling. Be sure to wear your work gloves and a long-sleeved shirt."

"Yes, Mother, I will."

Scott leaned against the railing a few feet from where Louise was sitting on a wooden bench that wrapped around two sides of the middle deck.

"Are you enjoying your classes this semester?" Louise took a pack of cigarettes from her sweater pocket.

"Jeez, Louise," said Scott, clearly surprised. "I've never seen you smoke. How long has this been going on?"

"Oh, well,"—tapping a cigarette from the pack—"I suppose I started when I was dating your father, but no more than once in a while on special occasions."

"This is a special occasion?"

"Well, yes, sweetheart, having you with us for the weekend is a very special occasion."

Scott took a pack of cigarettes and a book of matches from his shirt pocket. He lit Louise's cigarette, then his own.

Louise blew a stream of smoke. "You didn't answer my question, sweetheart."

"Which question?"

"Are you enjoying your classes this semester?"

"Not so much." Scott took a drag on his cigarette. "As a matter of fact, I'm taking the Air Force entrance exam when I get home Monday afternoon."

"You are?" Louise tilted her head. "What's that mean, sweetheart? You're going to enlist?"

"At some point, unlikely as that may seem." Scott extended his arm beyond the railing and tapped ash from his cigarette.

"My gosh, Scott." Louise cast her gaze into the middle distance. A moment later, she returned her eyes to Scott. "Will you be going to Vietnam?"

"Hell, no," said Scott, shaking his head. "That's why I'm enlisting in the Air Force. The test I'm taking on Monday has four parts—general, administrative, mechanical, and electrical. Depending on your scores in each category, you're eligible for specific jobs, which you choose from before you sign up."

"I'm not sure what you mean by 'specific jobs,' sweetheart." Louise shook her head slowly. "Doesn't everybody, I don't know,"—raising her eyebrows—"*go to war.*"

"Not in the Air Force. Which is why you have to wait at least a year after you take the test before you can sign up—*if* you qualify. Everybody's trying to enlist in the Air Force because nobody wants to go to Vietnam." Scott took a final drag on his cigarette; as he exhaled, he held up the butt with a quizzical look.

Louise reached beneath the bench and brought out an ashtray with a hinged lid. She held it out to Scott. "Do you have any idea what sort of job you'd be interested in, honey?"

"Meteorologist seems like the safest bet." Scott took the ashtray and tamped out his cigarette.

Louise furrowed her brow. "You want to be a weatherman?"

"I suppose that's a common misconception—meteorologist and weatherman—but one's not necessarily the other." Scott grinned. "To be more precise, a weatherman on TV is no more likely to be a meteorologist than a meteorologist is likely to be a weatherman on TV."

Louise moved her head from side to side.

"The thing about being a meteorologist in the Air Force," Scott continued, "according to the recruitment officer I met with, is you'll likely be stationed in Greenland, which is a good distance from Vietnam. And by 'good,' I mean 'good' in more ways than on. The bugaboo is that meteorologist is one of the jobs in the highest level of the General category, which means you pretty much have to get a perfect score on that part of the test to qualify."

"What happens if you don't qualify?" Louise tamped out her cigarette and placed the ashtray beneath the bench.

"Taking the test doesn't mean you're signing up. It lets you and Uncle Sam know what jobs you're eligible for, and then you take it from there. Do you want a job you're eligible for? Does Uncle Sam want you? I don't know if you've seen the posters, but that last one's pretty much a given."

"What's pretty much a given?" said Kathy, coming down the stairs.

"That Uncle Sam wants *you*," replied Scott, pointing his finger at Kathy.

"Why would Uncle Sam want me?" Kathy sat down a few feet short of Louise.

"He doesn't want you," said Scott. "But he sure as hell wants me."

"Yeah, but you're in school. So you're safe, right?" Kathy lifted her feet to the bench and hugged her knees.

"That's a mixed blessing," replied Scott, stepping over to a couple of chairs. He turned the closest one around and sat down. "Going to school in the land of the free and the home of the brave keeps a boy safe from harm, or so it would seem. But what good is keeping all your limbs when your brain's dying on the vine?"

"Is that some kind of weird poem?" Kathy screwed up her face.

"It wasn't meant to be." Scott shrugged. "But, you know, art happens."

"That remains to be seen,"—Kathy smirked—"or heard. Anyway, what's the deal? Are you dropping out of school?"

"That also remains to be seen." Scott crossed his legs. "The deal is, in two words or less, school's boring, profoundly boring.

All the same, I'd rather not visit the snake-infested countryside of North Vietnam. So, I'm taking the Air Force entrance exam on Monday, and I'll enlist if they agree to send me somewhere safe."

"Wow." Kathy frowned at the unexpected news. "Are you sure school's not the lesser of the evils?"

"It's all relative, don't ya know? And 'evil' is the operative word. School, no matter how dull, would be less evil than guerilla warfare in a tropical rainforest." Scott grimaced for effect. "But four years, all expenses paid, in Greenland, which is mostly snow-white, by the way, far surpasses the trials and tribulations of undergraduate endeavors."

"Nothing about school interests you, honey?" Louise leaned forward, inserting herself into the conversation.

Scott stood up more abruptly than the moment warranted. He started to say something, glaring at his mother, but then composed himself, breathing slowly as his features relaxed.

More to Kathy than Louise, Scott said, "I brought something that was passed out in my Psych 101 class yesterday as an example of 'perceived reality.' I think it'll amuse you. It cracked me up anyway. Okay, I'll be right back." Scott bounded up the stairs two at a time.

"How long are we staying here?" said Kathy.

"I don't know, sweetheart. Why? Do you have plans for this evening?"

"*No.*" Kathy exhaled. "I was just wondering."

"I suppose we'll be home by five or five thirty. We're going to have meatloaf for dinner, and it'd be much appreciated if you'd give your poor old mother a hand in the kitchen."

"Doing what?" Kathy tempered her tone with practiced precision.

"Well," Louise replied, tilting her head from side to side. "Do I need to present you with a list of options before you decide?"

"No. But I'd like to know if you mean setting the table or peeling potatoes?"

"Well, now that you mention it, sweetheart, scalloped potatoes sounds like a good idea."

"*Mom.*"

Scott returned somewhat short of breath, flourishing a sheet of letter-size paper.

"Okay," said Scott. "As I said, this was passed out by my psychology teacher, who received it from a friend of his who teaches linguistics at MIT."

Louise rolled her eyes and shook her head as a sign that Scott's introduction had landed with a thud. Louise looked at Kathy. "Did you understand that, Kathy Sue?"

" 'Linguistics' has to do with language, right?" Kathy looked at Scott.

"Yes," Scott replied, nodding slowly. "And 'MIT' is the Massachusetts Institute of Technology, one of our country's most prestigious schools, located a hop, skip, and a jump from Harvard University, with which I'm certain you're both familiar."

"Thank you, Scott," said Louise, shaking her head. "I think we get the picture. On another note, sweetheart, your mother's going to need a trip to the little girl's room in about three minutes, so you need to speed things up, or we need to take a break." Louise offered a look of desperation for emphasis.

"All right, all right," said Scott. "Let me read this before Mom has an accident." Scott lowered his voice to a deeper, professorial tone.

"In John R. Ross's linguistics dissertation 'CONSTRAINTS ON VARIABLES IN SYNTAX,' Mr. Ross begins with:
"The following anecdote is told of

William James. I have been unable to find any published reference to it, so it may be that I have attributed it to the wrong man, or that it is apocryphal. Be that as it may, because of its bull's-eye relevance to the study of syntax, I have retold it here.

"After a lecture on cosmology and the structure of the solar system, James was accosted by a little old lady.

" 'Your theory that the sun is the center of the solar system, and that the earth is a ball which rotates around it, has a very convincing ring to it, Mr. James, but it's wrong. I've got a better theory,' said the little old lady.

" 'And what is that, madam?' inquired James politely.

" 'That we live on a crust of earth which is on the back of a giant turtle.'

"Not wishing to demolish this absurd little theory by bringing to bear the masses of scientific evidence he had at his command, James decided to gently dissuade his opponent by making her see some of the inadequacies of her position.

" 'If your theory is correct, madam,' he asked, 'what does this turtle stand on?'

" 'You're a very clever man, Mr. James, and that's a very good question,' replied the little old lady, 'but I have an answer to it. And it's this: the first turtle stands on the back of a second, far larger, turtle, who stands directly under him.'

" 'But what does this second turtle stand on?' persisted James patiently.

"To this, the little old lady crowed triumphantly, 'It's no use, Mr. James—it's turtles all the way down.' "

Scott looked up to see Kathy forcing a smile and Louise blinking her eyes.

"That fell short of the mark," said Scott, "or vice versa."

Kathy at first looked puzzled but then narrowed her eyes.

"Well, Scott," said Louise, "that was fascinating."

"Talk about *fascinating*," said Scott. "You should look up the etymology of *that* word."

"What word?" said Kathy.

" 'Fascinating,' " said Scott, raising his brow.

"Can't you just tell us, Scott?" said Louise. "I'm sure we'll be fascinated, honey."

"Don't mind if I do, since you insist. 'Fascinate' derives from the Latin word for 'phallus,' which, of course, is a highfalutin term for 'penis.' There are several variations on the theme, but my favorite is the penis-shaped amulet worn as a preventive against witchcraft." Scott looked at Louise. "Now that I think of it, whenever you hear Nat King Cole singing 'Fascination,' don't you say to Allison, 'Oh, listen, Daddy, they're playing our song'?"

"All right, Scott." Louise looked bewildered and perturbed. "I imagine you could find something wrong with just about everything under the sun if you worked at it long and hard enough."

"Whoa, Nellie," said Scott. "I think the history of words is supremely interesting—as good as it gets in the realm of thought-provoking conversation. The problem with hard and fast rules about acceptable language is the wellspring of words that remain unspoken."

"Okay, Scott, whatever you say." Louise stood up. "I'm going to use the little girls' room. After that, I think we should put every-thing away and hit the road. Don't you agree, Kathy Sue?"

Kathy drew her head back in mock surprise. "I'm just along for the ride. Anything you say is fine with me."

"What time is it?" Scott asked.

Louise checked her watch. "Almost four o'clock, honey."

"That reminds me," said Scott. "I have another fascinating bit of trivia."

"Hold that thought," said Louise, starting up the stairs. "You can dazzle us when we're in the car on the way home. Okay, sweetheart?"

"Yes, sweetheart," said Scott, flaring his nostrils.

Twenty minutes into the drive home, the particulars of that night's dinner and the next morning's breakfast having been discussed ad nauseam, Louise turned to Scott and said, "Weren't you going to share something of interest with us, honey, once we were on the road?"

"Uh . . . yes," Scott replied, floating to the surface of a self-induced trance. " 'O'clock.' Did you know that 'o'clock' is a con-traction of the words 'of the clock'?"

"Well, no, honey, I didn't know that." Louise looked from Scott to Allison. "Did you know that, Daddy?"

"What else would it be, darlin'?" Allison smiled at Louise.

"I wouldn't say it's self-evident." Scott turned to Kathy. "Not to mention, I can't think of any other contraction that accounts for one word missing altogether. Anyway, I think it's a hoot. If we were in Elizabethan England, I might say, 'Why don't we meet at the Pig and Whistle for pork pie and stout at seven of the clock?' "

Kathy giggled.

"I don't know where you come up with this stuff," said Louise, turning around in her seat.

"I didn't come up with it, Mom. I'm just trying to keep things interesting." Scott turned his attention to the urban sprawl at the outskirts of Santa Rosa, not, however, before he saw Allison's eyes in the rearview mirror.

7:00 PM

Dinner for the first time as a guest at the Eddys' table provided Scott with the pleasure of serving himself large portions of what he liked (scalloped potatoes and sautéed mushrooms), a small portion of something unfamiliar (broccoli rabe), none of what he didn't like (carrots and peas). Scott had requested a different vegetable—"anything else"—but Louise had gone ahead with the lowbrow medley because it was one of Allison's favorites. When Louise handed Scott a platter of sliced meatloaf, he served himself the larger of two end-cuts, after which he all but winked at Allison, the Marquis de Sade of mealtime abuse.

After dinner, looking from Louise to Kathy, Scott suggested a game of Scrabble. Scott kept his eyes on Kathy when Allison used paperwork as an excuse for not joining in.

"You kids go ahead and play," said Louise, "while I clean up the kitchen. Kathy Sue, you can clear the table, sweetheart, all right?"

"Yes," said Kathy, sounding anything but enthusiastic.

"Or, Kathy Sue, you can do the dishes, and I'll play Scrabble with Scott. Which would you prefer?"

"Scrabble," said Kathy with a saccharine smile.

"Scott," said Louise, "as soon as the table's clear, you can set up the game right there. All right, honey?"

"Yes, honey," said Scott, bringing a stack of plates to the kitchen counter. "Where's the game?"

"In my bedroom," said Kathy, stepping off in that direction. "I have to use the little girl's room first. After that, I'll be back with the box."

Halfway through the game, Scott urged Louise to the play as she finished drying a Pyrex baking dish.

"We don't mind starting over," said Scott. "It's not like we're playing for money."

"Thank God," said Kathy, studying the board.

"Oh," said Louise, "thank you for asking, honey, but I'm going to set my hair and crawl into bed. It's been a long day for all of us, and we have quite a bit of sight-seeing planned for tomorrow. You kids should think about hitting the hay a little early yourselves. Scott, we're having waffles for breakfast, honey, so you need to be up and at 'em by eight o'clock."

"Sounds good," said Scott. He then arranged *E-M-E-N-T* after Kathy's *E-L*—the second *E* on a DOUBLE LETTER SCORE and the *T* on a DOUBLE WORD SCORE—for a total of twenty-six points.

"Cripes," said Kathy, recording the score. "Does anyone ever beat you?"

Scott looked sideways as if trying to remember. "It did occur once," he finally said, "but the son of a bitch was cheating."

"All right, Scott," said Louise, looking over Kathy's shoulder at her assortment of tiles. Louise reached down and rearranged Kathy's letters. "What about that, sweetheart?"

"Looks good to me," said Kathy, placing *V-I-O-L-A-S* with the *V* and *O* on DOUBLE LETTER SCOREs and the *S* at the end of *E-L-E-M-E-N-T* for a total of thirty points.

"Hey, hey, hey," cried Scott, "no fair ganging up. All I have to say after that maneuver is good night, Irene. And by 'Irene,' I mean 'Louise.' "

Louise giggled, lifted her shoulders, and tilted her head from side to side. She kissed Kathy on the cheek, blew a kiss in Scott's direction, told the children not to stay up until all hours, then walked from the kitchen to the master bedroom.

Half an hour later—Kathy, well and truly trounced—Scott fell into bed, exhausted from the push-pull tension of family dynamics. He opened *Siddhartha* to where he'd placed his boarding pass that morning when the plane began its approach into the San Francisco Airport, flying dramatically low above salt ponds, wetlands, low bridges, and wide stretches of open water.

Now, Scott picked up where he'd left off: Siddhartha fasting for twenty-eight days, "shriveling fingers" and "stubbly beard." And then, one of those surprise sentences Scott so much admired:

> He saw merchants doing business, princes leaving for the hunt, mourners lamenting their dead, whores offering their services, doctors busy with patients, priests determining the proper day to begin sowing, lovers in love, mothers nursing their children—and none of it was worth the trouble of a glance, it was all a lie, it all stank, it all stank of lies, it all gave the illusion of meaning and happiness and beauty, and it was all unacknowledged decay.

"Ain't that the truth," murmured Scott, turning the page. As much as he preferred to read to the end of a chapter, his eyelids would not comply. Scott looked at the clock-radio, then took a slow breath. He'd not turned the lights out before ten o'clock on a Saturday night since he'd left home on his eighteenth birthday.

Scott considered his options, which were pretty much the same as when he'd lived under Allison's roof. Whatever he chose to do, he'd be left to do it alone in his room, albeit Kathy's room on this occasion. Still, the parallels of isolation and proximity were enough to stir up the tamped-down emotions of frustration and fury that had been the leitmotif of his years with his mother and stepfather. What came next was equally familiar, the impulse to masturbate as a diversion, but Scott was accustomed to masturbating in the shower, which provided an immediate change of focus from the revulsion he knew would occur as soon as he climaxed.

Scott reached over and switched off the bedside lamp. He rolled onto his side, plumped his pillow, and closed his eyes. Well-practiced at suppressing his feelings, Scott visualized the first page of the second movement of the *Moonlight Sonata*. He recalled the motion of his head and shoulders as he "plucked" the melody from the keys, the mirror image of his hands as the staccato echoed in one register after the other. After he repeated the second section, his mind drifted to thoughts of reading the music while his arm had been in a cast . . . to thoughts of Mrs. Hudson, his first piano teacher . . . to his uncle swooping into his grandparents' living room when he'd first played *Mary Had a Little Lamb*. . . .

SUNDAY

SEPTEMBER 22, 1968

8:00 AM

Scott rolled onto his back. He'd been half-awake since seven fifteen, drifting in and out of dreamless sleep, delaying, as long as possible, his first full day with the family in almost two years. Now, however, Scott could no longer resist the smell of bacon wafting from the kitchen. He swung his feet to the floor, slipped on a flannel shirt over his T-shirt, a pair of khaki trousers over his low-rise briefs. Scott opened the bedroom door and shuffled through the hallway into the bathroom.

Two minutes later, Scott crossed the L-shaped living room and came to a stop beside the dining table, where Kathy was arranging flatware on blue-striped placemats.

"Good morning, sleepyhead," said Louise, smiling at Scott as she closed the oven door. "We were beginning to wonder if we'd see you before lunch, honey."

"Nobody in their right mind could stay in bed with the smell of frying bacon in the air." Scott inhaled and widened his eyes. "It's better than an alarm clock."

"Better, perhaps," Louise replied, "but a tad less convenient—not that I'm complaining. There's nothing I'd rather be doing than cooking breakfast for my family. And, although I'm not one to toot my own horn, I have to congratulate myself for preparing all of our favorite dishes—well-done bacon, scrambled eggs with cheddar cheese, waffles with fresh fruit and maple syrup."

"Holy cow," said Scott, steadying himself. "After our not so *petit-déjeuner*, we can all go back to bed and sleep through lunch."

"Oh, no, you won't, sweetheart," said Louise, turning strips of bacon. "After breakfast, we're taking you on a tour of the wine country, and then we're having lunch at a real cute sandwich place in the Valley of the Moon."

"Sounds good." Scott puffed out his chest. "I am, after all, a growing boy." Scott looked around, then asked, "What can I have to tide me over until breakfast?"

"How about a banana?" Kathy replied. "That should *appeal* to your monkey brain."

"Very good, Sue." Scott nodded. "You're almost as clever as you are cute."

Kathy was pleased by the compliment, despite her frown.

Having noticed the perfectly made bed in the master bedroom, Scott considered Allison's whereabouts, but four settings at the table indicated his imminent appearance. Just then, the front door opened, and Allison walked into the room, carrying a brown paper bag in one hand, a Sunday newspaper in the other.

"Good morning, Scott," said Allison, offering an oily smile.

Scott said, "Good morning," without looking at Allison.

"Would you like to see the paper?" Allison paused at the kitchen doorway.

"No." Scott frowned while shaking his head. "Unless they've started printing informative articles without socioeconomic bias."

Allison narrowed his eyes, then stepped into the kitchen.

"I would like to see the entertainment section," Scott called out, even though he could see Allison setting the bag on the kitchen counter.

"There's no need to shout, Scott." Allison fixed his eyes on Louise.

"I didn't see you standing there," Scott replied, testing Allison's self-restraint.

"Scott," said Louise, stepping to the kitchen sink with a frying

98

pan at arm's length, "Allison made a special trip to the grocery store, honey, because we didn't have enough syrup for your waffles."

Scott's reply was indifferent at most.

"Wasn't that nice of him?" said Louise, pressing the point.

"Hmm," said Scott, and nothing more. He turned away from the kitchen, indicating his unwillingness to participate any further in this particular exchange.

Allison walked into the living room. He placed the newspaper on the coffee table, removed the outer section, and continued into the master bedroom, where he closed the door behind him.

Remaining where he stood, Scott glanced at the coffee table but decided against perusing ads for newly released movies until he was back in Long Beach, where the information would be about theaters in his area. More and more often, Scott had driven to Los Angeles to see movies in limited release before Long Beach theaters were included in their wide release. One of his favorite limited-release experiences had occurred nine months earlier when he, his friend Andy Johnson, and Andy's friend Andy Thomas had driven to LA on Christmas Eve to see a movie Scott had seen advertised in the Los Angeles Times.

◆　◆　◆

It took some cajoling on Scott's part to get the guys to make the trip on Christmas Eve. When he offered to chauffeur the trio in his Porsche, they hit the road at seven o'clock.

They made it—Long Beach Freeway, Santa Monica Freeway, La Brea Avenue—to the 4 Star Theatre on Wilshire Boulevard in less than an hour. As they approached the theater, the boys expressed varying reactions to the line of people that extended down the side street as far as they could see. Scott pulled to the curb, and Andy Johnson asked a couple standing in line if they already had their tickets. When they nodded, Scott drove forward to where several cars were idling in front of the ticket booth. Andy jumped out of the car and joined the line of people waiting to buy tickets.

When Andy climbed back in the car, he said, "Drive me around the block and let me out before you park." Holding up three tickets, he continued, "These are three of the last tickets for this showing, as in they're going to be sold out in two minutes. Step on it, buster, or we're going to be sitting in the aisle."

Scott popped the stick into first gear. Noting a lull in traffic from both directions, Scott shot away from the curb into a tight U-turn and sped to the intersection, where he careened around the corner in front of an oncoming bus.

"Jesus Christ!" shouted Andy Thomas from the backseat. "I'd rather live to see what I got for Christmas than die in a car crash trying to see a movie."

" 'O ye of little faith,' " said Scott. "Sit back and enjoy the ride. I guarantee you'll live to see what's under your tree."

"This is good," said Andy Johnson, opening the passenger door as Scott slowed to a stop. Andy hopped out while the car was still moving. He hurried across the street and got in line behind a group of what appeared to be high school cheerleaders. The look on Andy's face was hilarious, lit up with impish glee and paralyzed by the proximity of a boyhood fantasy.

"Hold on," said Andy Thomas. "I'll get out here too."

"The hell you will," said Scott, pressing down on the accelerator. "I'm not doing all the dirty work alone. Drive you guys to LA and then look for a parking place *by myself*."

"Okay, okay," said Andy Thomas. "Quit your griping—wait a minute, wait a minute—I think someone's pulling out of a place right up there. Yes! That's what I'm talking about."

"There, you see," said Scott, slowing to a stop. "If you hadn't stayed in the car, I'd be driving around for who knows how long."

"Yeah, yeah, yeah," said Andy Thomas. "Hurry up and park so we can get in line."

Scott and Andy Thomas jogged up to join Andy Johnson just as the line began moving forward at a surprisingly brisk pace.

"I wonder if they're even checking tickets," said Scott, walking at his usual pace. As they approached the theater entrance, the question of the line's momentum was answered when they saw a pair of ushers at each of the main doors, ripping tickets in half as the single line separated into two streams of anxious fans.

"I need to pee like the future of mankind depends on it," whispered Scott.

"I think we should find our seats first," said Andy Johnson.

"You guys go ahead." Scott grimaced. "I'll find you after I make a deposit. I mean it, I'm barely going to make it through the doors." That said, Scott asked the location of the men's room as an usher ripped his ticket in half.

"To your right, sir."

"Thanks," said Scott, striding off in that direction.

Five minutes later, Scott pushed through the crowd gathered around the refreshment counter and made his way into the theater. Pausing for a moment to get his bearings, Scott then continued down the aisle, looking from side to side, searching for his friends. On the verge of running out of aisle, Scott turned around and looked into the house. When he heard his name called out from behind him, Scott turned around to see Andy Johnson waving from the left side of the middle section's front row.

Scott rolled his eyes. He walked down to the level ground in front of the screen and over to the empty seat beside Andy Johnson.

"I could've gotten good money for this seat," said Andy Johnson.

"Would it have been enough for cab fare home?" said Scott.

"All right," said Andy Thomas, leaning forward. "Now that we're here let's ixnay the squabbling. I, for one, have no idea what to expect, which usually works in my favor because the movie doesn't fall short of my expectations."

"Same for me," said Andy Johnson.

"Ditto," said Scott, stretching his legs straight out in front of him. "Hey, you can't beat these seats for the legroom."

"Shut the fuck up," said Andy Thomas.

"*Okay*," whispered Scott as the house lights began to fade.

One minute into the film, the opening strains of a single guitar were eclipsed by the dulcet harmony of two male voices:

"Hel-lo—dark-ness—my—old—friend . . ."

The boys, along with the rest of the audience, were taken by surprise. After the second line, harmonious and heartfelt as the first, members of the audience exchanged glances, some of them uttered asides. As the voices sped up and soared, the audience was transported to a slow-moving walkway, where they watched a young man on his way into an airport. By the end of the song—the young man at home, sitting in front of an aquarium—the audience had suspended their disbelief and settled in for the ride.

An hour and a half later, when Ben shoved the crucifix through the handles of the church doors, the theater swelled with whistles and cheers; Andy Thomas jumped to his feet; Andy Johnson pulled him back to his seat; Scott brushed tears from his eyes; but then, as if they themselves were sitting at the back of a municipal bus, the audience fell silent as Ben and Elaine contemplated their future. . . .

"I have to see this again," said Scott, leaning forward for Andy

Thomas's benefit. Andy Thomas met Scott's eyes, then raised his brow.

"Now?" said Andy Johnson.

"Why the hell not?"

"I'm game," said Andy Thomas. "Do you think we can stay in the theater? We have to get better seats, though."

"Absolutely," said Scott. "Middle section, middle row."

"Works for me," said Andy Johnson. "Not to mention, this movie is near the top of my all-time top ten. And the music—Jesus Christ. Simon and Garfunkel—who knew? This is the best Christmas present ever."

"I concur," said Scott. "*And* it'll be Christmas day by the time the next showing's over. So, merry Christmas, boys." Scott looked around and saw they were not the only people remaining where they were. "I think we should change our seats sooner than later. After that, who wants popcorn?"

The boys enjoyed the movie even more the second time around. Not for sitting a reasonable distance from the screen, but for the film itself: the acting, the dialogue, the set design, the cinematography, and it goes without saying the music.

On their way home, they deconstructed the film, scene by scene, pointing out their favorite moments, agreeing and disagreeing, joking, laughing, taunting, recollecting favorite parts of other movies, a freewheeling discussion of the silver screen.

When Scott mentioned sitting through two showings of Franco Zeffirelli's *Romeo and Juliet* a couple of weeks earlier, Andy made a wisecrack about "suddenly last summer" when Brooke showed up at the shoe store with an overnight bag on a Friday night.

"Do tell," said Andy Thomas, leaning forward.

After too long a silence, Andy Johnson turned his head and

said, "Things got off to a bumpy start and went straight downhill from there."

"That's not the whole story," said Scott, frowning at Andy Johnson.

"As I said," said Andy Thomas, "do tell."

"Things did get off to a rocky start," Scott allowed, "but then things heated up, and the ice melted."

Andy Thomas burst into laughter. "Things heated up, and *you smelled it?*"

Andy Johnson bit his tongue.

"No," cried Scott. "*The ice melted.*"

"Oh . . . right." Andy Thomas's laughter trailed off. After a moment, he pushed for details, but Scott offered nothing more as he followed the sweeping curve of the freeway's downtown exit.

Andy Johnson returned the discussion to recent movies with his take on the two James Bond films released the previous year, of which he'd seen *You Only Live Twice* three times and *Casino Royale* once.

Andy Thomas climbed out of the backseat in front of his house a few minutes past two o'clock. "Thanks for dragging me along," he said to Scott, speaking through the open door as Andy Johnson got back in the car. "And, by the way," he added, "ho, ho, ho."

"Back atcha," said Andy Johnson, fastening his seat belt.

"Happy Hanukkah," said Scott, pushing the stick into first gear.

"Talk to you later," said Andy Thomas. He stepped onto the sidewalk and gave the guys the peace sign.

Andy Johnson returned the gesture as they pulled away from the curb.

◆　◆　◆

Scott inhaled.

"Where were you, sweetheart?" said Louise. "I asked if you'd like some orange juice, but you didn't answer. Are you all right?"

"Yes," said Scott. "But, no. Orange juice gives me an upset stomach. Remember?"

"Your stomach's still giving you problems, honey?" Louise posed the question as if asking the time of day.

Scott inhaled, then said, "Not so much, now that I'm drinking a quart of milk every day."

"My gosh, honey." Louise looked at Scott with a puzzled expression. "I don't think we have that much milk in the house, sweetheart. If you'd told us yesterday, Allison could have picked up more milk this morning."

"Don't worry about it. It's not a requirement, just a preference." Scott stepped into the living room and shuffled the newspaper sections until he saw the Sunday magazine.

"Kathy Sue," said Louise, "would you be an angel and put the fruit salad on the table?"

"Yes," said Kathy, in the tone she used to mask insolence.

"Thank you, sweetheart," Louise replied, playing her part in their domestic routine. "All right, everybody," Louise called out, "come to the table, *please.*" She stepped into the dining area and placed platters of scrambled eggs and rashers of bacon near the head of the table. "Scott, honey, wouldn't you like to wash your hands before you sit down?"

"Why?" said Scott, tilting his head.

"Weren't you looking at the newspaper, sweetheart?"

"Yes, but I'll take my chances. We don't share the same mindset on the subject of germs, among other things."

"Oh well, Scott." Louise sighed. "I just thought, since you're going to use your fingers to eat your bacon, you'd prefer to have clean hands, honey." She leaned around the corner and raised her voice. "Daddy, breakfast is ready, sweetheart. Come to the table, please, before everything gets cold."

Allison entered the dining room with an audible sigh. He came to a stop at the head of the table as Louise placed a plate of waffles beside a pitcher of syrup. "Good Lord, Louise." Allison frowned as he surveyed the table. "There's enough food here to feed an army."

"It's been so long since the whole family's been together on a Sunday morning," replied Louise, "I thought it'd be nice to have a special breakfast, you know, as part of our celebration."

"What celebration?" said Kathy, eyeing Louise.

Louise looked from Kathy to Allison, then back to her daughter. "Well, Kathy Sue, we're celebrating because Scott's home for the weekend, of course."

Kathy looked from Louise to Allison, sensing more of an explanation than her mother had offered.

"Scott," said Louise, "come to the table, honey, before your breakfast gets cold."

As soon as he finished his breakfast, Allison said he'd be in the bedroom reading the paper until everyone else was ready to leave. Before Allison stood up, Scott forked the last waffle onto his plate, tipped the last of the fruit onto the waffle, emptied the pitcher of syrup.

"Well, Scott," said Louise, "that's one way to clear the table. Kathy Sue, would you be an angel and help your mother with these dishes. I'd like to get going before the morning's half over." With that, Louise started stacking empty dishes. Kathy stood up and carried her plate to the kitchen. "Take your time, Scott," said Louise, stepping over to the stove. "Us girls will have our hands full until it's time to collect your plate."

Scott extended a forkful of waffle and fruit in Louise's direction. "Thanks for breakfast, Mom. I liked all of it."

"Literally." Kathy shook her head. "As in, there's nothing left."

"I do my part," Scott rejoined, scowling for Kathy's amusement.

"Kathy Sue," said Louise, "is that what you're wearing for our outing?"

"*Yes.*" Kathy's tone registered easygoing defiance, which had become the bulwark against her mother's persistent imposition of outlook and preference.

"All right, darling." Louise leveled an impatient smile. "I just thought you'd be more comfortable in something a little nicer than blue jeans, is all."

Scott chimed in, "Is there anything more comfortable than blue jeans?" He stood up and carried his plate to the kitchen.

"I've never thought of blue jeans as being particularly comfortable," Louise replied, taking the dish from Scott's hand.

"That's why they call it the generation gap." Scott put his arm around Louise's shoulders. "And, just to be clear, you're on the wrong side of the abyss."

"Oh well," said Louise, basking in Scott's proximity. "That's why they call it a difference of opinion."

"*Touché,*" said Scott. "And now, please excuse me while I change into my 501s."

"What are 501s?" said Louise.

"Blue jeans," replied Scott and Kathy at the same time.

Half an hour later, as Allison was backing out of their parking space, Louise said, "Let's take Montgomery Road, sweetheart. It's so much prettier than the highway. . . . All right, darling?" she added, uncharacteristically decisive.

Allison did not respond, but by the tone of Louise's voice, when she asked how long it would take to get to their first stop, it was clear Allison had adjusted their route accordingly.

"Oh look, Scott," said Louise, leaning closer to the windshield.

"On that telephone wire, honey, three chicken hawks. Do you see them? Oh my gosh, Scott. Another one just landed. Aren't they majestic?"

"Uh-huh," said Scott, leaning forward to see the birds in question. "Are they really called 'chicken hawks' . . . ? That doesn't sound very majestic."

"I believe those are red-tailed hawks," said Allison. "They're the most likely species in our area. A couple of other varieties are commonly referred to as 'chicken hawks'—the Cooper's hawk and the sharp-shinned hawk—but we don't see them as often as the red-tailed variety."

"The 'sharp *what* hawk'?" said Scott.

"*Shinned*," said Allison, "like the front part of your lower leg, as in 'shin splints.' "

"Ah, yes," said Scott, "I'm well acquainted with shin splints. I enrolled in Track and Field last semester, thinking it would be less demanding than tennis, which may have been true, but I developed a continuing case of shin splints after the first month of training for a half marathon."

"A half marathon," said Kathy. "How far is that?"

"Half as far as a full marathon," Scott replied with a straight face.

Kathy punched Scott in the arm.

"Yeow," cried Scott, rubbing his arm. "Thirteen-point-one miles, and, believe me, that 'point-one mile' can really bring a guy to his knees."

Kathy said, "I don't understand."

"It's simple math, *Kathy Sue*. A full marathon is twenty-six-point-two miles. Therefore, a half marathon is thirteen—"

"No, you idiot," Kathy interrupted. "I don't understand why you're taking PE classes in the first place. You hate PE."

"That is correct," Scott allowed with a minimal shrug. "But the institution of higher learning I attend requires every student to complete three units of physical education, which is a bitch because—"

"Scott," said Louise, "watch your language, honey."

Scott rolled his eyes. "Every student has to complete three units of physical education," he repeated, "which is a *drag* because the classes are pretty much two units each, so you have to take two classes to satisfy the requirement."

"You've taken other PE classes?" Kathy furrowed her brow.

"As a matter of fact," Scott replied, "I have. I took Tennis for Beginners, my first semester last year, Track and Field, my second semester. I dropped out of Track and Field because of shin splints, so this year I'm taking Folk Dancing to complete my three units."

"Folk Dancing?" said Kathy and Louise. Louise turned partway around to look at Scott.

"Yessiree Bob," said Scott. "Ain't that a hoot? And, all the more surreal, we've been learning square dancing steps since the class began."

"Like 'swing your partner' and 'do-si-do'?" Kathy smiled in disbelief.

"Exactly like that. But it's a college class, so we learn about the history and evolution of the dances as well. The who, what, and where, so to speak."

"That's very interesting, Scott," said Louise. She then leaned forward. "Oh look, honey, two more chicken hawks . . . or are those turkey vultures?"

Allison chuckled. "Those are turkey vultures, darlin'."

"Oh, drat," said Louise, taking the information personally. She then perked up. "Scott, Spring Lake Park's right over there, honey. It's too bad you don't like to fish."

"Not really," said Scott.

Louise clicked her tongue. "Anyway, we've had some real nice picnics by the water. After lunch, we usually rent a boat. Allison spends an hour or two fishing, and I go along for the scenery. It's a real pretty area, with the mountains in the background."

"I wouldn't call those mountains," Allison corrected.

"Oh well," said Louise. "You know what I mean."

Everyone kept their eyes on the scenery as Allison drove through the gated entry of the Chateau Montelena Winery and parked within a few yards of the eponymous structure. As striking as the building's ivy-covered facade was, Scott found the arrangement of twenty-nine large casks—each holding 252 gallons of wine— on the courtyard in front of the chateau equally impressive.

"I want you to see the bridges, honey." Louise put her arm through Scott's and tugged him in the direction of a sign that featured an arrow and the words "Jade Lake." They walked along a gray-brick path until they reached two Chinese-motif bridges that continued in different directions to small islands, each with an oriental pavilion. Louise tightened her hold on Scott's arm. "Which one do you want to see first, honey?"

"I can see both well enough from here," said Scott, less enchanted by the scene than Louise expected.

"Oh, Scott," cried Louise. "Look at the swans, honey. Aren't they serene?"

Scott could not help but laugh. "Mom, you really put the 'bash' in 'unabashed.' "

Louise looked perplexed for a moment, then turned her attention back to the swans.

Allison and Kathy walked up.

"Are you going to a pagoda?" said Kathy.

"I think I've seen enough," said Scott.

"All right." Louise tilted her head from side to side. "Maybe we should get back on the road. What do you think, Daddy."

"I'm just along for the ride." Allison grinned. "Whatever you decide is fine with me."

"Kathy Sue," said Louise, "have you seen enough, sweet-heart?"

"Yes," Kathy replied, blinking slowly.

"Okay," sighed Louise. "I guess that settles it." She smiled at Allison. "Where to next, darling?"

Allison fixed his eyes on Louise for a moment, then said, "I believe you wanted Scott to see the Charles Krug Winery."

"Oh, yes." Louise turned to Scott. "It's the oldest winery in the Napa Valley, honey. The man who started it—well, I guess that was Charles Krug. Anyway, more than a hundred years ago, Charles Krug started making wine using a cider press. You know, like they use to make apple cider. Isn't that interesting, Scott?"

"Uh-huh," said Scott, which made Kathy giggle.

The drive from Chateau Montelena to the Charles Krug Winery took all of fifteen minutes. After Allison parked the bus, Louise and Kathy got out and walked toward the main building, a three-story stone structure with dormer windows and a small cupola that looked more like an afterthought than a flourish. Scott headed off in the opposite direction, intrigued by the smaller, more elaborate building that revealed itself as the carriage house. Passing conversation with a groundskeeper informed Scott of the common name for the ornamental trees flanking the building's entrance.

"What do you think, honey?" said Louise, as Scott joined the family at one of the picnic tables beneath a shade tree.

"I don't know," said Scott. "I mean, I'm enjoying the sightsee-ing and all, but this place looks like a resort for people of the cloth. The main building looks like a monastery, and the landscaping is a little sparse for my taste. I do think the carriage house is kind of cute, you know, as in every estate should have one. The skyrocket junipers in front of the carriage house are my favorite part of the trip so far. When I grow up, I'm going to have trees just like those."

"Well, hallelujah, Scott." Louise brought her hands together. "I'm glad something finally meets with your approval."

"All right, Mother," said Allison. "There's no need for that."

Kathy shot a look at Scott, never having heard Allison come to her brother's defense.

"Oh, for goodness' sake," said Louise. "I wasn't serious. Did you think I was serious, Scott?"

Scott inhaled as he considered any answer other than the one Louise expected. Finally, no alternative worth the blowback, he answered, "No."

"Well, of course not." Louise looked from Scott to Kathy. "All right, then. We have one more stop before lunch,"—smiling broadly—"so I suggest we get this show on the road."

The next leg of the trip took less than ten minutes.

"Last, but not least," said Louise, "is the Inglenook Winery."

No sooner had Louise announced their destination than Allison turned onto the two-lane road leading toward the Inglenook Chateau. A few minutes later, walking from the bus to the chateau, Scott remarked on the panoramic view of the surrounding vineyard and the mountains in the distance.

After a beat, Scott added, "If those qualify as mountains."

Louise put her arm through Scott's and pulled him close, reined him in, as it were, as they continued walking.

"Isn't this gorgeous, Scott?" Louise slowed to a stop so they could admire the turn-of-the-century, French-style chateau.

"I'd live here," said Scott, "with a full staff, of course."

"Who wouldn't?" said Louise, continuing toward the building.

"Have you been inside?" Scott disengaged from Louise's arm.

"Oh well, you know." Louise looked mildly vexed. "The tours are expensive, honey, and we aren't interested in tasting all those wines."

"Okay." Scott stopped walking. "Does that mean we're getting close to the lunchtime part of our outing? I have to say sightseeing really works up an appetite. What time is it, anyway?"

"Now that you mention it, Scott,"—looking at her watch— "I'm a little hungry myself. It's almost twelve o'clock, honey. Why don't we see if Allison and Kathy are ready to leave?"

Lunch was agreed to, if not by a consensus, by a majority of three. Allison could have gone either way, which evoked a thin-lipped smile from Louise.

"As you wish," said Allison, "I'm only here to please." That said, everyone got back in the bus, and Allison drove them to the next stop on their itinerary.

12:00 PM

Louise's "real cute sandwich place in the Valley of the Moon" did not disappoint. Nestled between a stand of cedar trees and an outcrop of gray-streaked stone, the shingled structure had six tables inside, six tables outside. Orders were taken at the counter from a blackboard menu that described the daily fare. Louise and Kathy decided to split a Black Forest ham and Swiss cheese sandwich on rye bread with a side order of potato salad; Allison requested tuna fish salad on a bed of greens; Scott ordered a patty melt, well-done onion rings, a side order of coleslaw. Everyone took their glass of iced tea outside, sat down at a table, and discussed the sights they'd recently seen.

The second time slow-drifting clouds passed in front of the sun, Louise suggested they move to a table inside, where the temperature didn't waver between warm and cool. The idea was shot down, however, as the days for dining al fresco were coming to an end.

The sun was shining through a break in the clouds when the owner's daughter (apple cheeks and blond pigtails) set overloaded paper plates and a basket of onion rings at the center of the table.

"Thank you, honey," said Louise. "Now, would you be an angel and bring us another plate. My daughter and I are going to share the ham and cheese sandwich."

"Sorry, I meant to bring one," said the teenager, her cheeks all the more florid. "Anything else?"

"Some mustard, please" said Scott. "Not French's, if possible."

"I'll bring what we have," the girl replied, unable to look Scott in the eye.

The food was good enough to curb conversation. Louise telegraphed her satisfaction by raising her brow as she chewed her first bite. Kathy smiled at Scott as she swiped an onion ring from the plastic basket. Scott moved the basket out of Kathy's reach. He then tucked into his patty melt as if he'd missed his last meal. Allison focused on his mixed greens as if he were eating alone.

Although Scott had the largest order, he was the first to finish his lunch. He wiped his hands with a few paper napkins, stood up and carried his trash to the waste can at the side of the building. Scott returned to the table but remained standing while Louise and Kathy finished eating. When they were done, Kathy carried their trash to the waste can. Allison, making a show of taking his time, chewed every bite methodically, wiped his mouth more often than necessary. Scott caught Kathy's attention as she was returning to the table. He tilted his head toward the outcrop, and the two of them walked to the jutting limestone.

"Now what?" said Scott.

"Now what, what?" Kathy replied.

"What are we doing for the rest of the day?"

"At this rate,"—looking toward the picnic table—"we're going to be here a while."

But then, preternaturally contrary, Allison stood up and carried his plate to the waste can.

Louise stood up, brushed a few crumbs from the front of her sweater, and called out, "Okay, you two, this train's about to leave the station."

Louise and Allison were walking hand in hand toward the bus, which looked to Scott like a loaf of bread on wheels, when their rosy-cheeked waitress stepped out of the restaurant and invited them back whenever they were in the neighborhood.

"Thank you, sweetheart," said Louise. "We don't live that far away, honey, just in Santa Rosa. But our son's visiting from Long Beach—you know, in Southern California."

The girl nodded, keeping her eyes on Louise. "Come back soon, okay?"

"Yes, honey, we will." Louise smiled. "We think this place is so cute, and the food is delicious. You be sure to tell your parents. Okay, sweetheart, bye-bye."

On the drive home, everyone was quiet except for the occasional comment from Louise about something that caught her eye: a farm stand with baskets of apples, horses in a small field, a calico cat sitting in a driveway. "Oh, look, Kathy Sue, isn't that cat adorable?"

When Kathy didn't respond, Louise persisted. "Did you see it, honey?"

"Yes," said Kathy.

"Didn't you think it was adorable?"

"Uh-huh," said Kathy, flaring her nostrils.

Louise accepted Kathy's response as sufficient, knowing they'd be home in a few minutes.

When everyone shuffled through the front door, each of them continued in a different direction. Allison walked into the master bedroom and closed the door behind him. Louise stepped into the kitchen and started washing her hands. Kathy went into the hallway bathroom. Scott sat down on the sofa.

Louise stepped into the living room as Kathy returned from the bathroom.

"Maybe you kids would like to see a movie." Louise stood beside her Hammond organ (replete with 25-note pedalboard), rubbing lotion into her hands. "Is there something you'd like to see, Scott? Something that would be suitable for your little sister?"

"I'd like to see *Funny Girl*." Scott shrugged. "But we'd have to fly to New York for that."

"Why don't you look in the newspaper, honey, and see what's playing in Santa Rosa?"

Scott said, "*Bonne idée*," without accent or inflection.

"Is 'bunny day' a movie you'd like to see? Would it be appropriate for Kathy?"

"No, Mom," said Scott, laughing to himself. " '*Bonne idée*' is French for 'good idea,' as in looking in the Santa Rosa newspaper for showtimes is a '*bonne idée*.' "

Louise inhaled.

Scott leaned forward and rifled through the newspaper until he found the schedule of movie showtimes. "Here we go," he said, studying the ads for recently released films. "Aha! How about *The Thomas Crown Affair* with Steve McQueen and Faye Dunaway?" He looked at Kathy, who nodded in response. Scott continued, "I'm sure it'll be good, and . . . it's playing with *How Sweet It Is!*, which is as safe as it gets for Kathy's tender sensibilities."

"Who's in the second one?" said Louise.

"Uh, Debbie Reynolds, for one, and . . . here it is, oh, yeah, James Garner. Debbie Reynolds and James Garner. It's sure to be sweet enough to rot one's teeth."

"That's a revolting endorsement," said Louise, hypersensitive to the subject of dental health. "Kathy Sue, honey, what do you think about those two movies?"

"They sound good to me," said Kathy. "When does the first one start?"

"Let's see." Scott pulled the newspaper closer. "*How Sweet It Is!* starts at one fifteen. *The Thomas Crown Affair* starts at three thirty."

"My gosh, Scott," said Louise, "it's almost one fifteen now. Where are they playing, honey? What theater?"

Scott studied the newspaper for a moment, then said, "At the Park Cinema on Summerfield Road."

"That's about ten minutes from here," said Louise. "It's next to Howarth Park, which is next to Spring Lake."

"And the leg bone's connected to the thigh bone," said Scott. "Okay, let's go. I don't care if we miss the coming attractions. And, just to prove what a good brother I am, I'll pay for Kathy as a belated birthday present."

"Can I have a belated bag of popcorn too," said Kathy, "or should I bring my wallet?"

"Sky's the limit," said Scott, heading for the door.

Four hours later, a few minutes past five fifteen, Louise pulled to the curb in front of the theater as people started walking out of the building. Scott and Kathy did not appear until almost five thirty, which had Louise on the verge of going inside to find out why.

"Where were you two?" said Louise, as Scott and Kathy climbed into the bus.

"*The Thomas Crown Affair* started a few minutes late," Scott replied. "We're the last ones out of the theater because I made us sit through the credits so we could listen to the music. The theme song was *a*-mazing."

"It really was," Kathy agreed. "The movie was good too."

"I concur," said Scott. "*But* I would've walked out after fifteen minutes of 'how sweet it wasn't' if we hadn't been waiting to see Steve McQueen."

"Scott thinks Steve McQueen looks like our dad," said Kathy.

"Now that you mention it," said Louise, "I suppose there is a resemblance. They both had blond hair and blue eyes, that's for sure."

"Steve McQueen still does," said Scott.

"Well, yes, of course," said Louise, shaking her head. "Now, enough of this. As soon as we get home, the two of you need to change your clothes. Allison made a seven o'clock dinner reservation at a good restaurant, so you need to wear something nice."

"Wow," said Kathy. "This is a first."

"What's that, honey?" Louise glanced at Kathy while they were stopped at an intersection.

"Going out to eat twice in one day."

"I have to agree," said Scott. "Going to Der Wienerschnitzel wouldn't be all that surprising for a second meal out, but dressing up for a restaurant that takes reservations is a horse of a different feather. What's the special occasion?"

"Oh well," said Louise, turning into their cul-de-sac. "Sometimes it's nice to celebrate, even if it's not a special occasion per se."

"*Per se*," said Scott, considering the implication.

"So this *is* a celebration," said Kathy. "But you're not going to say any more than that."

"All right, Kathy Sue." Louise pulled into their parking space and turned off the engine. She set the emergency brake even though they were on level ground. "Let's not make a big deal out of this. We just thought it'd be nice to have a pleasant dinner with the family since Scott's here and all." Louise got out of the bus. "Make sure your doors are locked."

"Mine's locked," said Scott, preempting his mother's request for verbal confirmation.

"Mine too," said Kathy, following her brother's lead.

"Now," said Louise, indicating a need for further conversation. "Kathy, you had a bath this morning, so you can change clothes in your bedroom while Scott takes a shower. You should be done by the time Scott needs to use the room. Scott, did you bring anything a little bit dressy?"

"Does the Pope shit in the woods?" Scott smiled at Kathy.

"All right, Scott." Louise shook her head. "A simple 'yes' will do."

"Yes," Scott allowed, "but what's the fun in that?"

Louise addressed herself to Kathy. "Does the plan work for you, sweetheart?"

"Yes," said Kathy, meeting her mother's eyes. "Can we go inside now? I need to use the bathroom before Scott takes a shower."

6:00 PM

Scott pulled on a pair of corduroy bell-bottom pants, tucked in a long-sleeved penny-collar shirt, fastened the buckle of a wide leather belt, slipped on brown suede, stacked-heel shoes. He checked his appearance in the mirror before joining Kathy in the living room, where she was sitting on the sofa, leafing through the latest issue of *House & Garden.*

"You look very mod," said Kathy, smirking at Scott as he entered the room.

"I am very mod." Scott flopped down beside her with enough bounce that the magazine fluttered closed.

"*Scott*," whined Kathy as she'd done countless times before.

"All right, you two," said Louise, entering the room.

"Wow, Mom," Kathy enthused. "When you said 'wear something nice,' you weren't kidding."

Louise struck a pose to show off her two-piece suit in the style of Coco Chanel. "Well, Kathy Sue, thank you—I think. Was that supposed to be a compliment, sweetheart?"

"Yes," said Kathy, shaking her head. "I mean, you know, after you spent a year sewing that suit, I thought you'd wear it more often than once a year."

"Oh well." Louise mugged for her audience of two.

Allison emerged from the bedroom wearing a suit and tie.

"I don't believe this," said Kathy, darting her eyes from Scott to Louise to Allison. "When was the last time you wore a suit and tie to dinner with us?" Kathy paused for a moment, then said, "Let me rephrase that. Have you ever worn a suit and tie to dinner with us?"

"All right, Kathy," said Louise. "Everybody looks very nice, including Scott in his up-to-date outfit."

"Mom," said Scott, "it's just pants and a shirt."

"And high heels," said Kathy, pursing her lips.

"Kathy Sue," said Louise, smiling uncertainly. "What's gotten into you?"

"Nothing." Kathy sighed. "I just don't understand why we had to get dressed up."

"*Kathy Sue.*" Louise smiled broadly. "Try not to be a party pooper before the party begins."

"That's what I mean," said Kathy, making a face. "You keep saying it's not a celebration, but then you say it's a party." She took a short breath, then blurted out, "Are you pregnant?"

The ensuing silence was awesome but short-lived.

"Wow," said Scott, "I didn't see that coming."

Allison looked at no one in particular.

"Oh, honey," said Louise, walking over to sit on the edge of the sofa. "No, sweetheart. Oh, my gosh, no." Louise started to giggle. "I'm sorry, honey. I know this isn't funny. I'm in a state of shock—a little bit, anyway. But, no, I'm not pregnant."

"That would be a cause for concern," said Allison, "not celebration."

"Now, Daddy, no need to make any more of this than it already is."

"Yes, dear," Allison replied, suppressing a grin. "You're absolutely right."

"Okay, then," said Scott. "Now that that's settled, who's ready for dinner?"

Louise bent forward and kissed Kathy on the check. She stood up and walked over to stand beside Allison. "Come on, you two," she said, raising her brow. "We don't want to be late for our reservation."

"Where are we going?" said Kathy.

"That new restaurant in the Montgomery Village Shopping Center," Louise replied. "Cattlemens. It looks like a real nice steak house, and I'm sure they have seafood and pasta, or whatever else you might be in the mood for."

"All right, Louise," said Allison. "Instead of discussing what they might have to offer, why don't we go to the restaurant and have a look at the menu?"

"Yes, of course, dear. I just need to get my handbag. Is everybody else ready?"

Scott and Kathy stood up and followed Allison out the front door.

Louise was heard closing the door as the others reached the bottom of the stairs.

Cattlemens was chockablock at six forty-five. People waiting to be seated were standing three deep at the bar or sitting on benches outside the front door. Allison made his way to the hostess station and was pleased to hear that a booth was ready for Dr. Eddy's party of four.

"Carolyn will show you to your table," said Mary Lou, according to her name tag. Mary Lou handed four menus to Carolyn, who smiled at Allison and said, "Are you ready to be seated?"

"By all means," replied Allison. Allison stepped aside so Louise, Kathy, and Scott could follow Carolyn into the dining room. When Carolyn stopped at the only empty booth in the room, Louise slid across one bench as Kathy slid across the other. Scott slid in beside Kathy, Allison beside Louise. As soon as they were settled, Carolyn handed each of them an oversized menu.

"Can I bring you something to drink while you're deciding?"

Carolyn looked around the table until her eyes settled on Louise.

Louise looked at Allison, widened her eyes, and smiled.

Allison turned to Carolyn and said, "Do you serve champagne by the glass?"

"I don't believe this," whispered Kathy.

"I'm sorry," said Carolyn, "but we don't serve champagne. We do have a California sparkling wine, if you'd like to order that by the glass."

"It's not too dry, is it?" Louise wrinkled her nose.

"I couldn't say," Carolyn replied. "I'm not old enough to drink. But everyone who's ordered it has enjoyed it. I could bring a sample if you'd like."

"I'm sure it'll be fine," said Allison. "We'll have two glasses of the sparkling wine. One for my wife and one for myself."

"And for you," said Carolyn, looking at Kathy.

"I'll have water," said Kathy, looking from Carolyn to Louise.

"Same for me," said Scott, looking somewhat amused. He then opened his menu and considered which dinner option (served with soup or salad, choice of potato, and dish of ice cream) would be the largest portion for the least amount of money.

Kathy turned her attention from her mother to her menu with an eye on the prices as well.

Louise opened her menu. After a moment, she cleared her throat and said, "You kids go ahead and order anything you like—soup to nuts. I'm going to have the filet mignon. Scott, I bet you'd enjoy one of the Beef and Reef Combos—maybe the sirloin steak and lobster tail. Oh look, honey, the New York Steak and Jumbo Shrimp sounds yummy. What do you think?"

Scott looked at Louise as if she were speaking in tongues. Never, while living with his mother and Allison—not from ages six through nine, nor thirteen through eighteen—had Scott been allowed carte blanche when ordering in a restaurant. Limitation had sometimes been a matter of cost ("order whatever you want up to three dollars"), sometimes a matter of quantity ("you can have two hotdogs or one hotdog and an order of French fries"), but "order anything you like" had never been uttered before that evening.

Kathy nudged Scott's thigh.

"What?" said Scott, drawing unwanted attention to his sister.

"I just wondered what you're going to order," said Kathy, ignoring Allison's glare.

"I don't know yet," said Scott. "But I'm going to start with the 'All-You-Can-Eat Salad and Warm Sourdough Bread.' "

"Ooh," said Louise, rocking her shoulders, "that sound's good. I think I'll start with that too. Kathy Sue, you can have some of my salad, sweetheart, unless you have something else in mind."

"I was going to order a shrimp cocktail," said Kathy, rebuffing her mother's invitation to share.

"Oh my," said Louise, shifting her eyes from one section of the menu to another. "Maybe you'll let your poor old mother have one small shrimp. If you're feeling generous, that is."

Kathy kept her eyes on her menu.

"That's redundant," said Scott, " 'one small shrimp.' I prefer 'jumbo shrimp,' which is an oxymoron."

"Which reminds me of you," said Kathy. "The 'oxymoron' part, not the 'jumbo shrimp.' However—"

Scott elbowed Kathy's arm.

Allison cleared his throat.

Louise turned to Allison. "What looks good to you, darling?"

"Well, Mother, I'm considering grilled salmon with a twice-baked potato or teriyaki chicken with sautéed vegetables."

"Those both sound delicious." Louise smiled uncertainly. "Don't you think the salmon would be more like a special occasion, sweetheart, since we have chicken at home so often?"

125

Just then, Carolyn arrived with their beverages. She set tumblers of water in front of Kathy and Scott, glasses of wine in front of Louise and Allison. "I'll be back in a moment to take your order." Carolyn smiled at Louise as she stepped away from the table.

"Thank you, dear," said Louise. She then turned toward Allison, holding out her glass. Allison lifted his glass and clinked Louise's. They paused for a moment, then raised their glasses and took a sip.

"Mmm," said Louise, beaming at Allison. "Isn't that *delicious*?"

"Yes, darlin'." Allison tilted his glass in Louise's direction. He said, "Here's to you," and took another sip.

"And to you," said Louise, taking another sip as well.

"This is weird," said Kathy.

"What is, honey?" Louise placed her glass on the table.

"Why are you toasting each other?" Kathy frowned. "And why are you drinking wine? You never have wine when we go out."

"Well, Kathy Sue," said Louise, "I wouldn't say we *never* have wine when we go out."

"You've never ordered wine when you were with me," Kathy rejoined. "I know that for a fact. Never once."

"All right, Kathy," said Allison. "I think you've made your point. Why don't we change the subject?"

"Yes," said Louise, smiling at Kathy. "What are you going to order for dinner, sweetheart?"

"Shrimp cocktail and filet mignon." Kathy closed her menu with a fifteen-year-old's flourish of finality.

"That sounds very sophisticated," said Louise, raising her brow. "Scott, what about you, honey? Have you decided what you're going to order?"

"No," said Scott, considering the options by cost and quantity.

Carolyn returned to the table and asked if they were ready to order?

"Yes, dear." Louise smiled brightly. "I'd like to start with an all-you-can-eat salad, which will be wasted on me, but I can't resist the idea of warm sourdough bread. I'd like ranch dressing on the side, honey, and then I'll have your petit filet mignon." Louise turned to Kathy. "I can't eat a whole baked potato, Kathy Sue. Don't you think half a potato would be enough for you?"

"Yes," said Kathy, thinking agreement the lesser of the evils.

"Thank you, sweetheart." Louise turned back to Carolyn. "And a baked potato, honey. Maybe a large one since my daughter and I are going to split it. If that's possible." Louise broadened her smile.

"I'll do my best," said Carolyn. "How would you like your steak?"

"Medium-well," said Louise. "And could you bring some horseradish, dear?"

"Horseradish sauce. Yes, of course." Carolyn turned to Kathy. "Have you decided?"

"Yes," said Kathy. "I'd like a shrimp cocktail and the filet mignon."

"Petit or ten-ounce?"

"Petit, please."

"How did you want that cooked?"

"Medium."

"Perfect," said Carolyn, turning to Scott. "And for you?"

Scott glanced at the menu, then asked, "Is it possible to get a Caesar salad with warm sourdough bread?"

"Sure," said Carolyn, pencil poised. "Would you like to start with that?"

"Yes, please. And then I'd like the steak and lobster—the steak medium-rare, and a baked potato with sour cream and chives."

"Anything else to drink."

"No, thank you. Water's fine."

"And for you, Dr. Eddy?" Carolyn smiled.

Allison was not expecting to be addressed by name. He grinned like a teenage boy, covered his mouth, and suppressed a cough. "Excuse me." He took a sip of water, then said, "I'd like the broccoli soup, Carolyn—just a cup, not the bread bowl." Smiling still, he continued, "For my entrée, I'd like the grilled salmon and your signature twice-baked potato."

"Would you like sour cream and chives as well?"

"No, no, butter will be fine."

"All righty, then." Carolyn collected everyone's menus. "I'll be back in two shakes of a lamb's tail with your salad, salad, soup, and shrimp."

"Isn't she adorable?" said Louise before Carolyn was out of earshot. When no one confirmed her appraisal, Louise looked at Scott and asked, "Are you still seeing that girl from New York, honey? What was her name? The one who wore so much eye makeup?"

"Melissa," Scott replied. "And, no, I'm not seeing her anymore."

"My gosh," said Louise, shaking her head, "I've never seen anyone with that much eye makeup. I thought she was wearing glasses when you brought her by to meet us."

"Yes, Mom," said Scott. "That's what you said to her when I introduced you."

"Oh my god," muttered Kathy, in commiseration.

"All right, Kathy," said Louise. "You had to be there to believe it. And the skirt she was wearing, if you can call something that short a skirt. It was the size of two dinner napkins with a zipper up the back."

"Not to put too fine a point on it," said Scott, ever amazed by his mother's provincial bent. "Melissa is from an old-money New York family. She has her hair cut by Vidal Sassoon. She buys her clothes in London and Paris. She goes to school at USC because she's tired of East Coast society—New York and Palm Beach. Melissa went out with me because she was bored with young men of suitable social standing. In light of this, you might rethink looking down your nose at what you don't understand."

Unswayed by Scott's advice, Louise leaned in with, "Am I supposed to know who Vidal Sassoon is?"

Kathy said, "He cut Mia Farrow's hair for *Rosemary's Baby*."

"That real cute pixie cut?" said Louise, somewhat impressed.

"Yes," replied Scott, "among other celebrities, including Mary Quant, who made the miniskirt what it is today. Melissa was probably wearing one of Mary Quant's miniskirts. Anyway, I'll tell you a funny story about Melissa and me that will close the book on this discussion. Okay?"

"Yes, please," said Kathy, before anyone else could speak.

"Melissa and I went to see a late showing of *Wait Until Dark* at the Crest Theater, which everyone here knows all too well."

"Ugh," said Kathy, recalling years of Sunday mornings spent in the Crest Theater for Church of Religious Science services.

"Exactly," said Scott. "All the same, it's a world-class theater regardless of the heresy perpetrated therein."

"All right, Scott," said Allison. "If you have a story to tell, please do."

"Yeah, well,"—looking from Allison to Kathy—"it started with everyone having to wait in line longer than expected because a couple of elderly people from the previous showing had heart attacks while watching the film."

"What kind of film was this?" said Louise, registering concern.

"A thriller—that's for sure." Scott widened his eyes. "A thriller starring Audrey Hepburn, so, you know, who could ask for anything more. Anyway, we finally got inside the theater, twenty minutes late at least, and the house wasn't as full as I'd expected. I think some people got their money back after seeing the ambulance at the front of the theater."

"Seriously, Scott?" said Louise. "An ambulance was called for someone who'd just seen the movie."

"Yep." Scott nodded. "Two of them, in fact. Anyway, we finally got inside the theater, and we found really good seats. The movie started, and I could not have been happier. It was a good production, and Audrey Hepburn was amazing. Okay, so . . . an hour and a half went by, and everything was fine. I mean, the movie was a thriller, and I was on the edge of my seat, so to speak, but I was holding Melissa's hand, and we were making comments every once in a while. But then something happened. I won't tell you what, but something happened that scared the bejesus out of me, and Melissa pulled her hand away. I said, 'Okay, okay, I won't squeeze so tight. I know the scary parts are coming now. I promise I'll be okay.'

"Melissa said, 'No way, Jose. I saw the play on Broadway, and you need to keep your hands to yourself until the lights come up.' I said, 'Are you serious?' And she said, 'As a heart attack. I mean it, buster, keep your hands to yourself until the movie's over.' "

"I like this girl," said Kathy.

"Right," said Scott, rolling his eyes. "Anyway, I crossed my arms and slid lower in my seat. I was a little antsy from sitting still for two hours, so I threw my feet over the seat in front of me."

"Oh, Scott," said Louise, shaking her head.

"Yeah, yeah, I know, but that's what makes the story interesting. Okay. So, this big climax happened, and the scary part was over. I was starting to calm down when suddenly, the bad guy, who we thought was dead, lunged out of the dark, and everyone in the theater screamed. I was so freaked out that I flung myself forward and ended up standing in the seat in front of me. By the time I got back in my seat, Melissa was laughing so hard she said it was all she could do to keep from wetting her pants."

"All right, Scott," said Louise, "I don't think that's a story for the dinner table."

"I do," said Kathy. "I wish I'd met this Melissa person."

"Yeah, well," said Scott, "I think she plays better as an anecdote than as a person."

Carolyn arrived at the table with a large tray balanced on one hand above her shoulder. She flipped open a portable stand she'd carried in her other hand, set the tray down, and began to place or pass various assortments of plates and bowls. "I think that's everything," Carolyn finally said, directing her smile around the table. "Can I get you anything else?"

"Oh, you know," said Louise, "I'd love a dab of that 'pecan nut butter' that comes on your baked sweet potato, if that's possible, honey. I wouldn't want you to get in trouble." Louise winked as if this were just between the two of them.

"I think I can manage that," said Carolyn. "Anything else?"

Louise looked around the table, then spoke on everyone's behalf. "No, dear, I think that will do it."

After a busboy made a second pass at clearing dishes from their table, Carolyn arrived to ask if everyone had enjoyed their meal?

"Oh my gosh, honey," said Louise. "I haven't eaten that much since Thanksgiving."

"Does that mean you don't have room for dessert?" Carolyn teased, grinning like a Cheshire cat.

Louise gasped, then managed to say, "I couldn't eat another bite if you paid me."

"I could," said Scott, leaning forward. "I'd like a large piece of your pistachio carrot cake with two scoops of vanilla ice cream."

"I'll have a bite of yours," said Kathy, smirking at her brother. Scott narrowed his eyes.

"Well, now that you mention it," said Louise, giggling a bit. "I might have a small bite of Scott's carrot cake as well."

"Hold on," said Scott. "The two of you can get a piece of your own."

"I don't think we can eat a whole piece of cake," said Louise. "Do you, Kathy Sue?"

"Not really," Kathy replied.

"That's okay," said Scott. "I'll finish whatever you don't eat."

"Good heavens, Scott." Louise frowned. "It sounds like you have a hollow leg."

"As a matter of fact," said Scott, "I have two." Scott glared at his mother, who had for years doled out food to her teenage son as if he were a prepubescent girl.

"All right, dear," said Louise, feigning ignorance of the struck nerve. She smiled at Carolyn. "We'll have two pieces of carrot cake, honey, one with vanilla ice cream. And could you bring four forks?" Looking at Allison, she added, "You should have a bite of dessert with the rest of the family, sweetheart. Think of it as the frosting on the cake of our little celebration."

"Well, all right," said Allison. "But just a bite."

"Good," said Louise, looking to Carolyn. "That should do it, honey. Two pieces of carrot cake and four forks."

"Would anybody like coffee?" Carolyn looked around the table.

"Good heavens, no," said Louise, shaking her head. "We'd be up the rest of the night. Just a little more ice water, honey, when you come back with our dessert."

"And the check," said Allison.

"Absolutely," Carolyn replied, picking up a dish of butter pats.

Several minutes later, Scott took his first bite of ice cream as

Kathy reached across the table and lifted a forkful of cake from the plate in front of her mother. Louise took two bites, singing the praises of whoever came up with the idea of adding pistachio nuts to the recipe. Kathy took one more bite, then Louise slid the plate in front of Allison. Allison took several bites, commenting on the pistachios as well, then pushed the plate to the middle of the table, halfway between himself and Scott.

Scott finished his cake and ice cream, took a sip of water, wiped his mouth, leaned back, and exhaled.

Louise cleared her throat. "There's still more cake, *Scott*, if you have any room left in one of those hollow legs of yours."

"I'm good," said Scott, to no one in particular. He would have finished the cake if Louise had left Allison out of the mix. But he was unwilling to eat from the same plate as his stepfather.

"Oh well, that's all right." Louise caught the attention of a passing waiter. "Could you ask Carolyn to put this in a doggie bag for us?" She handed him the plate. "Thank you, honey."

Carolyn returned a few minutes later with Allison's change and a small paper bag. Directing her smile around the table, Carolyn said, "We hope to see you again real soon. Get home safe and enjoy the rest of your evening."

"Thank you, dear, we will," said Louise, sliding along the bench as Allison stood up. Carolyn stepped away as Scott stood up. Kathy slid out, and the group made their way through the restaurant to the parking lot.

"That was delightful," said Louise, fastening her seat belt. "Thank you, Daddy, for taking the family out to dinner." She turned her head. "Didn't you kids think that was delightful?"

"Uh-huh," said Kathy, tempering her tone.

"How about you, *Scott*?" Louise poked the bear, undeterred by precedent or probability.

"I enjoyed the meal," said Scott. "What time is it, by the way?"

"Eight thirty-five," Louise replied, checking her watch. "Why, sweetheart, is there somewhere you need to be?"

"No." Scott looked out the window as Allison pulled into slow-moving traffic. "I was wondering who's on Ed Sullivan tonight, but it doesn't matter. It'll be over by the time we get home."

"It's a repeat," said Kathy, "with Liza Minnelli and The Fifth Dimension."

"Okay," said Scott. "I've seen it."

"Kathy," said Louise, "have you finished your homework?"

"Sort of," said Kathy. "I was going to read for a while because I have a book report due on Wednesday."

"What are you reading?" said Scott, genuinely interested.

"*To Kill a Mockingbird*," Kathy replied. "And I love it. I love the children, especially the little girl. Her name is 'Scout.' And I love the father. His name is 'Atticus.' "

"Cool names," said Scott. "When was it published?"

"1960, I think." Kathy turned to Scott. "You know, Harper Lee was best friends with Truman Capote."

Scott narrowed his eyes. "Harper Lee's the author?"

"*Yes.*" Kathy registered disbelief at her brother's ignorance of contemporary writers.

"Well," said Scott, curling his lip, "admitting to a close personal relationship with Truman Capote says little for the . . . woman, right?"

Kathy nodded.

Scott continued, "Says little for the woman, in my book, anyway. That guy's a twerp."

"Don't knock it till you've read it," said Kathy, her feathers slightly ruffled.

Scott poked Kathy in the ribs until she giggled. "I'm not talking about the book," he said. "I'm sure it's fine. I'm not talking about Harper Lee, either. But that Truman Capote creep is a creep."

Kathy stuck out her tongue. "So, what are you reading, mister smarty pants?"

Scott snorted, then said, "I'm a few chapters into *Siddhartha* by Hermann Hesse."

"What's it about?"

"Life and the pursuit of self-discovery during the time of the Gautama Buddha. You know, same old, same old. No, wait a minute, that's not fair. I'm liking it a lot. So much, in fact, I'm planning to read a different book by Hesse as soon as I finish this one."

"Are you reading this one for school?"

"Yep, for a discussion group."

"A discussion group sounds like more fun than a book report."

"The grass is never greener, Sue." Scott raised his brow. "You'll find that out soon enough. College-wise, anyway."

Allison pulled into the apartment complex driveway. He proceeded to their parking space, turned off the engine, and set the emergency brake. Scott took a slow breath, looked at Kathy, and rolled his eyes. Kathy stifled a laugh. Louise darted a glance in Kathy's direction.

"Home again, home again, jiggety-jig," said Louise, sliding out of her seat. "Daddy and I are going to stay in our bedroom and catch up on some paperwork after we get out of these clothes. Scott, do you want to read your book in the living room with your sister?"

"No," said Scott, poking Kathy in the ribs. "I'll read in bed, which allows, in my opinion, the preferred posture for expanding one's worldview."

"Whatever you say, Scott." Louise turned to Kathy. "You change your clothes right away, Kathy Sue, so Scott can lie down and expand his worldview. Okay, sweetheart?"

"Yes," said Kathy, swatting Scott's hand away.

9:00 PM

Allison knocked at Kathy's bedroom door.

Scott looked up from his book. "Yes?"

The door opened wide enough for Allison to lean in and say, "Your mother would like you and Kathy to come to our bedroom."

"All right." Scott frowned at the prospect of visiting the master bedroom just when he'd thought he was going to make it out of Santa Rosa unscathed.

Allison left the door ajar. Scott set his book aside. He walked into the hallway and followed Kathy into the master bedroom, where the maple bedroom set from the Long Beach apartment had been squeezed into a less than ample space.

Waiting to learn why they'd been summoned, Scott and Kathy stood near the doorway as Allison got in bed beside Louise, both of them sitting with their backs against upright pillows. The sight of Louise with a stretch turban holding her curlers in place, wearing a long-sleeved nightgown buttoned to the neck, sitting beside Allison with his ridiculous sideburns and dingy white T-shirt, set Scott's teeth on edge. Not only Louise and Allison's provincial appearance but also the distinctive smell of Allison's breath added to the unsettling atmosphere of the overcrowded room.

"Scott," said Louise, "you go ahead and sit in the rocking chair, honey. Kathy Sue, you can make yourself comfortable at the foot of the bed. Would you like a couple of pillows, sweetheart?"

Looking from Louise to Scott, Kathy said, "No," then crawled onto the bed and stretched out with her head propped on her arm.

"Scott," said Allison, "please close the door before you sit down. We like to keep this room a little warmer than the rest of the house."

Scott turned around before rolling his eyes. He closed the bedroom door, stepped back to the rocking chair, and sat down with his legs crossed and arms folded. Scott looked at his mother with curious expectation.

"Okay," said Louise, looking at her hands, then at Scott. "Well, the best place to start, of course, is at the beginning, so that would be when I was going through the cupboards on our first weekend at Oakcrest."

Scott swung his head as if reeling from unexpected news, which, in effect, he was.

Unfazed by Scott's theatrics, Louise continued: "The previous owners had left quite a few board games and jigsaw puzzles in a hallway closet. For the most part, they were in pretty bad shape. I looked inside the game boxes and saw pieces were missing, and some of the boards were damaged. The thought of getting to the end of a jigsaw puzzle to discover a piece had been lost in the shuffle answered the question of what to do with all of the puzzles anyway." Louise looked at Allison. "It wasn't much of a discussion before Daddy and I agreed we might as well throw everything out. I mean, none of it was good enough to donate to Goodwill or a thrift shop. So I packed everything in a cardboard box—which didn't have a top, by the way—and put it on the front porch with everything else we were taking to the dump.

"Now, here's the first *unusual* thing that happened." Louise widened her eyes. "When I started to walk away, the box of games fell to the deck. I thought I'd put it smack dab on top of another carton. But there it was, sideways on the deck, with a dozen games scattered this way and that." Louise paused for effect. "When I put the half-empty box back on the other carton," she continued, "I noticed one of the games inside the box was The Mystifying Oracle Ouija Board."

Scott unfolded his arms and focused his attention.

Louise smiled at Scott. "Well, I'd never played with a Ouija board before. I didn't even know what you were supposed to do if you wanted to. Anyway, I put the rest of the games back in the box and went to the kitchen to make lunch. I set out everything I needed to make tuna fish sandwiches—two cans of tuna, a jar of mayonnaise, a jar of pickle relish, a loaf of rye bread."

Scott's head fell forward as if he'd nodded off.

Ignoring Scott's theatrics, Louise continued, "But I couldn't stop thinking about that darned Ouija board.

"You know how that is. You tell yourself not to think about something, and all you can do is think about that very thing. Well, hard as I tried, I couldn't stop thinking about the Ouija board. Finally, I decided to put the game somewhere out of the way, so I could look at it without Allison seeing what I was up to." Louise placed her hand on Allison's thigh.

Allison smiled.

Scott looked away.

Kathy pulled her knees closer.

"That night," said Louise, "the sound of rushing water kept me awake. At least, that's what I thought was keeping me awake." Her wide-eyed smirk telegraphed otherwise. "After tossing and turning for almost an hour, I came out to the kitchen and made myself a cup of tea. While I was waiting for my tea to cool, it seemed like the perfect time to pull out the Ouija board and read the instructions. I put the board and the *planchette* on the table. I didn't know that's what the gadget was called when I opened the box. The planchette is the piece that moves around on the board and points to a letter or an answer. You know, like the words 'YES' and 'NO,' which are already spelled out. Anyway, like I said, I put the board and the planchette on the table in front of me, and then I read the instructions. One of the rules was 'Always say goodbye.' I thought that was a little funny, but what did I know? Another rule was 'Never use the board in your home.' Well, Oakcrest wasn't really my 'home,' so I felt okay in that regard. The next part was a little odd—something like 'What about rule number four?' But they didn't even list a rule number four." Louise furrowed her brow and shook her head. "They did say some people have asked about rule number four, which is about one person using the board. But the booklet pointed out that rule number four doesn't really matter because most people aren't psychic enough when they're alone. It also said, 'No group, nothing happens.' "

Allison leaned forward and adjusted his pillows.

"Are you all right, sweetheart?" said Louise.

Allison replied with an oily smile. He then leaned back and said, "Go ahead with your story, sweetheart."

"Okay, well, there I was, all alone with me, myself, and I, and the Ouija board, of course. So, I thought, 'What the heck? I might as well give it a try. If nothing happens, I'll put everything away, turn out the lights and go to bed.' I checked the instructions one more time and saw they recommended a dark, candlelit room. The previous owners had left several jar candles in case of a blackout. I lit a couple of the tall ones and put them on the table. I turned out the overhead light, put my teacup in the sink, sat down at the table, and tried to clear my mind of any negative thoughts."

"Mom," said Kathy, "I'm sorry to interrupt, but I have to go to the bathroom."

"Okay, sweetheart."

"So do I," said Scott.

"Okay, then," said Louise, patting Allison on the thigh. "This seems like a good time for a short break. Kathy, you can use our bathroom, honey. Scott, you can use the bathroom in the hallway."

"Right-o," said Scott, standing up from the rocking chair. Before going into the bathroom, Scott stepped into Kathy's bedroom, shrugged off his flannel shirt, and threw it over the chair at his sister's desk.

When Scott and Kathy were back in their places, Louise picked up where she'd left off: "I was sitting at the table, like I said, trying to clear my mind. When I felt calm and relaxed, I placed the planchette in the middle of the board. I didn't have a specific question in mind, and there wasn't anyone in particular I wanted to contact. You know, anyone who'd passed away. I just wanted to see if anything would happen on its own—what with my being alone and all. So, I took a deep breath and closed my eyes. I placed my fingertips on the planchette, and"—looking from Scott to Kathy—"it started to move."

"This is giving me the creeps," said Kathy, hugging her knees.

"Oh, Kathy Sue," said Louise. "There's nothing for you to worry about. Nothing's going to happen to you. I'm just sharing what happened to me." Louise smiled bravely. "All right, sweetheart?"

"I guess so." Kathy inhaled, shaking her head. "Where's the Ouija board now?"

"It's on the top shelf of our bedroom closet at Oakcrest, honey. And, just so you know, it hasn't been used for almost a month. Like I said, sweetheart, you have nothing to worry about. Okay?"

"Yes," Kathy allowed, sounding unconvinced.

"All right, honey, just relax." Louise looked from Kathy to Scott. "How are you doing, Scott?"

"You have my full attention," Scott replied. "Please continue."

"Okay, honey, like I said, I put my fingertips on the planchette, and right away, it started to move. Well, my gosh, I wasn't expecting that. I pulled my hands back, and"—winking at Kathy—"I

140

took a deep breath told myself to relax. After a minute or so, I put my fingertips back on the planchette, and it started moving more slowly than before, almost like it was trying not to frighten me. I managed to keep breathing as I watched the planchette slide to the letter *H*, then to the *E*, then to the *L*, to the *L* again, and then the *O*."

"This is weird," said Kathy.

"I think it's far out," said Scott. "Literally."

"I don't understand how that stuff happens," said Kathy.

"Well, Kathy Sue," said Louise. "If you'd allow me to continue, I might clear that up for you."

Kathy tilted her head back and studied the ceiling.

"Actually, sweetheart, it looks like you might be getting a sense of this on your own. You know"—looking from Kathy to Scott—"the four of us have exceptional psychic powers."

"We do?" said Kathy.

"Yes, honey, if we'd just allow ourselves to realize them."

"All right, Mother," said Allison. "Let's continue with your story."

"Yes, dear," said Louise. "Well, obviously, the planchette had spelled out 'HELLO,' which, I have to say, gave me a chill. But I wasn't willing to stop at that point. I mean, I certainly wanted to know *who* had said 'hello.' So, I put my hands on the planchette and whispered, 'Who are you?' In no time at all, the planchette moved to the *J*, then to the *E*, then to the R, to the *R* again, then to the *Y*."

"Wow," whispered Scott, nodding slowly.

"Are you saying it was our father?" Kathy looked from Scott to Louise.

"Yes, sweetheart. Jerry was telling me he was there."

Kathy exhaled.

"Okay," said Scott. "What happened next?"

Louise tilted her head from side to side. "Well, Scott, it was slow-going from that point on. I mean, I'd ask a question out loud, and that went fairly fast. But it took a while for the planchette to spell out Jerry's answers."

"What did you ask him?" said Scott, sitting forward in the chair.

"Oh, you know, honey, pretty much what you'd expect. 'Are you all right?' 'How do you pass the time?' Questions like that."

Scott laughed through his nose. "Our father's been dead for six years, and you asked if he's all right?"

"Well, yes, Scott." Louise shook her head. "What would you have asked?"

Scott screwed up his face. "I'd have asked what the hell's going on over there, wherever 'over there' is?"

"All right," said Louise, sitting up straight. "There's no need for that kind of talk. And, yes, of course, I asked Jerry what it was like 'beyond the veil,' as they refer to it."

"And . . . ?"

"Like I said, honey, every answer took several minutes, sometimes ten minutes if it was a long explanation. Also, excited as I was with the exchange, my eyelids were starting to droop. You know, the whole thing was taking a lot out of me. After an hour or so, I told Jerry I was going to say goodbye, like the instructions said, that I'd check in with him when I was back at Oakcrest the following weekend."

"You waited a week before trying again?" Scott pulled back his head.

"Yes," said Louise, nodding slowly. "Remember, Scott, one of the rules was never use the board at home, honey, and I needed some time to digest everything that was happening."

"Okay," Scott groaned. "What happened the next weekend?"

"On Saturday," said Louise, "Allison and I spent most of the day trimming overgrown shrubs and trees. That night, both of us were bushed—"

"Ha!" said Scott. "Good word choice, Mom."

"What's that, honey?" Louise looked baffled.

"You were 'bushed' after trimming shrubs and trees all day."

"Oh, yes, I see." Louise cleared her throat. "Well, it wasn't intentional. Anyway, we were so worn out that we barely made it through dinner. I told Allison I'd do the dishes in the morning, and we both went straight to bed."

"Where was I during all of this?" said Kathy.

"This was the first week of August, honey. You were in Long Beach, staying with Karen Diotte."

"Oh, right." Kathy nodded. "How could I forget that?"

"Anyway," said Louise, "even though I could barely keep my eyes open at dinner, I couldn't get to sleep once I was in bed. The creek was really full that night. It sounded like it was going to wash the mountain away. To tell the truth, I knew I wouldn't be able to fall asleep without seeing if Jerry was still there. So, I came out to the kitchen, made myself a cup of tea, and set up the Ouija board. Oh,"—shaking her head—"I just remembered this. You know, your father could always make me laugh. Well, when I asked if he was still there, the planchette started moving so fast, I could barely keep my fingertips on it. I was laughing to myself by the time it finished spelling out 'WHAT TOOK YOU SO LONG.' " Louise finished with a flourish, expecting some degree of mutual amusement.

No one rose to the occasion. Allison, having heard everything before, was looking into the middle distance. Kathy, breathing more slowly than usual, was lying on her back. Scott, considering the story so far, was looking at Louise, but an indication of amusement was not forthcoming.

"Anyway," said Louise, smoothing the covers across her lap,

143

"the next thing I knew, the planchette was racing around the board, and it was all I could do to keep track of the letters. When the planchette finally stopped, the message was 'THIS IS TOO SLOW GET PAPER AND PEN.' Well, I thought Jerry wanted me to start taking notes, but that wasn't what he had in mind."

"You talk like you were having an actual conversation with our father," Scott interjected. "Like you knew it was Jerry on the other end of the line—so to speak."

"Not 'so to speak,' " Louise replied. "I know Jerry well enough to know that that's who I was communicating with."

"Okay," said Scott, "but, really, Mom, of all the people 'beyond the veil,' why would Jerry answer your call?"

"I'm coming to that, Scott." Louise smiled. "But first, honey, the next thing Jerry conveyed was 'START AUTOMATIC WRITING,' which I didn't understand at all. After thinking about it for a minute, I asked, 'What do you mean by that?' Right away, the planchette spelled out 'GET BOOK.' Just to be sure, I said, 'You want me to get a book on automatic writing, whatever that is?' Well, the planchette went directly to 'YES,' and then straight down to 'GOODBYE.' I laughed a bit at how abrupt Jerry was being with me. But, like I said, Scott, I knew your father well enough to know that that's who I was communicating with. I said, 'All right, Doctor Henry. I'll get a book, and I'll check in with you next week.' I waited for a response, but after a minute or so, I said, 'Goodbye,' and put everything away for the night."

"Mother," said Allison, sliding his feet to the floor. "I'm in need of a bathroom break."

"All right, darling, take your time. We're not going anywhere." Louise looked across the room and said, "*Scott*," in a saccharine tone, "would you be an angel and get your mother a glass of water?"

Without answering, Scott stood up and went to the kitchen. He returned to the bedroom, closed the door behind him, walked around the bed, and handed Louise a tumbler.

"Thank you, sweetheart." Louise took a sip of water as Allison crossed the room and got back in bed.

Scott returned to the rocking chair and sat down with his legs stretched out and his hands behind his head.

"All right," said Louise. "Are you boys comfortable?"

Scott and Allison waited for the other to say something in response until Louise accepted their mutual silence as answer enough. Louise took another sip of water, cleared her throat, and started again with a brief recap: "Like I said, Jerry wanted me to get a book about automatic writing. I didn't know if I should go to the library or a book store. Monday afternoon, we had a couple of cancellations at the office, so I told Allison I had to run a couple of errands.

"I went to this real cute bookstore in the St. Francis Shopping Center, but after explaining what I was looking for, the saleslady suggested I try the bookstore on Third Street, across from Courthouse Square. When I got to that store, the manager—an older gentleman, who remembered helping me track down a book on antique sewing machines for Allison—said he thought he had just what I was looking for. He walked me to a small selection of books about metaphysical subjects. He ran his finger across several volumes before he pulled out Ruth Montgomery's *A Search for the Truth*. He turned to the table of contents and pointed out 'Chapter 3. The Pencil Writes.' I said, 'By George, I think you've got it.' " Louise reached over to a stack of books on her bedside table and pulled out the second book from the top. "And here it is," she said, holding up a hardcover edition of the book in question.

"After purchasing the book," Louise continued, "I drove across town and did some grocery shopping. I mention this because I wanted to hide the book in the bag of groceries so Allison wouldn't see what I was up to. You know, I still wasn't sure about any of this, and I didn't know how I'd explain it if Allison saw the book." Louise took a sip of water. She returned the glass to her nightstand, reached a bit farther, and plucked a tissue from a decorative box. Although Louise rarely blew her nose in anyone else's presence, necessity trumped convention on this occasion. Holding the tissue in place, Louise blew her nose twice, applying pressure to one nostril after the other, and finished by rearranging the tissue before one last insistent wipe. Louise tucked the tissue in the sleeve of her nightgown, composed herself, and continued telling her story.

"That night, after doing the dishes, I wanted to wash and set my hair. By the time I finished with that, Allison was already asleep, and I could barely keep my eyes open. I really wanted to look at the book, but it would have to wait one more day.

"Tuesday night, I was raring to go, but Allison asked me to help him with some paperwork. Well, that kept us busy until we both shuffled to bed around eleven o'clock. Wednesday night was the charm. Allison was still involved with the paperwork, so I told him I was going to treat myself to a long hot bath."

"Was I in Long Beach all this time?" said Kathy.

"Yes, sweetheart." Louise smiled. "The Wednesday I'm talking about was during the third week of August. You came home the following Monday, August 26, right?"

"Technically," said Kathy, "it was Tuesday the twenty-seventh because the bus didn't arrive until after midnight."

Louise broadened her smile. "Yes, honey, you are correct. Now that we've settled that, I'll get back to telling my story. Like I said, Wednesday night was the charm. I read the third chapter of Ruth Montgomery's book two times while I was in the bathtub. By the time I came into the bedroom, Allison was already asleep. I thought about it for a minute and decided there was no time like the present. I got a pad of paper and one of my favorite pens and went back into the bathroom where I wouldn't be disturbed. I sat down with my back against the door. I placed the pad in my lap and held the pen against the paper like I always do when I'm beginning to write. I took a slow breath and tried to clear my mind.

"It wasn't long before I began to feel warm, pleasantly warm like a summer morning. I felt warm and calm and protected, and then I felt the pen moving across the paper. I didn't look down, but I could feel my hand traveling from side to side faster than it ever had. I could hear the pen scribbling at a speed I was certain could only produce gibberish. When my hand stopped, I waited a few seconds to catch my breath.

"When I did look down,"—pausing for effect—"I couldn't believe my eyes. The piece of paper was halfway covered with my handwriting, my handwriting the way it always looks. All the i's were dotted, all the t's were crossed. The lines were straight, and the margins were even."

"Okay, Mom," said Scott. "We know you have baroque penmanship. I, for one, don't know how you manage it under normal circumstances. That said, what the hell was the message?"

"You know, *Scott*," Louise replied, signaling her particular brand of irony. "It's interesting that you keep referring to hell. We'll come back to that in a few minutes, honey, and I think you'll see what I mean."

"Okay," said Scott, clenching his teeth. "But what the hell was the message?"

Louise chuckled to herself. She was enjoying her moment in the sun, albeit sitting in bed on a September night. She tucked a wisp of hair beneath a curler, then said, "The message, Scott, was from your father. He congratulated me on the new format, the automatic writing. He told me it was going to make everything so much easier."

"What did that mean?" said Kathy, looking perplexed.

"All it meant, honey, was that automatic writing was easier than spelling things out on the Ouija board."

"I understand *that*," Kathy replied. "What I don't understand is why you need an easier way to communicate with our dead father."

"That's what I'm trying to explain, Kathy Sue, but you keep interrupting me."

"O*kay*," said Kathy, rolling onto her side, facing Louise.

"Anyway," said Louise, tilting her head in Kathy's direction. "Jerry went on to say he wasn't the only one who was glad to hear from me."

"Oh boy," said Scott. "This is going to be interesting."

"Yes, Scott," said Louise. "This is very interesting."

"Let me guess," said Scott, "Grandma Taylor, Uncle Pete, Amelia Earhart, JFK, and Buddy Holly."

"Not exactly," said Louise. "In the first message, Jerry didn't mention anyone by name, other than telling me that Grandma Taylor sends her love."

"I knew it," said Scott.

"Jerry did say they'd been waiting for me to make contact."

"What did that mean?" said Kathy. "That they'd been waiting a long time?"

"And who are 'they'?" said Scott.

"Those were my exact questions," Louise said as if discovering something in common with newfound friends. "As for your question, Kathy Sue, 'had they been waiting a long time?' Jerry explained that time as we know it does not exist in their dimension."

"Sounds like something Rod Serling would say," said Scott.

"The guy from *The Twilight Zone*?" Kathy looked at Scott.

Scott dropped his head to his chest, designating Kathy's question too inane to answer.

"All right, you two," said Louise. "Please stop clowning

around. It's important that you understand what I'm telling you. Okay?"

"Yes," said Kathy.

"Okey-dokey," said Scott.

"Thank you," said Louise, shaking her head.

"Are you going to tell us who 'they' are?" said Scott.

"Yes, Scott, I'm coming to that." Louise inhaled. "But who they are wasn't made clear to me until the following night. As for that night, I told Jerry I was already on overload, that I needed to get some sleep. He told me that was fine. He'd be there whenever I was ready. We had all the time in the world, which he pointed out was an inside joke in his neck of the woods."

"Were those his words—'his neck of the woods'?" said Scott.

"Not exactly," answered Louise with an impish shrug.

"Does he refer to where he is?"

"Yes, Scott, but I think I need to use the bathroom before I go into that."

"Oh, come on," said Scott. "Just when things are getting interesting."

"I'll only be a minute," said Louise, dropping her feet to the floor. "And, Scott, if you think this part is interesting, hang on to your hat, honey."

"Yes, ma'am," said Scott, standing up. "But first, I'm going to get something to drink."

"Me too," said Kathy, following Scott out of the room.

"Okay," called Louise, "but don't be long. We still have a lot of ground to cover."

ELEVEN

10:00 PM

Scott and Kathy returned from the kitchen, where they'd whispered misgivings and concerns over glasses of farm-stand apple
cider. As the unfolding situation weighed more heavily on Kathy,
she'd implored Scott to rein in Louise. Not quite sure where
Louise's story was going, Scott had convinced Kathy to bide her
time until sufficient cause for an intervention presented itself.

Louise was back in bed beside Allison, the two of them holding
hands. Scott closed the bedroom door and sat down in the rocking
chair as Kathy stretched out at the foot of the bed.

"Oh, Kathy Sue," said Louise, "I can smell the apple cider on
your breath, honey. Scott, did you have some too? Isn't it delicious?"

Scott recognized the look on Allison's face, the inclination to
pounce for the slightest violation of his tyrannical rule. The
memory of living under Allison's roof, where opening the refrigerator had been strictly forbidden, was precisely why Scott—first
time as a guest in the Eddys' apartment—had offered apple cider
to Kathy. Kathy, feeling insulated by her brother's current status,
had accepted for the same reasons.

"Yes," said Scott, ignoring Allison, "I had two glasses."

"Oh, I know." Louise removed her hand from Allison's. "Fresh
apple cider is one of my favorite things about this time of year."
Louise patted Allison on the thigh, folded her hands, and placed
them in her lap. "Okay, well, where were we?"

"You were about to tell us where Jerry and his friends are hanging out," Scott replied. "Their 'neck of the woods,' as it were."

"Yes, Scott. But before I go into that, I wanted to say I understand why you're making jokes about all of this. You know, honey, it wasn't a walk in the park for me when everything started happening. It was all I could do to keep from blabbing to Allison, but I didn't want to say anything until I had a better idea of what was going on. Even Jerry advised me to keep things to myself for the time being. He said there was going to be a lot of information coming through, and I needed to have a level head before I started sharing any of it with Allison or anyone else."

"You're sharing it with us," said Scott.

"Yes, honey," Louise replied. "A lot's happened since those first couple of nights, which is why I'm sharing it with you and Kathy now. All right?"

Scott exhaled.

"Be patient, honey." Louise offered a blissful smile. "Everything will be revealed to you in good time." Louise paused as though collecting her thoughts, then said, "I suppose I should come right out with it. . . . Gosh,"—turning to Allison—"I don't know why I'm so nervous. I guess it's because I'm talking to my family, not some strangers on the street."

"You're doing fine, Mother." Allison smiled. "Tell your story the way it happened, darlin', just like we discussed."

"All right, dear." Louise straightened her back, relaxed her shoulders, and said, "Let's see now. . . . Oh yes. On the second night, I did ask Jerry if he could describe where he was. He answered, 'Not exactly, but it does have a name that will be familiar to you, and that name is heaven.' "

"Our father's in heaven?" said Kathy.

"Our father who art in heaven," said Scott.

"Yes, Scott," Louise replied as if a matter of fact. "Jerry's in heaven, along with the other people I've already mentioned."

"The only other person you've already mentioned is Grandma Taylor," Scott rejoined.

"Oh well." Louise shook her head. "I was getting ahead of myself when I mentioned Grandma Taylor, but this is a good time to clarify that point. Like I said, Jerry told me how happy everybody was that I'd started the automatic writing."

"Everybody?" said Scott.

"Yes, Scott." Louise composed herself. Her voice became full-throated and resonant as she said, "Heaven is home to countless beings, some of them known to us, like Jerry and Grandma Taylor, some of them familiar to us, like angels and prophets, all of them enraptured by the glory of God."

"Wow," said Scott, nodding slowly. "Jerry told you this?"

"Yes, honey. Jerry told me this and many other wondrous things. Many of his revelations came as a surprise, but none of them more than this. Reincarnation is a part of God's plan for every sentient being."

"Every what?" said Kathy, glancing at Scott.

"Every sentient being, sweetheart. That means any form of life that's able to perceive or feel things."

"Does this mean Buddha is the one true God?" said Scott. "Or the one true God is a Buddhist?"

"No, Scott." Louise smiled. "Neither of those possibilities is true, which is why everybody in heaven was so happy when I finally made contact. The purpose of all this, the reason Jerry reached out to me, is that I'm the person who will provide the answers to mankind's most compelling questions. 'Does God exist?' 'Was Jesus real?' 'Is there a heaven?' 'Is there a hell?' "

"Whoa, whoa, whoa," said Scott. "I think you just changed lanes without signaling. Are you saying that you . . . uh—what *are* you saying?"

"I think you're asking if I'm going to be one of God's prophets.

152

If that's what you're asking, honey?" Louise smiled. "The answer is 'yes.' "

"What's that mean?" said Kathy.

"What that means, Kathy Sue, is that your mother's been chosen to transcribe an updated version of God's written word."

"A new, improved Bible," said Scott. "Every home should have one."

"Yes, Scott." Louise met Scott's gaze. "Despite your sarcasm, you're correct on both counts."

"Holy moly, Mom. You say you've been chosen for this. Chosen by whom?"

"Who else?" Louise replied as if stating a fact. "I've been chosen by God."

"And Jerry told you this?" Scott furrowed his brow. "What's his role in this joint venture?"

"Jerry," said Louise, "was chosen by God as the go-between. He would be transmitting the word of God, and I would be receiving it. That's why everyone in heaven was rejoicing when I started the automatic writing."

"By what arcane process would God choose Jerry to be his intermediary?"

"It just so happens, Scott, God chose Jerry on many occasions for important assignments, long before he chose him to be your father."

"Jerry was *chosen* to be my father?"

"Yes." Louise turned toward Allison for a moment, then to Scott. "The members of our family—you, me, Allison, Kathy, Jerry, and others, like Grandma and Grandpa, who were saints for you in particular, honey. All of us have been chosen by God for important missions, important incarnations, throughout the ages."

"Okay," said Scott. "Can you give me an example? One of Jerry's better-known incarnations, for instance?"

"Yes, Scott, as a matter of fact, I can. One of Jerry's more interesting incarnations, according to him, was Abraham Lincoln."

Thinking they had reached a tipping point, Kathy glared at Scott.

Ignoring Kathy, Scott asked, "Anyone else of note?"

"Well, Scott, since you're so fond of puns and such, I'd say Jerry's incarnation as"—pronouncing the name phonetically— " 'Richard Wagner' was *someone of note.*"

Scott was silent as he considered Louise's pronunciation of the name in question. "Do you mean"—pronouncing the name properly—" 'Ricard Vagner,' the German composer?"

"Yes, I suppose," said Louise. "I only read the name in a message from Jerry when we were discussing past lives. This one I do know how to pronounce, though . . . Frédéric Chopin."

"Dad was Chopin as well?" Scott twisted his face for Kathy's benefit.

"No, sweetheart." Louise laughed lightly. "*I* was Chopin."

"Oh. Well. Right," said Scott. "That makes more sense."

Kathy snorted.

"All right," said Allison, fixing his eyes on Kathy. "We'll have none of that."

"It's okay, darling." Louise patted Allison's thigh. "This is going to take some getting used to for everyone concerned. Truth be told, Kathy's reaction is better than I'd expected. Now, let's get back to the question of reincarnation."

"Jerry told you about these past lives?" said Scott.

"Yes, Scott." Louise adopted a serious tone. "Previous incarnations are discussed by sentient beings in heaven, much the same as classroom studies are discussed by students at school. Each individual, for lack of a better description, carries the imprint of their previous lives. An individual's past-life information can be accessed by any other individual, but that only occurs when all the parties involved, whether two or twenty-two, benefit from the exchange."

"Holy cow, Mom," interjected Scott. "You're beginning to sound like a lecture on comparative religion."

"I've been reading my notes, which is the whole point of this, as you say, 'joint venture.' I mean, if I don't understand what I'm putting on paper, how can anyone else be expected to?"

"Fair enough," replied Scott. "But don't you think it's time to acknowledge the elephant in the master bedroom?"

"I'm not sure I follow your meaning, honey." Louise tilted her head.

"You've told us this fantastic story, Mom, about the circumstances that have presented you with a new career opportunity. But you haven't shown us how it works, how you communicate with our father who art in heaven."

"Oh," said Louise, picking up the pad and pen from her bedside table. "Is there something in particular you'd like to ask?"

"Uh . . . I'm not sure what I think about everything so far, but I have to admit, I keep having this feeling that Jerry's standing behind me. Is Jerry standing behind me?"

"Well, Scott, I already know that Jerry's here. He was very excited to see you—both of you, Kathy Sue. Okay, I'll go ahead and ask what Jerry's doing right now."

Louise placed the pad of paper in her lap. She exhaled; her head fell forward, and she began to write. Her hand tracked across the pad with astonishing speed, left to right, left to right, left to right.

The episode stopped as abruptly as it had begun. After Louise's hand stopped moving, her head returned to its upright position. Louise read what she'd written, looked up, and smiled at Scott.

"It just so happens, Scott, that your father's been standing behind the rocking chair since you first sat down. He wants you to know how happy he is to see you, how proud he is of you—and you, Kathy Sue. Although, since he's been spending time with me, he's been enjoying the side-benefit of seeing Kathy as well. More than once, sweetheart"—smiling blissfully—"your father mentioned how pleased he was to see what a fine young woman you've become." Louise looked at Kathy with expectation.

Realizing a response was unavoidable, Kathy said, "That's nice."

"Kathy Sue." Louise affected surprise, "Is that all you have to say to your father after all these years?"

Kathy glared at Scott.

"This may sound strange," said Scott, "but I'm feeling claustrophobic. Would it be all right if I open the door?"

Allison laughed. "Yes, Scott, that would be fine. I'm laughing because, as your mother's about to tell you, this room is packed to the rafters with visitors from heaven."

Kathy pushed herself up to sit cross-legged, facing Louise. Louise was watching Scott as he opened the bedroom door and returned to the rocking chair.

Kathy said, "Mom . . . ?"

"Yes, dear?" Louise looked at Kathy.

"Does that mean this room's full of angels?"

Louise thought for a moment, then said, "Well, yes and no, sweetheart, which is to say, 'angels,' as we commonly refer to God's heavenly creatures, are in actuality the lowest order of divine beings. I've received quite a bit of information on this subject, but I'm not conversant with the particulars yet. I can tell you there are three 'spheres of angels,' and each sphere contains three 'orders' or 'choirs.' Isn't that pretty, Kathy, 'choirs of angels'?" Louise paused.

After a beat, Kathy said, "Yes."

"I *have* memorized the three orders in the First Sphere," Louise

156

continued. "Now, let me see,"—looking up and to the right—"the First Choir are the Seraphim, the 'burning ones' who continuously chant, 'Holy, holy, holy is the Lord of hosts. The whole earth is full of His glory.' Next are the Cherubim, the Second Choir, who guard the tree of life in the Garden of Eden, as well as the throne of God. And then, of course, the Thrones, who present the prayers of men and listen to the will of God."

"Of course," said Scott, making a face. He then smiled and said, "A-plus, Mom. I can't wait to hear the next installment."

Louise exhaled; her head fell forward, and she began to write. She filled one sheet of paper, tore it from the pad, and continued writing as the first sheet of paper floated to the bed. Louise's hand was halfway down the second sheet of paper when it came to an abrupt stop. Her head returned to its upright position. She picked up the first sheet of paper and spent a moment reading what she'd written.

Louise looked up and said, "Well, Scott,"—a self-satisfied smile—"ask, and it shall be given you."

"Okay?" said Scott, not quite sure of what she meant.

"The Second Sphere of Angels," said Louise, reading from the first piece of paper, "includes the Dominions who oversee the duties of lower angels, the Virtues who manifest signs and miracles in the world, and the Powers who supervise the movements of all the heavenly bodies—stars, planets, and moons—to maintain order in the cosmos." Louise looked at Scott.

"Ah, so," said Scott, nodding slowly.

Louise looked back to the paper she was holding and continued: "The Third Sphere is made up of the Principalities who guide and protect nations or large groups of people such as major religious organizations. The next choir is composed of the seven Archangels who are known by name and associated with days of the week—Michael for Sunday, Gabriel for Monday, Raphael for

Tuesday, Uriel for Wednesday, Raguel for Thursday, Remiel for Friday, and Sariel for Saturday." Louise picked up the second piece of paper and continued, "Last but not least—"

"Is that what it says?" said Scott. "On the paper?"

"Well, no, Scott." Louise smiled. "I'm ad-libbing a bit to lighten things up."

"Speaking of the devil," said Scott. "Where does Lucifer fit into all of this?"

"Let's not get ahead of ourselves," Louise replied, looking as if a cloud had passed in front of the sun. "Like I was saying, last but not least, the third order of the Third Sphere is the Choir of Angels. These are the angels we're most familiar with because they're involved with all living things. Also, Kathy Sue, the Choir of Angels is the group that includes all of the guardian angels." This last tidbit was delivered with a flourish, as if the messenger derived a sense of importance from knowledge of the fact.

"Wow, Mom," said Scott. "Where were you when I needed research information for my school assignments?"

"All right, Scott." Louise exhaled. "I'd appreciate it if you'd stop making wisecracks."

"No, no, no," said Scott, holding out both hands. "Don't get me wrong. I think this is fantastic. All of it—really phenomenal. But what are you going to do with it?"

"Well, Scott," Louise replied, feigning frustration. "That's what we wanted to share with you and Kathy. Why we called you into the bedroom tonight."

"Okay, then," said Scott. "I'm all ears." Scott looked at Kathy. "How about you, Sue?"

"I think I should go to bed."

"Oh, no, sweetheart," said Louise. "This concerns you as much as anyone else, honey."

"It does?" Kathy glared at Scott.

"Yes, Kathy," said Allison. "Your mother needs you to hear the rest of her story tonight."

"Why tonight?" Kathy replied, testing Allison's patience.

"Kathy Sue," Louise cut in, preempting a display of Allison's authority. "You can stay awake another half hour or so. Can't you, sweetheart?"

"I guess so." Kathy narrowed her eyes.

"Thank you, dear." Louise composed herself, then said, "Let's see now, where was I?" She turned to Allison. "Do you remember where I left off, darling?"

"I believe you were telling the children about Jerry's previous incarnations."

"Oh, yes, that's right." Louise inhaled. "Another one of Jerry's important incarnations—this one especially difficult for obvious reasons—was Pontius Pilate."

"Who was Pontius Pilate?" said Kathy.

"Pontius Pilate?" echoed Scott. "Pontius Pilate in the Bible, Pontius Pilate?"

"Yes, Scott." Louise looked from Scott to Allison, then to Kathy. "Pontius Pilate, honey, was the Roman governor of Judaea who presided over the trial of Jesus Christ and gave the order for his crucifixion."

"Ugh," said Kathy.

"Nail on the head," said Scott, "if any of that were true. I think *crucifixion* should be spelled with *ct* instead of an *x*."

"All right, Scott," said Allison with a stern look. He then turned to Louise and said, "Perhaps it's time to tell the children some of their past lives, darlin'?"

"Yes, dear," said Louise, "this would be the perfect time."

Louise exhaled; her head fell forward, and she began to write. A minute later, Louise tore a sheet of paper from the pad but did not continue writing. There was a moment of indecision as

Louise's hand remained poised at the top of the pad, but then her head returned to its upright position. Louise picked up the sheet of paper from the bed and read what she'd written.

"Oh my gosh, Kathy Sue," Louise exclaimed. "You were Elizabeth, the mother of John the Baptist."

"I was?" said Kathy, considering the implications.

"And Scott," Louise continued, "you were John the Baptist."

"*Eww*," said Kathy, reaching a conclusion.

Louise looked at Kathy. "Like I said, sweetheart, the four of us have been chosen throughout history for important incarnations."

"Anything other than characters from the New Testament?" said Scott.

Louise gave Scott a look of beneficent restraint. She then looked down and read more of what she'd written. After a moment, she looked up and said, "Kathy Sue, you were Ponce de León, the Spanish explorer who named Florida and became the first governor of Puerto Rico. He was also famous for believing there was a 'fountain of youth,' but that was more a myth that became associated with his name after his death."

"Who are you?" interjected Scott. "And what have you done with my mother?"

Louise giggled, then said, "I'm just a messenger."

"So said Gabriel," said Scott, somewhat bemused.

"As a matter of fact, Scott, I didn't want to tell you this until later, but now that you've brought it up. When I asked if Jerry was in the room, I was told that he *and Gabriel* were standing right behind you."

"What are the odds?" said Scott. "But then, it's a small world, as they say in Anaheim."

Louise did not dignify Scott's remark with a response. She looked down at her recent revelation, then to Kathy.

"Kathy Sue," Louise enthused, "you were Marie Antoinette."

"*Marie Antoinette*," said Scott, frowning. "That's a dubious distinction."

"Well, Scott," said Louise. "She *was* the Queen of France."

"Yes," said Scott, nodding agreement. "And as such, Her Most Christian Majesty was responsible for inciting the French Revolution, which was the first domino to fall in the collapse of European aristocracy. So, hmm, okay, not bad, Sue." Scott gave Kathy a thumbs up.

"All right, Scott," said Louise. "Maybe you'll be a little less sarcastic when you hear about some of your previous incarnations, such as Frederick the Great."

"I was Frederick the Great?" Scott made a face. "Are you sure it's 'Frederick,' not 'Alexander'?"

"This isn't like ordering off the menu, Scott." Louise exhaled; her head fell forward, and she began to write. At a speed that brought to mind the contradictory definitions of the word *awesome*, Louise's hand moved from margin to margin several times and then stopped. Louise appeared to be unaffected by the rigors of each episode, regardless of its duration or output. Her eyes now followed the same path on the paper that her hand recently had. Her smile registered self-satisfaction when she said, "Well, Scott, I don't think you'll have a problem with the fact that you were Ludwig von Beethoven."

Scott raised his brow. "That would explain why I can play the first movement of the *Moonlight Sonata* with my eyes closed." He inhaled, then added, "The trouble I have with the third movement doesn't jibe so well with this revelation."

"All right, Mother," said Allison. "We should get back to the matter at hand."

"Yes, of course, darling." Louise smiled at Allison. "Let's see, where was I?"

"Jerry told you he was going to be away for a couple of days."

"That's right," said Louise. "But he also told me to continue checking in while he was away."

"Where'd he go?" said Kathy.

"Well, Kathy Sue, at the time, I wasn't sure where Jerry had gone. But he wanted me to keep up with the automatic writing. You know, to improve my ability before I started receiving the information for my book. The funny thing is, I expected Grandma Taylor would be the next person I'd hear from, but when I received the first message from Jerry's stand-in, I could tell it wasn't someone I knew. I mean, they knew me, knew things about me and my life. They mentioned Allison by name, but, like I said, I didn't know who they were."

Allison interjected, "Which probably has to do with why this was when I discovered Louise asleep on the bathroom floor, surrounded by sheets of paper covered in her handwriting. You can't imagine how bizarre that seemed to me. I'd woken up at two in the morning because I needed to use the bathroom. At first, I thought your mother must be in the bathroom for the same reason, but after five minutes or so, I realized I should get up and see what was going on. I knocked at the door and called her name, but there was no answer. I turned the knob, then opened the door wide enough to see Louise lying on the floor. When I stepped into the room and saw all that paper scattered on the floor, my mind went blank. Truly, this was one of those rare moments in life when you have no idea of what you're seeing."

"It was quite a sight," said Louise. "It had been one of my more"—turning to Allison—"would you say *productive* nights."

"For want of a better word." Allison shook his head. "You can't imagine the scene. I counted the pieces of paper as I picked them up—thirty-eight full-size sheets of unlined paper completely covered with Louise's handwriting."

"*And*," Louise chimed in, eager to embellish, "if that wasn't enough to give a person pause, some of the sheets had notes in the margins and writing on the back." She grimaced playfully. "Not to mention, I'd already hidden a batch of papers from earlier that evening."

"When I heard that," said Allison, ". . . well, what can I say, I was already speechless."

"Allison 'speechless,' " said Louise, "is a rare thing, as we well know. So, I took advantage of the situation to tell as much of my story as possible without interruption." Louise telegraphed a look of personal triumph, while Allison maintained his characteristic reserve.

"I started at the beginning," Louise continued, "back at Oakcrest with the Ouija board. And I have to say, even with the doubtful look on Daddy's face, he didn't say a word until I got to the part about Jerry leaving for a couple of days and my communicating with someone new. I haven't told you kids yet, but when I asked the new person who he was, he told me he was Allison's uncle.

"Now, this is someone I'd never met. I'd heard his name once or twice, but nothing more than that. Even so, when I described him to Allison, read some of the things he'd told me about his past, Allison said there was no doubt about it. This was his Uncle Frank who'd died of a heart attack"—looking at Allison—"how long ago, sweetheart?"

"Nineteen years," said Allison.

"That's right," said Louise, confirming the fact. "Uncle Frank died nineteen years ago before I even knew who Allison was. But there we were, having a conversation in the bathroom like we'd just met at a family picnic. Isn't that something?

"Yes, Louise," said Scott. "That is something."

"Well, *Scott*," said Louise, "Allison certainly thought it was. I mean, how could I know all the things Uncle Frank was telling me, things about his wife, Eileen, and their children, Sam and Janey?"

"You'd never heard their names?" said Scott.

"Well, no," said Louise, shaking her head. "Uncle Frank died before Allison and I knew each other."

"That doesn't mean you never heard the names of his wife and children," Scott rejoined.

"If I had," said Louise, standing her ground, "I certainly don't remember it. Anyway, Scott, it wasn't only the names he mentioned. He also told me about a fishing trip he'd taken with Sam and Allison and Allison's brother, Albert, and their father, John, Frank's younger brother. And I'm pretty darn sure I'd never heard anything about that."

"The fishing trip she's talking about was more than forty years ago," said Allison. "I didn't remember it myself until Louise told me Frank had mentioned it."

"So, you see," said Louise, "this was when Allison started considering the *veracity* of what I was telling him." Louise looked to Allison for confirmation; whether for his acceptance of her story or her co-opting one of his fifty-cent words was unclear.

"Yes," said Allison, tilting his head, "to some degree." Allison inhaled as he considered what he'd say next. Louise put her hand in Allison's. Allison smiled in response, then said, "I couldn't deny Louise's knowledge of events that even I'd forgotten. I still don't have a reasonable explanation for that, other than what she was telling me was God's honest truth." Allison broke into a self-conscious grin.

Louise clapped her hands together and giggled.

Scott and Kathy exchanged glances of uncertain anxiety.

"That apple cider went right through me," said Scott, standing up. "I need a bathroom break."

"All right," said Louise. "I think everyone could use a moment to digest what's been said so far." She turned to Allison. "Don't you agree, Daddy?"

"Yes, darlin', I do."

Louise turned to Scott. "Take your time, honey. We'll be right here collecting our thoughts. Kathy Sue, do you need to use the bathroom, sweetheart?"

"No," Kathy replied, rolling onto her back.

11:00 PM

Scott came back to the master bedroom and sat down without closing the door. Kathy returned from the living room, having excused herself for a minute because she didn't want to be alone with Louise and Allison. Kathy sat down at the foot of the bed with one leg curled beneath her, one leg over the side.

"Okay," said Louise. "Are you kids comfortable?"

"Bug in a rug," said Scott.

"Kathy Sue?" Louise tilted her head.

"I'm fine," Kathy replied, making no attempt to sound convincing.

"All right, then." Louise looked at Allison. "Where were we, darling?"

"I believe you were apprising me of your late-night activities."

"Yes, that's right." Louise smiled. "And you listened without interruption until I told you about Uncle Frank, which made you think I was really on to something."

"Yes, darlin'," said Allison, not quite smiling. "To some degree."

"Oh well." Louise slapped Allison's thigh. "I didn't mean hook, line, and sinker, sweetheart, although it was me telling you about your fishing trip that reeled you in."

"Mom," said Scott, "enough with the fishing metaphors."

"Really, sweetheart?" Louise made a face. "I thought those were keepers."

"Ugh." Scott shivered theatrically. "That is sufficient comic relief, Louise. Let's get back to the business at hand, your hotline to heaven."

Kathy stifled a laugh as she stretched out on the bed, head propped on her arm, facing Louise.

"I agree," said Allison.

"All right, sweetheart." Louise looked from Allison to Scott. "Like I said, I'd explained everything to Daddy, from the first weekend at Oakcrest to Uncle Frank's arrival six weeks later."

"At this point," said Allison, "I convinced your mother to discontinue her practice of sitting on the bathroom floor until all hours. I told Louise she could sit in the living room if she needed to be alone, or she could sit in bed as long as she turned her light off by midnight. Either way, she had to start getting at least six hours of sleep every night, or she'd start to come apart at the seams, which, by all appearances, was already happening."

"As much as I appreciated Allison's offer to sit in the bedroom," Louise resumed, "I wasn't ready to communicate with the spirit world in front of an audience." Louise smiled at Allison. "So I set up shop in the living room and agreed to come to bed no later than midnight. That first night, sitting on the sofa with my pad in my lap, I had a list of questions for Uncle Frank about Allison's family. But wouldn't you know it?" Louise shook her head. "That's when Jerry returned with some pretty big news."

"How convenient," said Scott, "as for not having to prove Uncle Frank's credibility."

Louise paused for a moment but decided against responding to Scott's innuendo. She continued, instead, from where she'd left off: "I knew God had requested Jerry's presence. Jerry told me that before he went away. I didn't tell Allison any of this when I was explaining what was going on because I wasn't sure myself what God had in mind. That's what Jerry had gone to discuss.

"Well, the first thing Jerry told me came as a bit of a surprise"—tilting her head from side to side—"that the process of receiving new information would continue for at least *five years*. Well, I didn't know what to say to that. I mean, Lord knows I wanted to participate, but I'd never considered being involved *for five years*. Then it dawned on me, what's the difference? Five days, five weeks, five years? I shared this thought with Jerry, and he replied, 'That's the spirit. And, by the way, that's exactly how it feels over here. Five days, five weeks, five years? What's the difference?' " Louise set the pad and pen on her bedside table.

"Does this mean you'll be taking dictation from nine till midnight for the next five years?" said Scott.

"Not exactly, Scott, which brings me to the next bit of unexpected news from Jerry's meeting with God. They think the transmission of this much information will require more of my time than a couple of hours a day."

"What's that mean?" said Kathy, now sitting cross-legged.

Louise put on a brave face. "Well, sweetheart, it means I'll be devoting more time to the project. Actually,"—leaning slightly forward—"it means I'll be devoting most of my time to the project." Louise looked into Kathy's eyes as if the last clarification was specifically for her.

"I still don't understand what that means," said Kathy, her voice wavering.

"What that means, Kathy Sue,"—leaning closer—"is that this undertaking is so important—not just for me, sweetheart, but for, well, *everyone*. It's so important that it will require as much time as I have to give."

"Does that mean you're going to stop working at the office?" Kathy swallowed hard.

"Yes, sweetheart." Louise paused as Kathy considered her answer.

Kathy looked at Allison, thinking he might have something to say about losing his all-in-one office staff, but he remained silent.

Struggling with the shifting terrain, Kathy asked Louise, "Are you going to stay home all day while you're working on this?"

"Not necessarily." The sparkle in Louise's eyes belied her tentative tone. "Which is why we wanted to celebrate tonight with the whole family, why we wanted to share the news with you kids while Scott was here."

Scott crossed his legs at the knee and leaned against the upholstered arm farthest from the bed.

"Yes," said Allison, "but, darlin', I think you may be getting ahead of yourself. That is if you want to share the whole story with the children."

"Well, of course, I do," Louise replied. "All right, then. Uh,"— turning to Allison—"do you remember where I was, sweetheart?"

"I believe you were in the living room for the first time when you realized Jerry had returned from his meeting."

"Oh yes, that's right." Louise arranged herself and the bedclothes as she picked up from where she'd left off: "Like Daddy said, I was in the living room—let's see, now . . . it was Sunday night. I remember it was the first of September because Kathy had returned from Long Beach, and I had to wait until she went to bed before I set things up in the living room. So, after I saw the light go out in Kathy's room, I sat down on the sofa with my pad and pen and the list for Uncle Frank—well, you knew that already. Okay, like I said, I was more than a little surprised when I realized Jerry was back. And also, right away, I could tell he was excited."

"How could you tell he was excited?" said Kathy.

"Oh well, Kathy Sue." Louise furrowed her brow. "You can tell by someone's words, honey, even if you can't hear their voice. It's like reading a letter from someone you know really well. You know what I mean, don't you, sweetheart?"

"No," said Kathy with an edge to her voice.

169

"Okay," said Scott, "you knew that Jerry was excited."

"Yes, honey, by the words he was using."

"All right, Mother," Allison cut in. "I think we can agree that Jerry was excited. Why don't you tell the children why?"

"I'd be happy to." Louise tucked a wisp of hair behind her ear. "You remember that Jerry had to leave because he had an audience with God."

"Sounds like something from the Brothers Grimm," said Scott, "an audience with the almighty king."

"It wasn't an audience with the almighty king," Louise replied. "It was an audience with the Almighty."

Louise raised her brow for emphasis.

"The first thing Jerry told me," she continued, "was that I needed to do as much automatic writing as possible to improve my speed. He said I was already doing really well. In fact, he said his only complaint since we started communicating this way was hearing from everyone how fantastic my writing was coming along."

"They must have thought it heavenly," said Scott.

Louise smiled at Scott, then narrowed her eyes. "Anyway,"—looking at Kathy—"the next thing your father told me *really* took me by surprise, and I'm still trying to come to grips with it. He said I needed to gain some weight, at least ten pounds. 'Why ever for,' I blurted out." Louise looked flummoxed, shaking her head. "But Jerry didn't answer. At least for longer than usual, he didn't answer. Finally, Jerry communicated, 'Sorry. I was laughing.'

"Right away, I whispered, 'Well, I'm glad one of us finds this amusing because I certainly don't.'"

"Why did Jerry want you to gain weight?" said Kathy.

"Jerry didn't want me to gain weight, sweetheart," said Louise. "God did."

"Okay," said Scott. "I'll bite—uh, sorry, sounds like we're

back to fishing metaphors. Anyway, why did God want you to gain weight?"

"Evidently," said Louise, "people in the past who've communicated through automatic writing for extended periods start to have physical problems, especially if they drink alcohol or smoke cigarettes."

"Lord knows you don't drink more than once or twice a year," said Scott.

"Yes, Scott, he does."

"But you smoked a cigarette with me at Oakcrest yesterday." Scott inhaled. "How's that figure in the scheme of things?"

"Well, Scott." Louise glanced at Allison. "I decided to have my last cigarette with you when you were here visiting. I thought it was something we could share. Not that I support your smoking habit, honey, because, of course, I don't. But I knew I had to stop smoking altogether, so I chose to have my last cigarette with you on the deck at Oakcrest. That in mind, sweetheart, maybe you'd consider stopping with me."

"Sorry to disappoint," said Scott, "but no can do. As a matter of fact, this seems like an excellent time for a cigarette break."

"Oh no, honey." Louise leaned forward. "You can wait a little longer, can't you, sweetheart? It's just that it's getting so late, and I'd like to go on with my story,"—changing her tone—"if that's okay with you."

Scott considered Louise's request, then said, "All right. But I'd like to step outside sooner than later, so keep an eye out for a convenient stopping point."

"Yes, dear, I will." Louise smiled briefly. "Now . . . oh, gosh, I'm having such a time remembering where I left off."

"You were telling us why God wanted you to gain weight," said Scott.

"That's right." Louise pursed her lips. "Well, like I already told you, in the past, people who practiced automatic writing over a long period very often suffered from ailments including severe exhaustion, nervous breakdowns, mental disorders, and, in some instances, cancer. So, you see, the reason God wanted me to gain some weight—I really don't think it has to be ten pounds, though——was because it would help to insulate me from the negative effects of that much psychic energy passing through my body." She looked to Scott for a sign of comprehension. "Do you understand, sweetheart?"

"Well enough, I suppose." Scott raised his brow. "Too much of a good thing can be a bad thing."

"Precisely." Louise leaned back against the headboard. "God was looking out for my best interests, which wasn't much different than a businessman protecting an asset, when you think about it." Louise adjusted the neck of her nightgown. "Anyway," she concluded, "I've been eating more than usual as well as more often— snacks in the afternoon and whatnot—in hopes of satisfying *our Heavenly Father's* unusual request."

"How does *our Heavenly Father* feel about you making light of his name?" said Scott. "Isn't there something or other about eternal damnation and hellfire?"

"Actually, Scott." Louise smiled softly. "That would be 'eternal hellfire and damnation,' neither of which will be visited upon me because God likes my sense of humor."

"God told you this?"

"Yes, Scott, more than once, as a matter of fact."

"I don't think you understand what those words mean."

"Which words, honey?" Louise looked at Scott with calm curiosity.

" 'A matter of fact,' " said Scott. "A matter of fact is something that's indisputably true, which, it seems to me, is the polar opposite of a faith-based experience, such as a thumbs up from God—

twice, as if once weren't enough. If God had given me a pat on the back, I'd be walking on air for the rest of my life, however long or short that might be. Isn't that how it works? Like with Moses, for example, or Joan of Arc?"

"I doubt this will support the point you're trying to make," said Louise, "but I can't help mentioning, since you brought it up, that I was Joan of Arc in one of my past lives."

"Of course you were," said Scott, blinking slowly. "Man, oh, man, this gives 'preaching to the choir' a whole new meaning. Okay, well, never mind. What else did Jerry have to say when he got back from his meeting with I Am That I Am, or does that moniker only apply to his stint with the Children of Israel?"

"All right, Scott," said Louise. "I don't think this is the time and place for you to exercise your intellect. You'll be back at school tomorrow, honey. Why don't you save your wisecracks for the teachers who are getting paid for the privilege of listening to them? Okay, sweetheart?"

"You bet." Scott pulled an imaginary zipper across his lips.

"Now I understand why Jerry wanted me to enroll in a public speaking class," said Louise, shaking her head.

"Excuse me," said Kathy. "Jerry wants you to take a public speaking class?"

"Yes, sweetheart."

"Why?"

"Part of the reason," Louise replied, "has to do with discussions like this being hijacked by smart alecks like your brother."

"Humph," was heard from Scott.

"Jerry told me that not only will I be receiving revelations from God," Louise continued, "I will also be lecturing and conducting discussion groups as the information becomes known to me. The public speaking classes are meant to bolster my confidence when I'm speaking to, well,"—breathes in, then sighs—"the public."

"I, for one," said Scott, "would pay to see a lecture demonstration. The automatic writing alone would be worth the price of admission."

"Now, Scott," said Louise, sitting up straight, "I thought you were taking a time out. If not, I'll thank you in advance for keeping your comments to yourself unless I ask for them."

"Holy cow, Mom, you don't need a public speaking class to gain confidence. Keep doing like that just now, and you'll be fine."

"Thank you, dear." Louise shook her head. "But standing in front of an auditorium full of strangers is a tad different than sitting in bed talking to my family, wouldn't you agree?"

"Absolutely." Scott leaned forward. "Then again, what can higher education teach you that a higher power can't?"

"Well, sweetheart, I guess I'll find out soon enough. As for whether or not a class will help, I've already signed up for one at Santa Rosa Junior College."

"You have?" Kathy made a face. "When? What class?"

"Aren't they teaching you to speak in complete sentences at that school of yours?" said Scott.

"Shut up," Kathy rejoined.

"Case in point."

"All right, you two, behave yourselves." Louise looked from Scott to Kathy and said, "In answer to your first question, Kathy Sue, I went to the campus on Friday afternoon. Even though classes had started three weeks earlier, the woman in the admissions office said she'd put the paperwork through if the instructor agreed to a late enrollment. So, I sought out the teacher, a nice older gentleman named Harvey Thomas, and we really hit it off. Mr. Thomas said he'd be pleased to include me in his Mastering Public Speaking class, and if our chat was any indication, he reckoned he might learn a thing or two from me."

"Wow, Mom," said Scott. "You, a college coed. Who'd a thunk it?"

"It's only one class, Scott, but it is exciting." Louise rested her hand on Allison's thigh. "And a little daunting, what with everything else I'm supposed to be doing."

"What else are you supposed to be doing?" said Kathy.

"My gosh, Kathy Sue." Louise furrowed her brow. "Aren't I doing enough already? Watching what I eat, abstaining from alcohol and tobacco, getting more exercise, improving my writing."

"Now that you're listing your do's and don'ts," said Scott, "I don't remember God telling you to get more exercise, number one. And, number two, it occurs to me, if you add caffeine to your list of don'ts, it would be eerily close to the religious persuasion of your childhood."

"Maybe I forgot to mention it, Scott. After all, this story has a lot of moving parts—"

"You can say that again." Scott rolled his eyes.

"Yes, dear, but I won't." Louise smiled briefly. "Anyway, when Jerry advised me to gain some weight, he also told me to start walking for at least forty-five minutes every day, preferably in the morning, which I've been doing for the last three weeks. As for the caffeine remark and how it relates to The Church of Jesus Christ of Latter-day Saints. Throughout history, religious factions have tried to control their followers' conduct, from dietary restrictions to sexual abstinence, but that's nothing more than small-minded men exercising control for the sake of lining their coffers. God isn't concerned with what people eat or drink or how they express their love as long as they don't harm themselves or anyone else."

"I've already said this," said Scott, "but I have to say it again. Who are you, and what have you done with my mother?"

"I think you may have to get used to the idea, Scott, that I'm no longer speaking as your mother. I'm speaking as the messenger of God."

"So far," said Scott, "your God seems like a nicer fellow than everyone else's, especially when it comes to sexual abstinence. I can't wait to hear what the Catholic Church has to say about that after two thousand years of cruel and unusual punishment."

"Shedding new light on these issues," Louise replied, "is precisely why God decided to reveal himself, here and now, without confusion or interpretation. His word, transmitted through me, will be clear and concise. Finally, after millenniums of conflict and discord, mankind will know the mind of God."

"As well they should," said Scott. "Do we get to meet him? Is he here tonight, with his heavenly host?"

"Before I answer that question," said Louise, looking from Scott to Allison, "let me get back to Jerry's checklist of what God was expecting from me. Last on the list, and the most difficult to understand, was the need for me to be in different locations—different cities and different countries—when I receive the transmissions from heaven."

Kathy looked at Scott, then back to Louise.

"I didn't know what to think when I heard that," Louise continued. "Aside from the time I was expected to put in, the thought of gallivanting around the country, let alone different countries, all I could say was I didn't know what to say. And, of course, how would I pay for the travel and lodging?"

"And . . . ?" said Kathy.

Louise laughed to herself. "This is where it gets very interesting and very confusing at the same time."

"To say the least," said Scott.

"I'm sure everyone's experienced something to that effect," said Louise, looking at Kathy. "But getting mixed signals from God has to qualify as above and beyond your everyday dilemma."

"I wouldn't be so sure about that," said Scott. "Getting mixed signals from God sounds very much like an everyday dilemma to me." Scott raised his hands, palms up. "I'm just saying."

"Anyway," said Louise, shaking her head, "Jerry told me not to worry about where the money would come from. He assured me it would appear, in the right amount, at the right time. And then,"—looking bewildered—"Jerry told me I should communicate with my father and left it at that. After a few seconds of silence—when I'm not writing, you know, it seems like there's silence on the other end. Anyway, after a few seconds of silence, I asked, 'Why should I communicate with my father? Is that where you think the money will come from? If it is, if that's who you think will provide financial support for me taking this show on the road, someone's got another think coming.' "

"That means you did not talk to Grandpa?" said Scott.

"Not right away." Louise pursed her lips. "I mean, I knew that Grandma and Grandpa were financially secure, not wanting for anything anyway. All the same, there was never any indication of more money than necessary to live as simply as they do. To tell the truth, I think Uncle Donald helps out from time to time. Not that he'd feel the pinch, in between buying motorboats and airplanes."

"All right, Louise," said Allison. "Let's not dredge up family issues."

"Yes, you're right, *of course.*" Louise smiled at Allison. "We need to be looking ahead."

"Hold on a minute," Scott cut in. "You said 'not right away,' which means you did talk to Grandpa. Now that would have been an interesting conversation. There's no way you could have explained all of this to Gus. He would have sputtered something or other after hearing you were communicating with your dead ex-husband, not to mention"— jerking his thumb toward the ceiling.

"No, Scott, you're right. I knew better than to tell Grandpa everything I've told you—well, you, Kathy, and Allison. I told Mother more than I told Daddy, but they're pretty much set in their ways when it comes to discussing God and religion."

"I know you don't get out much," said Scott, "social gatherings and such, but you should know by now that everyone on this planet is pretty much set in their ways when it comes to discussing God and religion."

"For crying out loud, Scott. We're not shut-ins."

"No," said Scott, raising his shoulders, "you just stay in. But that's not my point."

"What is your point?" Louise folded her hands in her lap.

"You've enrolled in a public speaking class with the intention of lecturing to large groups of people about the word of God. That's all well and good in that those people will come to hear you because they are, for the most part, like-minded individuals. It's everyone else I'm worried about. History has proven, time and again, that religion is the powder keg with the shortest fuse. What I mean to say is you sound like you expect to be welcomed into the fold, but I think you need to allow for the possibility of being left out in the cold. Sorry, I wasn't aiming for a rhyme. In other words, you're touting yourself as a messenger of God, but that may be nothing more than a fool's errand."

Louise took a slow breath, then said, "You make it sound like this is my plan, Scott. But this is not my plan. None of this is my plan. This is God's plan, and I have to believe that I will be directed to what is right and good, that I will be welcomed by, as you say, like-minded individuals, that God has chosen me because I'm up to the task. This is God's plan, Scott, and he's doing it for the betterment of mankind."

"Exactly," said Scott. "That's exactly what I'm saying. This is God's plan for the betterment of mankind. It was also God's plan

178

when he sent his only begotten Son for the betterment of mankind, in response to which mankind nailed him to a cross."

"All right, Scott," said Allison. "That's enough." Looking at Louise, he said, "Please get back to telling your story, darlin', after you'd spoken to Gus and Marguerite."

"Yes, sweetheart." Louise looked from Allison to Scott and said, "Mother and Daddy were confused by what little I told them. They made it clear they'd do whatever they could if I were in trouble. But they were in no position to, as Daddy put it, 'send me on a trip around the world.' " Looking slightly miffed, Louise added, "I'm sure he said more than that after he hung up."

"Oh yeah," said Scott, "you can take that to the bank. But God love him—whoops, sorry—anyway, Gus would give you the shirt off his back if you were in trouble."

"Yes, dear, your grandfather's been very good to you."

"In the sense that he's *been* a grandfather to me." Scott fixed his eyes on Louise.

"I don't know how much longer I can stay awake," said Kathy.

"What time is it?" said Scott.

Allison looked toward his bedside table and said, "A few minutes before midnight."

"Oh my gosh," said Louise. "I had no idea it was that late. Maybe we should call it a night."

"No way," said Scott, sitting forward. "I have to catch a bus in eight hours. I'm not going to bed until I've heard the whole story. However,"—standing up—"I'm going to start biting my nails if I don't go outside and have a cigarette."

"I'm going with him," said Kathy, lowering her feet to the floor.

"I don't know," said Louise, turning to Allison.

"We're only going out to the sidewalk," said Kathy. "Right?"

"Right," said Scott. "If we're attacked, Kathy will protect me."

"All right, Scott." Louise exhaled.

"Not to worry," Scott replied over his shoulder. "We'll be back before you know it. Ha! Remember what Jerry said about time? Not really a thing."

"Kathy Sue," called Louise, "put on your wool coat, sweetheart."

"I am," Kathy called from her bedroom.

Scott slipped on his flannel shirt, checking the pocket for cigarettes and matches. He waited by the front door until Kathy appeared, wearing a long wool coat over her pajamas.

"Love the shoes," said Scott, commenting on Kathy's red leather Mary Janes.

"Me too," said Kathy, waiting for Scott to open the door.

"I'm serious." Scott stepped out to the concrete landing.

"So am I." Kathy closed the door behind her.

MONDAY

SEPTEMBER 23, 1968

12:00 AM

Scott tapped a cigarette from his pack as he and Kathy walked to the sidewalk. He slowed to a stop, struck a match, and lit the cigarette. After a beat, Scott exhaled with a sigh of relief.

"Yuk," said Kathy, walking a few steps farther than the square of sidewalk Scott had claimed for himself.

"Don't knock it till you've tried it."

"I may not be as smart as you, but I'm not stupid." Kathy folded her arms, as much for emphasis as the late-night chill. "So, you're taking folk dancing. That's really neat. I'd take folk dancing if it were offered. How many boys in the class?"

"Uh. . . ." Scott looked down the lamp-lit street. "It's been different from class to class. I think a couple of guys have already dropped out. I don't know, six or seven."

"How many girls?"

Scott thought about it for a moment, then said, "That number also changes from class to class. I've only been in college for a few weeks, and it's not like high school. People show up after a few classes. People disappear after a few classes. I'd say,"—shrugging his shoulders—"twenty girls, give or take."

"What kind of dances do you do? Anything I'd know?" Kathy did a time step with the tongue-in-teeth concentration of a three-year tap student.

"It's a bit weird with people deciding whether or not to stay enrolled. All we've done for the last two weeks is square dancing."

" 'Square dancing'?" Kathy repeated, mildly surprised.

"Yes, ma'am. I can swing my partner with the best of 'em."
Scott stepped closer. "If you'd like a demonstration, I'd be happy
to oblige."

"No, thank you." Kathy stepped back.

"All right. But don't come to me later tonight and say you've
changed your mind. That was a one-time offer."

Kathy smirked, then asked, "Is square dancing really a folk
dance?"

"Not in my book." Scott performed a do-si-do with an imaginary partner as he said, "But the teacher justified her fondness for
square dancing by informing us that its roots were firmly fixed in
Western Europe, not only England and France but also Scotland
and Spain."

"*Olé*," said Kathy, snapping her fingers like castanets.

"More or less." Scott nodded. "More interesting to me is that
'do-si-do' comes from the French words 'dos-à-dos,' which mean
'back-to-back.' It's a small world . . . but I wouldn't want to paint
it."

"What?" Kathy looked confused.

"It's a joke." Scott shook his head. "When someone says 'it's
a small world,' you reply, 'but I wouldn't want to paint it.' Get
it?"

"I guess so." Kathy sighed. "We should go back inside."

Scott flicked his cigarette to the street, where it landed with a
burst of sparks.

Kathy made a face.

Scott shrugged. "What am I going to do? Bring it in the house
and throw it in the trash?"

"No."

"Okay, then." Scott extended his arm toward the building. "No
way around it, I'm afraid—unless you'd like to make a run for it."

"Where would we go?" Kathy's tone gave Scott pause.

"Sorry, Sue." Scott put his arm around Kathy's shoulders. "I believe we have no alternative but to go inside and find out what God has in store for holy Louise, mother of you and me."

Kathy laughed and frowned at the same time.

Scott kept his arm around Kathy's shoulders as they made their way to the staircase, two flights of concrete slabs with a concrete landing halfway up. Every few stairs, Scott pulled Kathy one stair back until she complained, bubbling with laughter, that she was going to wet her pants. Their playfulness subsided when Kathy opened the front door and preceded Scott into the apartment.

"All right, you two," Louise called out from the bedroom. "It's already past midnight, and everybody's got a big day tomorrow."

"Yes, Mother, we know," said Kathy, following Scott into her bedroom.

Kathy hung her coat in the bedroom closet. Scott threw his flannel shirt on the chair and followed Kathy into the master bedroom. Kathy resumed her position, stretched out with her head propped on an elbow at the foot of the bed. Scott sat down in the rocking chair with both feet on the floor and both arms on the chair.

"Is everybody comfortable?" Louise patted Allison's thigh as she said, "Daddy?"

"Yes, darlin', I'm fine."

"Kathy Sue, wouldn't you be more comfortable with a pillow, sweetheart?"

"No."

Louise looked from Kathy to Scott, but before she said anything, her head dropped back; the muscles in her neck stood out, and her hand began to move across the pad in her lap. Little more than a short burst of frenetic energy, the episode ended as abruptly as it had begun. When Louise lowered her head and read what she'd written, she smiled. She then looked up and said, "Scott, your father wanted you to know that the way you're sitting right now reminds him of his memorial in Washington, DC."

Scott was silent as he considered Louise's words. He then chuckled and said, "The Lincoln Memorial, right?"

"Yes, honey." Louise smiled like a Renaissance Madonna.

Scott crossed his legs at the knee.

"Mom," said Kathy, stifling a yawn. "I don't think I can stay awake much longer."

"Well, sweetheart," said Louise, "do the best you can." She smiled, then added, "But I'd rather you stay awake a little while longer, honey. Okay?"

Kathy nodded, then glared at Scott.

"All right, Mom," said Scott. "What happened next?"

"Let's see now." Louise closed her eyes for a moment, then looked from Kathy to Scott. "Like I said, honey, Jerry told me I should communicate with my father, which I had, but that didn't work out the way I'd hoped. Actually, it worked out exactly as I knew it would, but you know what I mean. Anyway, I have to say I was starting to lose faith in the idea of making myself available for this project. Jerry kept assuring me the financial support would manifest itself when the time was right, but I couldn't put everything else on hold until who knows when.

"So, I discussed my concerns with Allison, and I decided to tell Jerry that I'd need something more concrete than his assurance before I started making preparations to embark on this journey."

Kathy yawned.

"That night," Louise continued, "when I sat down with my pad and pen, I could tell something was different even before I began to write. Usually, I wait for a greeting before I start asking questions. But this was different, right from the start,"—looking at Scott—"right from the first word."

"What was the first word?" said Scott, sensing a shift himself.

"The first word was 'holy,' " Louise replied with a beatific smile.

"And . . . ?"

Louise leaned forward. She placed her hands in her lap, paused for a moment, then said, "The first words were 'Holy Mary, Mother of God.' "

Scott held his eyes on Louise. Unaware of his reaction, Scott's head began nodding almost imperceptibly as he contemplated Louise's words. After an eternity, Scott heard himself say, "So, that was not Jerry, right?"

"Yes, Scott. That was not Jerry." Louise appeared to be surrounded by an aura of white light. "Those were the first words directly from God."

Scott stared at Louise without seeing her. When she leaned back, he came to his senses and realized the halo-effect had been the result of lamplight from her bedside table reflecting off the pillowcases behind her. Scott cleared his throat. "God's communicating directly with you now?"

"Yes," said Louise without skipping a beat.

"And, if I may be so bold, why were those God's first words?" Scott steeled himself for Louise's answer.

"It was his way of greeting me." Louise reached over and put her hand in Allison's.

"By name?" Scott ignored the show of affection.

"Yes, Scott. It was God's way of greeting me by name."

"Greeting you by name," murmured Scott. He then said, "You were Mary, as in 'away in a manger?' "

Louise nodded. "Like I told you, honey, God has chosen the four of us for special incarnations throughout history. Not only people of religious importance but also artists and politicians."

"Right. Jerry was Abraham Lincoln, and I was Beethoven."

"Yes, dear." Louise squeezed Allison's hand. "Among others."

"Does that mean Jerry's one of the 'four of us' you keep referring to?"

"No, honey." Louise blinked slowly. "When I say 'the four of us,' I'm referring to the four of us in this room. But also, as I told you, Jerry and Grandma and Grandpa and other members of our family have played important roles throughout history. I know that Uncle Donald was Antonio Vivaldi in a previous incarnation, which explains his virtuosity on the violin at such a tender age. And Uncle Robert was Johann Sebastian Bach, which explains his prodigious musical talent."

"*Prodigious*. Have you been reading a dictionary?"

Louise smiled. "I'm not as simple as you might think, Scott."

"Certainly not in the eyes of God." Scott raised his brow as he lowered his chin. "I mean, you don't get much higher on the ladder of life than the Virgin Mary—as a woman, that is."

Louise exhaled; her head fell forward, and she began to write. When her hand stopped moving, her head returned to its upright position, and she studied the pad.

After a moment, Louise glanced at Scott, returned her eyes to the paper, and read aloud: "Greetings, Jerrold Scott Henry, prodigal son of the Blessed Mother, elder brother of Kathy Sue Henry and Jerrold Henry Giuliano. Honor thy father and thy mother, as I, thy God, hath commanded thee, that thy days may be prolonged, and that it may go well with thee, in the land which I, your God, giveth thee."

"Wow," said Scott, duly impressed. He leaned forward and said, "How do you do, . . . sir?"

Louise's head fell forward, and she began to write what Scott assumed would be a brief response. A moment later, Louise stopped writing as abruptly as she'd begun. She composed herself, studied the sheet of paper, and then read aloud: "I do good works, as one well knows. Rather than inquire the same of you, since I know the answer, I'll ask you to keep your comments to yourself and to show your mother the love and respect she so richly deserves."

"Really?" said Scott. "We're going from biblical prose to trite admonitions?"

As soon as Scott stopped speaking, Louise's head fell forward, and she began to write. The episode lasted less than a minute. It did, however, require a second sheet of paper after the first sheet was ripped from the pad and floated to the bed. As Louise's head returned to its normal position, she picked up the first sheet of paper and began reading aloud: "Whether lyrical or . . . *hackneyed*,"—looking at Scott—"do you know what that means, honey?"

Scott lowered his eyelids as he nodded slowly.

Louise said, "All right," then started again from the beginning: "Whether lyrical or hackneyed, prose or poem, whether taken at face value or with a grain of salt, the word of God illuminates the language of man, as the sun casts its light upon the earth entire. For nothing is secret, that shall not be made manifest; neither anything hid, that shall not be known and come abroad."

"Right on," said Scott.

Kathy stifled a nervous laugh.

Louise looked on with a Sphinx-like smile.

"So," said Scott, "I'm wondering if God's arrival on the scene was the reason for our big time in the little city? You know, sparkling wine and steaks all around?"

"Well, Scott," Louise replied, "not exactly, although God's arrival would have been cause for celebration."

"No kidding," said Scott. "Just ask the Seventh-day Adventists."

The reference was lost on Louise. She adjusted the collar of her nightgown, took a breath, then spoke as though continuing a

191

thought: "Like I said, Scott, Jerry assured me time and again the money necessary for our undertaking would manifest itself in the right amount, at the right time. Also, regarding the money, Jerry told me to communicate with 'Daddy.' Naturally, when Jerry told me to communicate with 'Daddy,' I thought he was referring to my father, to Grandpa. But yesterday,"—shaking her head—"well, *Saturday*, the day before yesterday, after everyone had gone to bed, I received a message from God that really threw me for a loop. When I asked for clarification about the money, God's reply was short and to the point. The financial support for our project would be provided by *Allison*." Louise telegraphed bewildered amazement.

Scott made a face and cocked his head. This was a revelation he found difficult to swallow, not that the presence of God was any more palatable. On more than one occasion, Scott had remarked that Allison could rub together the first two nickels he'd received as a weekly allowance. The thought of him parting with hard-earned cash for a scheme as suspicious as the one under discussion suggested unseen forces at work or, as the case may be, at play.

"I know," said Louise, shaking her head. "Isn't that *unbelievable*?"

"In a word," said Scott, nodding slowly.

Louise lowered her voice as if revealing a secret. "Jerry had misinterpreted one of God's instructions. When God told him I should communicate with 'Daddy,' Jerry thought that meant my father. That's why he told me to communicate with Gus, but God wanted me to communicate with Allison."

"*Okay*," said Scott, "I get it—I guess. Seems to me the angels in charge of public relations would come up with a better method of conveying God's instructions than a heavenly version of the Telephone Game. When it comes down to it, 1968 AD doesn't seem all that different from 1968 BC. Although considering time and place, Jerry's a better bet than a burning bush."

"Well, Scott," said Louise, "I think that's where I fit in."

"Good point." Scott raised his brow. "So, when are you taking your show on the road?"

Louise sighed. "As much as the whole idea overwhelms me, it seems that there's no time like the present."

"Which means what exactly?"

Kathy looked like she was waiting for the ax to fall.

"The first thing I need to do," said Louise, "is get Kathy situated."

"What's that mean?" said Kathy, her voice wavering.

"Well, sweetheart,"—smiling tenderly—"it won't be possible for you to stay here alone."

"What do you mean, 'stay here alone'?" Kathy looked from Louise to Allison. "Where's Daddy going to be?"

"That hasn't been decided yet, sweetheart." Louise rested her hand on Allison's thigh. "But we know a girl your age needs to have a sense of security about school and friends. Everything considered, honey, we think a move now is the best option before you get accustomed to this school and start making friends in Santa Rosa."

"What are you saying?" Kathy choked, her eyes brimming with tears. "You're going to send me away?"

Louise offered a sympathetic smile. "No, sweetheart, we're not sending you away. I mean, not really. We're making arrangements for you to live with Auntie Marguerite while you're still in high school, honey. That's only three years."

"*Three years,*" wailed Kathy, tears coursing down her cheeks.

"Now, Kathy." Louise leaned forward. "Auntie Marguerite and Uncle Don have a beautiful home and a loving family. Not only that, who wouldn't want to spend three years in Laguna Beach?"

"Me," said Kathy, her expression turning from blue to red. She pushed herself up to sitting cross-legged. Kathy wiped the tears from her face and said, "If you send me to Auntie Marguerite's, it'll be three years of cleaning the house and babysitting. I don't want to live with them. Maybe I can go back to Long Beach and live with Karen Diotte's family."

"That's not a good idea, sweetheart." Shaking her head, Louise knitted her brow and frowned. "Like I said, Daddy and I aren't exactly sure of where we'll be or what we'll be doing from one week to the next. We want to have a sense of security about you and your living arrangement. That's why we think it's important for you to be with members of our family, not the family of a school friend. You understand, don't you, sweetheart?"

"Daddy's going with you?" Kathy replied, more like an accusation than a question.

"Not right away, sweetheart." Louise placed her hand in Allison's.

"Does that mean Allison's been invited to participate in the project?" said Scott. "Or does he have visiting rights because he's paying the bills?"

Looking less serene by the minute, Louise tucked a wisp of hair behind her ear. "Like I said, Scott, we're not exactly sure of who will be doing what until everything's underway."

"But you'll be taking dictation, so to speak, and God will be handing down the word, right?"

"Yes." Louise nodded.

"What about Jerry?" Scott glanced over his shoulder. "Is he still in the mix, or has he been relegated to the sidelines?"

"I'm not sure what God has in mind for Jerry." Louise straightened the pad of paper in her lap. "I thought he was going to be the middleman, the, uh, go-between. But now that God's communicating with me directly, I'm not sure who else will be involved."

Scott glanced at the floor, lowered his chin, then raised his eyes to look at Louise. "Except for Allison."

"Yes, Scott." Louise removed the tissue from the sleeve of her nightgown. "I believe Allison will be involved. I'm just not sure in what capacity." She wiped the tip of her nose a couple of times, then tucked the tissue back in her sleeve.

"And you plan to move from city to city, country to country, pillar to post, something like a born-again nomad?" Scott folded his arms.

"I wouldn't say 'born again,' Scott." Louise frowned.

"Consider the facts," said Scott, shaking his head. "You were raised as a true believer in the Church of Jesus Christ of Latter-day Saints, from which you strayed when you married my father. Fifteen years later, you and Allison were married by a chiropractor in a movie theater, surrounded by members of the Long Beach chapter of the Church of Religious Science. If you'd spent time with L. Ron Hubbard, you would've hit a splinter-group trifecta."

Louise inhaled, then said, "I've always believed in a higher power, Scott, by whatever name you choose to call it. It's just that now I have a personal relationship with the higher power, and I know his name is God."

"Is it really?" said Scott. "I don't mean to quibble, but is his name 'God,' or is that his title? The same as Queen Elizabeth's name is 'Elizabeth,' not 'Queen,' and the Virgin Mary's name is 'Mary,' not 'Virgin'—no disrespect."

"None taken," said Louise, half-smiling. But then her head fell forward, and her hand began moving, left to right, left to right, across the pad. When her hand stopped, Louise brought her head to its upright position. She lowered her eyes as she collected herself, then focused her attention on the piece of paper. Louise began reading aloud in a curiously somber tone of voice: "What's in a name? That which we call a rose—"

"Ha!" said Scott. " 'By any other name would smell as sweet.' " Scott leaned forward, fixing his eyes on Louise. "Are you serious?" Scott tilted his head. "Is that the message?"

"If you'd be quiet, Scott,"—matching his intensity—"I'd finish reading what I wrote, all right?"

Scott nodded.

Louise started again from the beginning: "What's in a name? That which we call a rose, by any other name would smell as sweet." Louise looked at Scott for a moment, then continued. "Wise words written long ago by the one who at this time goes by the name of Allison Merlin Eddy."

"Oh boy," said Scott, leaning back and looking away.

"What's that mean?" said Kathy, looking from Scott to Louise.

"Well, Kathy," said Louise, savoring the moment, "that means Daddy was William Shakespeare, honey, in one of his previous incarnations."

"Oh," said Kathy, for lack of a better response.

Scott burst into laughter, then collected himself.

Louise raised her brow as an invitation for Scott to clarify.

"It's just that"—laughing through his nose—"you know how I like to come up with oblique interpretations of famous quotes?" Scott paused for a response.

"Yes," said Louise. "You're the poster child for abstract reasoning, as you've told us on numerous occasions."

"Okay, well." Scott scratched the back of his head. "Sort of like God using a quote from Shakespeare in reference to his name, it just occurred to me. With so many VIPs represented by the four of us, you could apply one of Churchill's famous quotes to our little group." Scott paused for effect, then said, " 'Never in the history of mankind has so much been owed by so many to so few.' "

Scott's bon mot fell on deaf ears, as was so often the case.

Louise exhaled; her head fell forward, and she began to write.

The episode lasted a few seconds longer than the previous one. When Louise's hand stopped, she raised her head and began reading aloud: "Not delivered in Parliament as cited by Jerrold Scott Henry for the presumption of primacy over my Son and his disciples. Therefore, it became 'Never in the field of human conflict has so much been owed by so many to so few.' Winston Leonard Spencer Churchill's transition occurred after these four began. He is not represented by any in this room. I offer this to Jerrold Scott Henry. Every famous person does not have vestigial lineage to a member of his family."

"*Vestigial lineage.*" Scott furrowed his brow. "Is that a thing?"

"That's a reference to the effect of previous incarnations," Louise replied as if discussing the weather. "The earlier experience is not a part of conscious memory, but the lessons learned are still in play—such as musical talent or political prowess. Somewhat the same as genetic inheritance, by which physical attributes are passed from one generation to the next, vestigial lineage allows personality traits to be passed from one lifetime to another."

"Whatever's going on here, Mom, you've definitely plugged into something phenomenal. A cosmic encyclopedia if not the mind of God."

"Or both." Louise smiled. "In that one is the other."

"Meanwhile, back at 1530 Boston Court. What's next?"

"What's next is getting down to nuts and bolts, so to speak."

"Care to elaborate?"

Louise squared her shoulders. "Since I'll be spending so much time on the road, Allison's giving me the Volkswagen Bus." She beamed a smile at Allison. "So, priority number one is getting the bus in shape for extended travel, setting up a rod for hanging clothes, getting some containers for towels and blankets and pillows. You know I prefer to travel with my own bedding. And writing supplies, of course. And some nonperishable foods. Tea that I like, dried fruits and nuts, crackers and peanut butter, things for snacks along the way."

"If you add all of God's creatures, two of each kind," said Scott, "this would be Louise's Ark. You could start with a couple of cats to keep you company."

"Good Lord, Scott." Louise put her hand to her throat. "The last thing I need is a couple of cats. Speaking of which, maybe I should invest in a small vacuum cleaner in case I need to touch up my motel room or if I spill something in the car."

"You know, Mom," said Scott, "that's why God created house-keeping staff and car washes."

"That may be so." Louise tilted her head from side to side. "But I'll be on a tight budget, honey, and anything I can do to keep expenses down will be much appreciated by my sponsor here." Louise patted Allison on the thigh.

"When are you leaving?" Kathy asked in a flat voice.

"I'm not exactly sure." Louise leaned forward. She moved her hand from Allison's thigh to Kathy's knee, lowering her head to look into Kathy's eyes. "Not until we get everything squared away with you and your new living arrangement, sweetheart. I'll spend some time with you at Auntie Marguerite's, helping you get your room set up and making sure everything's taken care of at your new school."

"You've already discussed this with them?" Kathy sounded more alarmed than surprised.

"No, sweetheart. But I'm sure everything will be fine."

Kathy straightened her back. "I wouldn't be so sure of that if I were you, starting with Janet having to share her bedroom."

"Well," said Louise, putting on a brave face, "we'll cross that bridge when we come to it. All right, sweetheart?"

Kathy wiped away a tear.

"Mom," said Scott, shifting focus. "How long have you been

in direct contact with God? When did he come a-knockin', as it were?"

"Tuesday night of last week," said Louise. "That's when we had our first conversation."

"That's when you found out you were Mary? That's when God greeted you as 'Holy Mary, Mother of God'?"

"Yes." Louise smiled serenely.

"And, I suppose,"—fixing his eyes on Louise—"Allison was Joseph?"

Louise placed her hand in Allison's. "No, Scott, Allison wasn't Joseph. Allison was Jesus."

Scott smiled. "And that would be where you crossed the line."

"Which line is that?" said Louise.

"The line between divine revelation and manifest lunacy." Scott continued smiling. "Was this tidbit revealed to Allison before or after he offered to finance the reappearance of God?"

Louise's head tilted back. The veins on her neck stood out as her hand began scribbling on the pad in her lap. When her hand stopped, her head returned to its upright position, and she began reading aloud: "Thou shall not scorn The Mother. Thou shall not scorn The Son. Cease thy mockery or lose thy tongue."

Scott chuckled, then narrowed his eyes. "Are you kidding me?"

"Scott," said Louise, "those are not my words."

"Yes, Louise, those are your words." Scott inhaled. "This was very interesting until three minutes ago. The automatic writing is awesome—awesome and astonishing. So is the information. Your subconscious mind should be studied by a team of Nobel laureates. Beyond that, and I say this with all due respect, you need to get a grip."

Louise's head fell forward, and she began to write. The episode was brief, no more than a few seconds. After her hand stopped, Louise raised her head and read aloud in a stentorian tone: "Jerrold

Scott Henry, heed me now, for this, I promise. Speak of this to anyone who listens, and you shall lose the gift of speech as they shall lose the gift of hearing."

"Okay," said Scott, standing up. "That concludes the show-and-tell part of this evening's entertainment. I have to catch a bus in a few hours, and Kathy has to go to school. Safe to say, a good night's sleep will do all of us a world of good." Looking at Kathy, he said, "Okay, Sue, let's go, let's go, *let's* really go."

Kathy stood up and followed Scott out of the room, neither of them saying a word until Scott closed the door.

"Jeez," whispered Kathy, following Scott into the living room.

"Don't get me started," said Scott. "And don't take Allison's name in vain."

Kathy punched Scott in the arm.

"Who's your daddy?"

"He's not my daddy." Kathy climbed into her makeshift bed.

"You mentioned his name."

"Cut it out, and I mean it."

"Yes, ma'am."

"What's going to happen now?"

"God only knows." Scott made the sound of a rimshot.

Kathy rolled her eyes. "Would you please go to bed? I have to get up in five hours."

"Okey-dokey, Sue. I'll see you mañana morning—actually, later on today."

Kathy groaned as she pulled the covers over her head.

FOURTEEN

7:00 AM

He couldn't tell if the alarm was for an actual fire or just a drill. From the looks on other students' faces, he wasn't the only person considering the question. . . . Scott started awake and remembered he was in Santa Rosa, having spent a few hours' fitful sleep in his sister's bed.

Scott reached over and switched off the alarm, thinking he'd stay in bed another few minutes when he also remembered Allison would be driving him to an Airport Express stop in half an hour. Scott pushed the bedclothes aside, swung his feet to the floor, and stood up. Stepping into one leg after the other of his corduroy pants, Scott wondered if his mother would speak to him before he left the apartment.

Twenty minutes later, Scott's question was answered when Allison stepped out of the master bedroom and closed the door behind him.

"Are you ready to go?" said Allison, crossing the room.

"Yep," Scott replied, employing the informal affirmation on behalf of Allison's countless rebukes for "slovenly speech."

Allison had too much on his mind to react, which brought a bemused expression to Scott's face.

"See ya later, sis," said Scott. "You know I'm not big on good-byes."

"All right," said Kathy. "See ya later." She widened her eyes and clenched her jaw.

Scott shrugged in response, indicating her guess was as good as his. Kathy heaved a sigh, walked to her bedroom, and closed the door.

After running the engine for two minutes, Allison kept the bus in first gear from the garage to the cul-de-sac, second gear for the length of Boston Court to the stop sign at Hoen Avenue.

Scott breathed slowly as Allison waited for an opening in on-coming traffic. When they were finally at cruising speed, Scott asked, "How are things with Mom?"

"That remains to be seen," Allison replied, slowing to a stop for a yellow light. After a moment, he added, "She was in the bath-room when I came back from the kitchen."

"Hmm." Scott focused on the scenery as they followed a one-lane road through a short stretch of undeveloped land. "Is she coming to the office today?"

"I don't know, Scott. After last night, anything's possible."

"Right," said Scott, considering his options. "So, I'll call you at the office when I get home from school."

"I have a full day, Scott. I doubt I'll have time for a conversation."

"That's okay. We don't need to have a conversation, but I'd like to know what's going on. I have a class from four to five. I'll give you a call around five thirty."

Allison said nothing more as he pulled to the curb. Scott grabbed his weekender from the backseat, stepped out of the bus, and joined a young couple standing amid their mismatched luggage. Scott offered a casual salute as he closed the door. Allison turned his head toward the street, pulled away from the curb, and merged into passing traffic.

The bus ride was uneventful, apart from three stops along the way, where a few more passengers of little interest to Scott boarded the half-empty vehicle. The same could not be said for one passenger who stopped in her tracks when Scott looked up from the book he was reading.

"Oh my," said the middle-aged woman, holding her hand to her chest. "For a minute, I thought you were Richard Chamberlain—you're not, though, are you? No, no, I can see you're too young. Are you related to Richard Chamberlain? You could be his younger brother. He's thirty-four, you know? How old are you?"

Scott smiled in response to the woman's enthusiasm. When she remained standing in the aisle with a look of expectation, Scott shifted his eyes upward and replayed her list of questions, honing in on two that put everything else in perspective.

"I'm eighteen years old, and my last name is Henry." Scott tilted his head and frowned as if sorry to disappoint.

"Well, there you are, your whole life ahead of you, looking like God's gift to women. You say your last name is Henry?"

"Yes." Scott smiled.

"Now, you see," the matron gushed, "when you smile like that, you're the spitting image. If I had a camera, I'd take your picture. I'm the recording secretary for the Richard Chamberlain Sonoma County Fan Club, and the other members would get such a kick out of how much you look like Richard's younger brother. Oh well, never mind. Where were we? Oh, yes, yes, you say you're a Henry. A Virginia Henry?"

Scott nodded slowly.

"Are you related to Patrick?"

Scott chuckled. "Yes, ma'am. According to a family tree my father had done in Ireland, Patrick Henry was my ninth cousin."

"Well, that's almost better than being a Chamberlain. Are you flying off to somewhere exotic?"

"Yes." Scott grinned. "Los Angeles."

The woman looked puzzled for a moment but then smiled as if

Scott's answer made perfect sense. "Have a safe trip, young man. It was a pleasure to make your acquaintance."

"Likewise," said Scott, "in both regards."

The woman made her way to the rear of the bus, where she settled herself and her belongings in the last row of seats.

When the bus pulled to a stop outside San Francisco airport's South Terminal, Scott made a point of disembarking without further conversation with the member in good standing of Richard Chamberlain's Sonoma County Fan Club. Walking through the terminal, Scott kept an eye out for the Pacific Southwest Airlines ticket counter, thinking it would be close to the gates for PSA flights. He already had his ticket, but negotiating an airport for the second time in his life had him paying close attention to everything in sight. Scott had taken no more than ten steps before he slowed to a stop and studied an electronic schedule board suspended from the ceiling. When Scott saw the gate listed for his flight, he headed toward the nearby walkway for gates 20–28.

In the waiting area for Gate 22, Scott stood in line behind two men of uncertain age—early thirties, more than likely—dressed in three-piece suits, discussing, much to their delight, Richard Nixon's significant lead according to a recent Gallup Poll.

"He's a shoo-in," the shorter man assured his associate.

"Your mouth to God's ear," the taller man whispered emphatically.

Scott inhaled. Above and beyond his opinion of politicians in general—pimps and hucksters perpetrating sleights of hand (except for the Kennedy brothers who'd fallen prey to the fat cats who were pulling strings)—Scott held a special place in his heart for Richard Millhouse Nixon, thinking him a perfect example of what can slither from the shallow end of the gene pool.

When the line moved forward, Scott allowed the businessmen

to advance a step without following suit in hopes of not hearing any more of their socio-toxic conversation. After they had checked in, the businessmen went in search of coffee and Danish. Scott stepped to the counter for a cursory inspection of his round-trip ticket. The young woman manning the station handed Scott a boarding pass and advised him to remain in the seating area as they would begin boarding the plane at ten o'clock.

Twenty minutes later, Scott was fastening his seatbelt when one of the businessmen from the check-in line—brush-cut brown hair, well-trimmed mustache, charcoal-gray pin-stripe suit (the one who'd praised God for Richard Nixon's imminent victory)—placed his briefcase in the seat beside Scott's. The man smiled at Scott before he turned his attention to his briefcase, rifling through an assortment of papers and folders until he pulled out what appeared to be a paperbound prospectus. The man slid the document into the pocket on the back of the seat in front of his. He placed his briefcase in the overhead compartment, removed his jacket, and placed it in the compartment as well.

Scott read the typeset title on the document's cover, *High-Tech IPOs*, but had no idea what it meant. Scott opened his copy of *Siddhartha* and began reading where he'd left off the previous evening when he'd been summoned to the master bedroom.

The businessman took his seat, fastened his seatbelt, unbuttoned his shirt cuffs, and rolled up his sleeves. Scott noticed the man's watch: rectangular black face, white roman numerals, "CARTIER" in small letters, black lizard band. Scott slid his eyes back to his book as the man turned toward him.

"That's some heady stuff you're reading there," the businessman said. "So, 'what's it all about, Alfie?' "

Scott thought for a moment, then said, " 'When you walk, let your heart lead the way.' "

The businessman smiled. "Well said, and I believe you hit both nails on their respective heads—the self-satisfied Cockney chauffeur and the self-effacing seeker of truth." He offered his right hand. "Name's Larry, by the way."

"Scott," said Scott, shaking Larry's hand.

"All right, then." Larry slid the prospectus from the seat pocket in front of him. "While you contemplate the big picture, I'll consider the little one." Larry flipped through the report, pausing now and again to study a pie chart, a list, a three-color graph. When Larry looked up, he saw Scott had been looking at the pages as well.

"Go small, young man," said Larry, sounding at once humorous and stern.

"Small?" Scott furrowed his brow.

"We've come as far west as possible,"—laughing to himself—"as far as this continent is concerned anyway. The next frontier is miniaturization."

"I thought the next frontier was outer space."

"No money to be made in outer space, kid. Not at this time anyway. But making things smaller—that's going to be a game-changer. Like I said, go small, young man, and the world will be your oyster."

"What's that mean, exactly? 'The world will be your oyster'?"

"Oysters offer pearls; pearls represent wealth; wealth provides opportunity; opportunity opens doors; open doors lay the world at your feet. I'm not quite sure that's what Bill had in mind, but that's how I see it."

"Bill?"

"Bill Shakespeare. Better known to you as William."

"As well as everyone else on the planet."

"Right you are, but what's the fun in making everything crystal clear?"

"Depends on whether you want to communicate or obfuscate."

Larry turned to Scott with a sly grin. "Well, well. You're not just a pretty face, are you?"

"Not even that if you ask me."

"False modesty much?"

"Everything's relative."

"I can't argue with that." Larry smiled, then returned to his document.

Scott returned to the page he'd just read and began again with the hope of being drawn into Siddhartha's current predicament.

When a stewardess rolled a beverage cart up to their row, Larry requested a Scotch on the rocks. "Might as well make it a double."

Scott asked for 7 Up and an extra bag of peanuts. Unlike the preferential treatment he'd enjoyed on the northbound flight, the service provided by the affable-while-multitasking young woman on the southbound flight left Scott with two bags of peanuts and a glass of pop.

"Care for a splash of this?" Larry held up a miniature bottle of Glenlivet.

"No, thanks."

"Do you drink at all?"

"Not really."

"If I didn't smell cigarette smoke on you, I'd guess you were a Mormon. You look like you've never had a cup of coffee in your life, not to mention the occasional beer."

"You're right about the coffee because I don't like the taste. But I have had the occasional beer, thank you very much."

"No need to be defensive, kid. I'm not accusing you of any-thing."

"Yeah, no, sorry. Kind of a knee-jerk reaction at my age." Scott made a desperate face. "No, no, really, we haven't been drinking."

"I get it, been there, done that." He chuckled. "It's up to you if you'd like to test the water. Nobody has to know but us chickens."

"I think that might be a mixed metaphor, and I've never trusted those chickens."

"I know what you mean. How about nobody has to know except you and me?"

"Good enough, but I'll pass." Scott took a sip of 7 Up.

Larry took a sip of Scotch, paused for a moment, then said, "All right, now that we've settled the beverage situation, I need to bury my nose in this." He held up the *High-Tech IPOs* document. "I'll check back with you when we get to LA."

"I'll be right here." Scott held up his copy of *Siddhartha.*

"Okay, then." Larry took a ballpoint pen from his shirt pocket, flipped to the first page of the brochure, and started making notes in the margins.

12:00 PM

Scott circled back to the LAX Theme Building for one more look before he left the airport. Traffic on World Way was stop-and-go, which provided a view of the Space Age structure from several vantage points. When Scott exited the airport proper, he had a hell of a time finding the Harbor Freeway. Once he did, traffic moved smoothly to the Los Angeles Street exit.

Scott followed Los Angeles Street to 11th Street and parked halfway down the block from the Armed Forces Examining and Induction Station, where he was taking the Armed Forces Qualification Test at one o'clock. An Air Force recruiter had advised Scott there was a one-year waiting list for induction, which did not require further explanation: Tens of thousands of draft-deferred college students disenchanted with higher education were opting for enlistment in the United States Air Force for the simple reason that that branch of the armed services had the lowest deployment of troops to Vietnam. The flip side of that particular coin—enlistment in the armed services or enrollment in college—was the unintended legacy of the Vietnam War because the trials and tribulations of academic pursuits were undeniably preferable to the hardships and atrocities of military aggression.

Scott locked the car door, lit a cigarette, and set off in the direction of the address stamped on the AFQT pamphlet. Inside the building, eerily quiet for all the comings and goings, Scott followed signs to the TESTING ROOM, where he was directed to a school desk with an attached chair in the middle of the third row.

Of the room's hundred desks—ten rows of ten, set wide apart—all but a few were occupied. Scott noted the range of skin tones from milk-and-honey to midnight-black, the buzz-cuts, shoulder-length mops, full-blown Afros, an American Indian with foot-long braids, T-shirts, sweatshirts, crew-neck and V-neck sweaters, several shirts and ties, a couple of sport coats, a three-piece suit. Scott slid into his seat and perused the instruction sheet he'd been handed when he entered the room: "PRINT LEGIBLY" (*as opposed to*?); "NAME, ADDRESS, DATE OF BIRTH, TELE-PHONE, SOCIAL SECURITY" (*nowhere to run to, baby, nowhere to hide*); MARK ANSWERS CLEARLY—ONE ANSWER PER QUESTION (*seriously*?). Scott looked around the room to gauge reactions to the "one answer per question" rule. Everyone else seemed to accept it as a reasonable request. Scott inhaled.

A well-groomed officer in a pristine uniform strode to the front of the room. He came to a stop facing the group and said, "Gentlemen, put your pencils down and pay attention." The officer waited for compliance, then continued: "I'm Lieutenant Hollis of the United States Army. I'll be supervising today's Armed Forces Qualification Test, with the assistance of the other two gentlemen in uniform. After everyone receives a test booklet, you'll have one minute to fill in the required information on the cover. Again, after everyone receives a test booklet, you'll have one minute to fill in the required information on the cover. Do not pick up your pencils before I tell you. Do not talk to anyone other than myself or one of the other officers. If you have a problem with your pencil, raise your hand, and you'll be given a new pencil by myself or one of the other officers. If you drop your pencil, do not pick it up. Raise your hand, and you'll be given a new pencil by myself or one of the other officers. If we suspect you're sharing answers, you'll be escorted from the room. If you're escorted from the room, you'll be able to take the test at a later date." Lieutenant Hollis paused as he looked around the room. He then asked if there were any questions?

No one risked drawing attention to himself.

"All right, my associates are going to distribute the test booklets now. They'll hand a stack of booklets to the person in the last seat of each row. That person will place one booklet on his desk, then pass the stack to the person seated in from of him until each of you has a booklet on your desk."

The rustle and squeak of shifting seats played out as booklets were passed from man to man. When the room fell silent, Lieutenant Hollis said, "All right, pick up your pencils and fill in your information on the front of the booklet."

A minute later, Lieutenant Hollis said, "You will have three hours to complete this test. If you have to use the men's room, one of my assistants will accompany you, but you won't receive any additional time. If you finish the test early, raise your hand, and one of my assistants will collect your booklet. After that, you're free to go. All right, you can break the seal on your booklet and proceed with the test."

Two hours later, Scott raised his hand. The nearest officer walked over and whispered, "Men's room?"

Scott shook his head. He held out his booklet and pencil and whispered, "I'm done."

The serviceman paused for a moment, then shrugged his shoulders. He took Scott's booklet and pencil and returned to his post at the rear of the room. Scott stood up and walked to the doors, noting the time as ten past three. If he sprinted to his car and drove like a madman, he might be on time for his four o'clock class.

4:00 PM

Scott jogged from the parking lot to the dance studio. He slowed to a walk as he passed through the open double doors, slowed to a stop as his eyes adjusted to the unlit room. The clock above the far set of doors showed the time as two minutes past the hour. Here and there, groups of students were discussing how long they should wait for their teacher to appear. As the various camps were reaching a consensus, one of the far doors swung open, and a small, energetic woman strode into the room.

At first glance, Scott thought of Louise. The fact that Scott had never seen Louise in a leotard and dance pants did not diminish the impression of this woman's upswept hair and deep-set eyes. When she smiled, the effect was all the more uncanny but for her perfect teeth, an attribute that had never been associated with Louise. Scott could not gauge a similarity of shape and form, having never seen his mother's figure so clearly exposed. However, as far as height and weight were concerned, one could have passed for the other.

"As you can see," the woman said loudly, "I am not Miss Perkins. Nor, for that matter,"—laughing lightly—"is Miss Perkins, who was married yesterday afternoon and will be on her honeymoon for the next several days." A nominal round of applause settled into uncertain silence. "My name's Miss Aston, and I'll be teaching this class until Miss Perkins—whoops, until *Mrs. Sare* returns." Miss Aston smiled.

"Dawn assured me," she continued, "that every one of you

would be terribly disappointed to miss out on one hour of folk dancing just because your teacher decided to tie the knot. So here I am to fill her shoes, as best I can. Now, who can tell me what you're working on?"

Someone called out, "Square dancing."

"Or," said Scott, "as we prefer to think of it, 'not-so-square dancing.' "

"Either way," said Miss Aston, "why don't we try something else?"

"Whatever you say," replied a self-anointed lothario in a suggestive tone.

Miss Aston narrowed her eyes and smiled in response, telegraphing zero tolerance for that sort of nonsense. "What I had in mind," she said, looking around the room, "is the Madison."

"*The Madison*" was repeated in various inflections, ranging from incredulous to scoffing.

"Yes," Miss Aston replied, offering a winsome smile, "the Madison. And I'll give you a very good reason why." She crossed the room and took a position in the middle of the studio, facing the mirrored wall. "Soon enough,"—addressing everyone's reflection in the mirror—"you and your closest friends will be attending one another's weddings. As you will discover at these happy events, the Madison's always a favorite, and anyone remotely good at it will be the hit of the party.

"That in mind, there's no time like the present to get some practice under your belt, and, thinking of this as the frosting on the wedding cake, let's give it our best effort in honor of our recently married absentee teacher. Now, everybody form a line on either side of me. It doesn't matter if you're boy-girl-boy-girl, which is good, since there are only . . . five, six, seven—seven boys in the class. What's your name?" Miss Aston asked, looking at Scott.

"Scott," said Scott, meeting Miss Aston's mischievous gaze.

"You look like you know what comes next." Miss Aston tilted her head as an invitation for Scott to prove her right.

Scott took one step forward, one step back, brushed his left foot back and forth in front of his right foot two times, took one step forward, clapped his hands, and stepped back to the first position.

"All right," Miss Aston exclaimed, beaming a smile. "You stand in the middle of the line on this side of me. That way, people can follow both of us. Does anyone else know the basic steps?"

Two African-American girls, who'd informed Miss Perkins on the first day of school that they were taking Folk Dance because it was the only physical education class that did not involve taking showers, raised their hands.

"Okay," said Miss Aston, "let's see what you've got."

The girls repeated the basic sequence, then proceeded to add hops, skips, full turns, changes of direction, shimmies, shuffles, and shouts. When they stopped, everyone burst into applause, including Miss Aston.

"Well, then." Miss Aston extended her arms. "I think I'll step back and let you two teach the class."

"All right," said the lankier of the two girls.

"No way," the other girl said, punching her friend in the arm.

"Oh well." Miss Aston stepped back in line. "Now, at least, everyone's had a preview of how good we'll look by the end of the hour. All right, let's get started."

By the end of the hour, the students' performance had fallen short of Miss Aston's prediction. All the same, a good time had been had by everyone in attendance, including their substitute teacher, who suggested the Bunny Hop as their next endeavor, should her presence be required in the future.

Miss Aston's statement was met with good-natured groans, except from five students, including Scott and the two African-

American girls, who formed a line and put their right foot out and back two times, their left foot out and back two times. By this time, Miss Aston had joined the line for one hop forward and one hop back.

Walking to his car, Scott considered stopping at Jack in the Box on the way home but then decided he should call Allison sooner than later. Scott took Clark Avenue to Anaheim Street, keeping an eye out for black-and-white cruisers, which he'd failed to do on two previous occasions when he sped across Spring Street as the traffic light changed from yellow to red. A different driver in a different car may have gotten off with a warning on one of the occasions, but an eighteen-year-old boy in a red Porsche was a simple equation for each of the officers who'd pulled Scott over: $X + Y$ = citation. No excuses. No discussion.

Scott stayed on Anaheim Street to Cherry Avenue, a better bet than Junipero Avenue, considering stop signs and traffic lights. He caught the green light at Broadway, downshifted into second gear, turned left onto Second Street, right onto Junipero, left onto Dodge Way, where he parked in front of his garage.

Inside his apartment, Scott dropped his weekender behind the partition wall. He made a quick stop at the toilet, splashed some water on his face, then walked back into the living room. Scott plopped down on the orange velvet chair. He pulled the telephone and his address book from the side table to his lap. Scott flipped through a couple of pages, lifted the handset to his ear, and dialed the number for Allison's office.

Allison answered the phone with pathological cheerfulness: "Doctor Eddy's office, this is Doctor Eddy. How may I help you?"

Scott vibrated with disgust, then steadied himself. "Hello, Allison. This is Scott."

Allison's tone shifted from saccharine to curt. "Yes, Scott?"

215

Scott raised a clenched fist. "I'm calling to find out what happened this morning after I left?"

"With your mother?"

Scott raised both fists, one clenched, the other holding the handset. He returned the handset to his ear and said, "Yes, with my mother."

"When I returned from dropping you off, Louise was standing at the curb, dressed in her uniform like any other workday morning."

"Did she say anything about last night?"

"She said she was putting the whole thing behind her, and she didn't want to discuss it any further."

Scott paused for a moment, biting his tongue. He then said, "And . . . that's it?"

"Yes, Scott. That's it. Was there anything else?"

"No."

"All right. I have quite a bit of paperwork in front of me."

"Right. Okay. Uh, good luck with, you know, *the situation.* I hope it really is over and done."

"Yes, Scott. All right, then. Goodbye."

Scott heard the line go dead. He held the handset at arm's length and said, "Goodbye, asshole. And, by the way, you're welcome."

THREE

A PLAY IN THREE ACTS

THE CHARACTERS

LOUISE EDDY, Allison Eddy's second wife, the receptionist, cleaning-staff, and laundress in Allison's office.

ALLISON EDDY, Louise's second husband, a chiropractor with a small private practice.

SCOTT HENRY, Louise's son from her first marriage, a college sophomore visiting for the first time since he left home on his eighteenth birthday.

KATHY HENRY, Louise's daughter from her first marriage, a high school sophomore grappling with the family's recent move to Northern California.

SCENE: *Late evening in the Eddys' master bedroom, a small rectangular room crowded with Early American furniture, situated at an angle to the front of the stage. A double bed is centered on the back wall with two sets of two standard pillows in white pillowcases resting against the headboard. The bed is made with white sheets, a green blanket, and a quilted bedspread in shades of brown. Two wood-framed prints of birds in trees are mounted above the headboard. Large windows with sheer curtains and heavy drapes bracket the headboard. There is a large nightstand with an oversized lamp on either side of the bed; an electric clock and various books and magazines on the stage-right nightstand; a decorative box of tissues, a stack of books, a pad of letter-size paper, and a ballpoint pen on the other. A spindle-back rocking chair, seat and back cushions tied in place, sits stage-right a few feet from the foot of the bed. Behind the rocking chair, a tall chest of drawers sits against the wall between the nightstand and the master bedroom doorway. A wide chest of drawers with an attached mirror sits against the other wall between the nightstand and the master bathroom doorway. A "wall-to-wall carpet" emphasizes the illusion of close quarters. Beyond the master bedroom doorway is a short hall with a ceiling light and two more interior doorways; one, five feet away, facing the master bedroom doorway, is the door to Kathy's bedroom; the other, in the middle of the connecting wall, facing downstage, is the door to the hallway bathroom. All the doors are closed.*

TIME: *September, 1968*

ACT ONE

When the curtain rises, Louise and Allison are sitting in bed with their backs against upright pillows. Louise, hair in rollers beneath a stretch turban, is wearing a lightweight flannel nightgown, buttoned to the neck. Allison, in metal-frame large-lens glasses, is wearing a dingy-white T-shirt. Allison gets out of bed, and we see he's also wearing dingy-white underpants. He walks to the master bedroom doorway, pulls the door open, and steps into the hallway. Looking toward the stage-right wings, Allison leans slightly forward.

ALLISON (*Voice raised*): Kathy, your mother would like to talk to you.

(*Small pause.*)

KATHY (*Offstage*): Okay.

(*Allison takes a few steps and knocks on Kathy's bedroom door.*)

SCOTT (*Offstage*): Yes?
ALLISON (*Opens the door and leans in*): Your mother would like to talk to you and your sister.
SCOTT (*Offstage*): All right.

(*Allison returns to the master bedroom. Kathy, in flannel pajamas and fuzzy slippers, appears from the stage-right wings. Scott, wearing an unbuttoned flannel shirt, a*

T-shirt, and sweatpants, steps through Kathy's bedroom doorway. Scott follows Kathy into the master bedroom, where they slow to a stop as Allison gets in bed beside Louise.)

LOUISE: Scott, you go ahead and sit in the rocking chair, honey. Kathy Sue, you can make yourself comfortable at the foot of the bed. Would you like a pillow, sweetheart?

KATHY: No.

(Kathy crawls onto the bed and stretches out with her head propped on her arm.)

ALLISON: Scott, please close the door before you sit down. We like to keep this room a little warmer than the rest of the house.

(Scott closes the bedroom door, then sits in the rocking chair, with his legs crossed at the knee, his arms across his chest.)

LOUISE: Okay.
      (Looks at her hands, then at Scott)
      Well, the best place to start, of course, is at the beginning, so that would be when I was cleaning out the cupboards at our cabin in the mountains.

(Scott swings his head as if reeling from unexpected news.)

LOUISE: The previous owners had left quite a few board games and jigsaw puzzles in a hallway closet. For the most part, they were in pretty bad shape. I looked inside the game boxes and saw pieces were missing, and some of the boards were damaged. The thought of getting to the end of a jigsaw puzzle to discover a piece had been lost in the shuffle answered the question of what to do with all of the puzzles anyway.

(*Looks at Allison*)

It wasn't much of a discussion before Daddy and I agreed we might as well throw everything out. I mean, none of it was good enough to donate to Goodwill or a thrift shop. So I packed everything into a cardboard box—which did not have a top, by the way—and put it on the front porch along with everything else we were taking to the dump.

(*Looks from Kathy to Scott*)

Now, here's the first *unusual* thing that happened. (*Widens her eyes*) When I started to walk away, the box of games fell to the deck. I thought I'd put it smack dab on top of another carton, but there it was, sideways on the deck, with a dozen games scattered this way and that.

When I put the half-empty box back on the other carton, I noticed one of the games inside the box was The Mystifying Oracle Ouija Board.

(*Scott uncrosses his arms and focuses his attention.*)

LOUISE (*Smiles at Scott*): Well, I'd never played with a Ouija board before. I didn't even know what you were supposed to do if you wanted to. Anyway, I put the rest of the games back in the box and went to the kitchen to make lunch. I set out everything I needed to make tuna fish sandwiches—two cans of tuna, a jar of mayonnaise, a jar of pickle relish, a loaf of rye bread.

(*Scott's head falls forward as if he'd nodded off.*)

LOUISE (*Ignores Scott's theatrics*): But I couldn't stop thinking about that darned Ouija board.

You know how that is. You tell yourself not to think about something, and all you can do is think about that very thing. Well, hard as I tried, I couldn't stop thinking about the Ouija board. Finally, I decided to put the game somewhere out of the way, so I could look at it without Allison seeing what I was up to.

(*Louise places her hand on Allison's thigh. Allison smiles. Scott looks away. Kathy pulls her knees closer.*)

LOUISE: That night, the sound of rushing water kept me awake. At least, that's what I thought was keeping me awake. Anyway, after tossing and turning for almost an hour, I came out to the kitchen and made myself a cup of tea. While I was waiting for my tea to cool down, it seemed like the perfect time to pull out the Ouija board and read the instructions.

(*Kathy rolls onto her back.*)

LOUISE: I put the board and the *planchette* on the table. I didn't know that's what the gadget was called when I opened the box. The planchette is the piece that moves around on the board and points to a letter or an answer, you know, like the words "YES" or "NO," which are already spelled out. Anyway, like I said, I put the board and the planchette on the table in front of me, and then I read the instructions. One of the rules was "Always say goodbye." I thought that was a little funny, but what did I know? Another rule was "Never use the board in your home." Well, the cabin wasn't really my "home," so I felt okay in that regard. The next part was a little odd—something like "What about rule number four?" But they didn't even list a rule number four.

(*Furrows her brow and shakes her head*)

They did say some people have asked about rule number four, which is about one person using the board. But the booklet pointed out that rule number four doesn't really matter because most people aren't psychic enough when they're alone. It also said, "No group, nothing happens."

(*Allison leans slightly forward and adjusts his pillows.*)

LOUISE: Are you all right, sweetheart?
ALLISON (*Looks at Louise with an oily smile*): Yes, darlin'. (*Leans back*) Go ahead with your story, sweetheart.
LOUISE: Okay, well, there I was, all alone with me, myself, and I, and the Ouija board, of course. So, I thought, "What the heck? I might as well give it a try. If nothing happens, I'll put everything away, turn out the lights, and go to bed." I checked the directions one more time and saw they recommended a dark, candlelit room. The previous owners had left several jar candles in case of a blackout. I lit a couple of the tall ones and put them on the table. I turned out the overhead light, put my teacup in the sink, sat down at the table, and tried to clear my mind of any negative thoughts.

(*Kathy raises her head and chest, pulls her elbows back*

to support herself, focuses her attention on the far wall.)

LOUISE: The first thing I did was place the planchette in the middle of the board. I didn't have a specific question in mind, and there wasn't anyone in particular I wanted to contact, you know, anyone who'd passed away. I just wanted to see if anything would happen on its own—what with my being alone and all. So, I took a deep breath and closed my eyes. I placed my fingertips on the planchette, and (*Looks from Scott to Kathy*) it started to move.

KATHY (*Hugs her knees*): This is giving me the creeps.

LOUISE: Oh, Kathy Sue. There's nothing for you to worry about, honey. Nothing's going to happen to you. I'm just sharing what happened to me.

> (*Smiles bravely*)
> All right, honey?

KATHY: I guess so.

> (*Inhales as she looks away, then back to Louise*)
> Where's the Ouija board now?

LOUISE: It's on the top shelf of our bedroom closet at the cabin. And, just so you know, it hasn't been used for almost a month now. Like I said, you have nothing to worry about. Okay, sweetheart?

KATHY (*A beat, then*): Yes.

LOUISE: All right, honey, just relax.

> (*Looks from Kathy to Scott*)
> How are you doing, Scott?

SCOTT (*Nodding slowly*): You have my full attention. Please continue.

LOUISE: Okay, honey, like I said, I put my fingertips on the planchette, and right away, it started to move. Well, my gosh, I wasn't expecting that. I pulled my hands back, and

(*Winks at Kathy*) I took a deep breath and told myself to relax. After a minute or so, I put my fingertips back on the planchette, and it started moving more slowly than before, almost like it was trying not to frighten me. I managed to keep breathing as I watched the planchette slide to the letter *H*, then to the *E*, then to the *L*, to the *L* again, and then the *O*.

KATHY: This is really weird.

SCOTT: I think it's far out. Literally.

KATHY: I don't understand how that stuff happens.

LOUISE: Well, Kathy Sue, if you'd allow me to continue, I might clear that up for you.

(*Kathy tilts her head back and studies the ceiling.*)

LOUISE: Actually, sweetheart, it looks like you might be getting a sense of this on your own. You know, (*Looks from Kathy to Scott*) the four of us have exceptional psychic powers.

KATHY: We do?

LOUISE: Yes, honey, if we'd just allow ourselves to realize them.

ALLISON: All right, Mother. Let's continue with your story.

LOUISE: Yes, dear. Well, obviously, the planchette had spelled out "HELLO," which, I have to say, gave me a chill. But I wasn't willing to stop at that point. I mean, I certainly wanted to know *who* had said "hello." I put my fingertips on the planchette and whispered, "Who are you?" In no time at all, the planchette slid to the *J*, then to the *E*, then to the *R,* to the *R* again, then to the *Y*.

SCOTT (*Nods slowly*): Wow.

KATHY (*Looks from Scott to Louise*): Are you saying it was our father?

LOUISE: Yes, sweetheart, Jerry was telling me he was there.

(*Kathy exhales.*)

SCOTT: Okay. What happened next?

LOUISE: Well, Scott.

(*Tilts her head from side to side*)

It was slow-going from that point on. I mean, I'd ask a question out loud, and that went fairly fast. But it took a while for the planchette to spell out Jerry's answers.

SCOTT (*Sits forward*): What did you ask him?

LOUISE: Oh, you know, honey, pretty much what you'd expect. "Are you all right?" "How do you pass the time?" Questions like that.

SCOTT (*Laughs through his nose*): Our father's been dead for six years, and you asked if he's all right?

LOUISE (*Shakes her head*): Well, yes, Scott. What would you have asked?

SCOTT (*Screws up his face*): I'd have asked what the hell's going on over there, wherever "over there" is?

LOUISE (*Sits up straight*): All right, Scott, there's no need for that kind of talk. And, yes, of course, I asked Jerry what it was like "beyond the veil," as they refer to it.

SCOTT: And . . . ?

LOUISE: Like I said, honey, every answer took several minutes, sometimes ten minutes, if it was a long explanation. Also, excited as I was to be communicating with your father, I could feel myself becoming very tired. You know, the whole thing was taking a lot out of me. After an hour or so, I told Jerry I was going to say goodbye—like the instructions said—that I'd check in with him when I was back at the cabin the following weekend.

SCOTT (*Draws back his head*): You waited a week before trying again?

LOUISE (*Nods slowly*): Yes, Scott. Remember, honey, one of the rules was never use the board at home. Not to mention, I needed some time to make sense of everything.

SCOTT (*Sits forward*): Okay, so what happened the next weekend?

LOUISE: On Saturday, Allison and I spent most of the day trimming overgrown shrubs and trees. That night, both of us were bushed—

SCOTT: Ha! Good word choice, Mom.

LOUISE (*Looks baffled*): What's that, honey?

SCOTT: You were "bushed" after trimming shrubs and trees all day.

LOUISE: Oh. Yes, I see.

> (*Clears her throat*)
>
> Well, it wasn't intentional. Anyway, we were so worn out that we barely made it through dinner. I told Allison I'd do the dishes in the morning, and we both went straight to bed.

KATHY: Where was I during all of this?

LOUISE: This was the first week of August, honey. You were in Long Beach, staying with Karen Diotte.

KATHY: Oh, right.

> (*Nods slowly*)
>
> How could I forget that?

LOUISE: Anyway, even though I could barely keep my eyes open at the dinner table, I couldn't get to sleep once I was in bed. The creek was really full that night. It sounded like it was going to wash the mountain away. To tell the truth, I knew I wouldn't be able to fall asleep without seeing if Jerry was still there. So, I came out to the kitchen, made myself a cup of tea, and set up the Ouija board and planchette.

> Oh,
> (*Shakes her head*)

I just remembered this. You know, your father could always make me laugh. Well, when I asked if he was still there, the planchette started moving so fast, I could barely keep my fingertips on it. I was laughing to myself by the time it finished spelling out "WHAT TOOK YOU SO LONG."

(*Looks from face to face*)

Anyway, (*Smoothing the covers across her lap*) the next thing I knew, the planchette was racing around the board, and it was all I could do to keep track of the letters. When the planchette finally stopped, the message was "THIS IS TOO SLOW GET PAPER AND PEN." Well, I thought Jerry wanted me to start taking notes, but that wasn't what he had in mind.

SCOTT: You talk like you were having an actual conversation with our father, like you knew it was Jerry on the other end of the line, so to speak.

LOUISE: Not, "so to speak," Scott. I know Jerry well enough to know that that's who I was communicating with.

SCOTT: Okay. But, really, Mom, of all the people "*beyond the veil*," why would Jerry answer your call?

LOUISE: I'm coming to that, Scott. (*Smiles*) But first, honey, the next thing Jerry conveyed was "START AUTOMATIC WRITING," which I didn't understand at all. After thinking about it for a minute, I asked, "What do you mean by that?" Right away, the planchette spelled out "GET BOOK." Just to be sure, I said, "You want me to get a book on automatic writing, whatever that is?" The planchette went directly to "YES" and then straight down to "GOODBYE." I laughed a bit at how abrupt Jerry was being with me. But, like I said, Scott, I knew your father well enough to know that that's who I was communicating with. I said,

"All right, Doctor Henry. I'll get a book, and I'll check in with you next week." I waited for a response, but after a minute or so, I said, "Goodbye," and put everything away for the night.

ALLISON (*Slides his feet to the floor without turning back the covers*): Mother, I'm in need of a bathroom break.

LOUISE: All right, sweetheart.

(*Allison crosses the room toward the master bathroom.*)

LOUISE: Take your time, darling. We're not going anywhere. (*In a saccharine tone*) Scott, would you be an angel and get your mother a glass of water?

(*Scott stands up and leaves the room.*)

KATHY (*Slides off the bed to her feet*): I need to check on something in my bedroom.

(*Scott crosses the hall, shrugging off his flannel shirt. He opens the door to Kathy's bedroom and tosses the shirt inside. Kathy closes the master bedroom door behind her as Scott turns around.*)

SCOTT (*In a low voice*): Boo!

(*Kathy flinches, then punches Scott in the arm. Scott leans in Kathy's direction.*)

KATHY (*In a loud whisper*): Cut it out!

(*Kathy pushes Scott out of the way. She steps into her bed-*

room and closes the door behind her. Scott disappears into the stage-right wings. Allison steps into the master bedroom, closes the bathroom door behind him, and crosses the room. Scott emerges from the wings, carrying a glass of water. He enters the master bedroom and proceeds to Louise's side of the bed. Allison gets in bed. Scott hands the glass to Louise, then returns to the rocking chair.)

LOUISE (*To Scott*): Thank you, sweetheart.

(Louise takes a sip of water as Allison gets settled. Kathy steps into the hallway and closes her bedroom door. She walks into the master bedroom, closes the door behind her, and resumes her place on the bed.)

LOUISE: All right. Is everyone comfortable?
    (Takes another sip of water, then clears her throat)
    Like I said, Jerry wanted me to get a book about automatic writing. I didn't know if I should go to the library or a book store. Monday afternoon, we had a couple of cancellations at the office, so I told Allison I had to run a couple of errands.
    (Tucks a wisp of hair behind her ear)
    I went to this real cute bookstore in the Saint Francis Shopping Center, but after explaining what I was looking for, the saleslady suggested I try the bookstore on Third Street, across from Courthouse Square. When I got to that store, the manager—an older gentleman, who remembered helping me track down a book on antique sewing machines for Allison—said he thought he had just what I was looking for. He walked me to a small selection of

books about metaphysical subjects. He ran his finger across several volumes before he pulled out Ruth Montgomery's *A Search for the Truth*. He turned to the table of contents and pointed out "Chapter 3. The Pencil Writes." I said, "By George, I think you've got it."

(*Reaches to the stack of books on her nightstand*)
And here it is.

(*Holds up a hardcover edition of* A Search for the Truth)

After purchasing the book, I drove across town and did some grocery shopping. I mention this because I wanted to hide the book in the bag of groceries so Allison wouldn't see what I was up to. You know, I still wasn't sure about any of this, and I didn't know how I'd explain it if Allison saw the book.

(*Louise takes a sip of water. She returns the glass to her nightstand, reaches a bit farther, and plucks a tissue from a decorative wooden box. She blows her nose twice, then tucks the tissue in her sleeve.*)

LOUISE: That night, after doing the dishes, I wanted to wash and set my hair. By the time I finished with that, Allison was already asleep, and I could barely keep my eyes open. I really wanted to look at the book, but it would have to wait one more day. Tuesday night, I was raring to go, but Allison asked for my help with some paperwork. Well, that kept us busy until we shuffled to bed around eleven o'clock. Wednesday night was the charm. Allison was still involved with the paperwork, so I told him I was going to treat myself to a long hot bath.

KATHY: Was I in Long Beach all this time?

LOUISE (*Smiles*): Yes, sweetheart. The Wednesday I'm talking about was during the third week of August. You came home the following Monday, August 26, right?

KATHY: Technically, it was Tuesday the twenty-seventh because the bus didn't arrive until after midnight.

LOUISE (*Broadens her smile*): Yes, honey, you are correct. Now that we've settled that, I'll get back to telling my story. Like I said, Wednesday night was the charm. I read the third chapter of Ruth Montgomery's book two times while I was in the bathtub. By the time I came into the bedroom, Allison was already asleep. I thought about it for a minute and decided there was no time like the present. I got a pad of paper and one of my favorite pens and went back into the bathroom where I wouldn't be disturbed. I sat down with my back against the door. I placed the pad in my lap and held the pen against the paper like I always do when I'm beginning to write. I took a slow breath and tried to clear my mind.

(*Pause*)

It wasn't long before I began to feel warm, pleasantly warm like a summer morning. I felt warm and calm and protected, and then I felt the pen moving across the paper. I didn't look down, but I could feel my hand traveling from side to side faster than it ever had. I could hear the pen scribbling at a speed I was certain could only produce gibberish. When my hand stopped, I waited a few seconds to catch my breath. When I did look down (*Little pause*) I couldn't believe my eyes. The piece of paper was halfway covered with my handwriting, my handwriting the way it usually looks. All the i's were dotted, all the t's were crossed. The lines were straight, and the margins were even.

SCOTT: Okay, Mom, we know you have baroque penmanship. I, for one, don't know how you manage it under normal circumstances. That said, what the hell was the message?

LOUISE: You know, *Scott,* (*Signaling her particular brand of irony*) it's interesting that you keep referring to hell. We'll come back to that in a few minutes, honey, and I think you'll see what I mean.

SCOTT: Okay. (*Clenches with impatience*) But what the hell was the message?

LOUISE (*Suppresses a laugh*): The message, Scott, was from your father. He congratulated me on the new format—the automatic writing. He told me it was going to make everything so much easier.

KATHY (*Perplexed*): What did that mean?

LOUISE: All it meant, honey, was that automatic writing was easier than spelling things out on the Ouija board.

KATHY: I understand *that.* What I don't understand is why you need an easier way to communicate with our dead father?

LOUISE: That's what I'm trying to explain, Kathy Sue, but you keep interrupting me.

KATHY: *Okay.*

(*Kathy rolls onto her side, facing Louise.*)

LOUISE: Anyway, (*Tilts her head in Kathy's direction*) Jerry went on to say he wasn't the only one who was glad to hear from me.

SCOTT: Oh boy. This is going to be interesting.

LOUISE: Yes, Scott, this is very interesting.

SCOTT: Let me guess—Grandma Taylor, Uncle Pete, Amelia Earhart, JFK, and Buddy Holly.

LOUISE: Not exactly. In the first message, Jerry didn't mention anyone by name, other than telling me Grandma Taylor sends her love.

SCOTT: I knew it.

LOUISE: Jerry did say they'd been waiting for me to make contact.

KATHY: What does that mean? That they'd been waiting a long time?

SCOTT: And who are "they"?

LOUISE: Those were my exact questions. (*Very matter-of-fact*) As for your question, Kathy Sue—"had they been waiting a long time?" Jerry explained that time as we know it does not exist in their dimension.

SCOTT: Sounds like something Rod Serling would say.

KATHY (*Hesitant*): The guy from *The Twilight Zone*?

(*Scott's head falls forward.*)

LOUISE: All right, you two. Please stop clowning around. It's important that you understand what I'm telling you. Okay?

KATHY (*A beat, then*): Yes.

SCOTT: Okey-dokey.

LOUISE (*Shakes her head*): Thank you.

SCOTT: Are you going to tell us who "they" are?

LOUISE: Yes, Scott, I'm coming to that. (*Inhales*) But who "they" are wasn't made clear to me until the following night. As for that night, I told Jerry I was already on overload, and I needed to get some sleep. He told me that was fine. He'd be there whenever I was ready. We had all the time in the world, which he pointed out was an inside joke in his neck of the woods.

SCOTT: Were those his words—"his neck of the woods"?

LOUISE: Not exactly.

SCOTT: Does he refer to where he is?

LOUISE: Yes, Scott. But before I go into that, I want to say I understand why you're making jokes about all of this. You know, honey, it wasn't a walk in the park for me when everything started happening. It was all I could do to keep from blabbing to Allison, but I didn't want to say anything until I had a better idea of what was going on. Even Jerry advised me to keep things to myself for the time being. He said there was going to be a lot of information coming through, and I needed to have a level head before I started sharing any of it with Allison, or anyone else.

SCOTT: You're sharing it with us.

LOUISE: Yes, honey. A lot's happened since those first couple of nights, which is why I'm sharing it with you and Kathy now. All right?

(*Scott exhales.*)

LOUISE: Be patient, honey.
　　　　(*Offers a blissful smile*)
　　　　Everything will be revealed to you in good time.
　　　　(*Appears to be collecting her thoughts*)
　　　　I suppose I should come right out with it . . . gosh, uh, I don't know why I'm so nervous. I guess it's because I'm talking to my family, not some strangers on the street.

ALLISON: You're doing fine, Mother. (*Smiles*) Tell your story the way it happened, darlin', just like we discussed.

LOUISE: All right, dear.
　　　　(*Sits up straight, relaxes her shoulders*)
　　　　Let's see now . . . oh yes, on the second night, I did ask Jerry if he could describe where he was. He answered, "Not exactly, but it does have a name that will be familiar to you, and that name is heaven."

241

KATHY: Our father's in heaven?

SCOTT: Our father who art in heaven.

LOUISE: Yes. (*In a matter-of-fact tone*) Jerry's in heaven, along with other people I've already mentioned.

SCOTT: The only other person you've already mentioned is Grandma Taylor.

LOUISE: Oh well. (*Shakes her head*) I was getting ahead of myself when I mentioned Grandma Taylor, but this is a good time to clarify that point. Like I said, Jerry told me how happy everybody was that I'd started the automatic writing.

SCOTT: Everybody?

LOUISE: Yes, Scott. (*Composes herself, then slowly and resonant*) Heaven is home to countless beings, some of them known to us, like Jerry and Grandma Taylor, some of them familiar to us, like angels and prophets, all of them enraptured by the glory of God.

SCOTT: Wow.

  (*Nods slowly*)

  Jerry told you this?

LOUISE: Yes, honey. Jerry told me this and many other wondrous things. Some of his revelations came as a surprise, but none of them more than this. Reincarnation is a part of God's plan for every sentient being.

KATHY: Every what? (*Glances at Scott*)

LOUISE: Every sentient being, sweetheart. That means any form of life that's able to perceive or feel things.

SCOTT: Does this mean Buddha is the one true God? Or the one true God is a Buddhist?

LOUISE: No, Scott. Neither of those possibilities is true, which is why everybody in heaven was so happy when I finally made contact. The purpose of all this, the reason Jerry reached out to me, is that I'm the person who will provide

the answers to mankind's most compelling questions.
Does God exist? Was Jesus real? Is there a heaven? Is
there a hell?

SCOTT: Whoa, whoa, whoa. I think you just changed lanes without
signaling. Are you saying that you . . . uh—what *are* you
saying?

LOUISE: I think you're asking if I'm going to be one of God's
prophets? If that's what you're asking, honey? (*Smiles*)
The answer is 'yes.'

KATHY: What's that mean?

LOUISE: What that means, Kathy Sue, is that your mother's been
chosen to transcribe an updated version of God's written
word.

SCOTT: A new and improved Bible—every home should have one.

LOUISE: Yes, Scott. Despite your sarcasm, you're correct on both
counts.

SCOTT: Holy moly, Mom. You say you were chosen for this.
Chosen by whom?

LOUISE: Who else? (*As if stating a fact*) I was chosen by God.

SCOTT: And Jerry told you this? (*Furrows his brow*) What's his
role in this joint venture?

LOUISE: Jerry was chosen by God as the go-between. He would be
transmitting the word of God, and I would be receiving it.
That's why everyone in heaven was rejoicing when I
started the automatic writing.

SCOTT: By what arcane process would God choose Jerry to be his
intermediary?

LOUISE: It just so happens, Scott, God chose Jerry on many occasions for important assignments, long before He chose
him to be your father.

SCOTT: Jerry was *chosen* to be my father?

LOUISE: Yes. (*Turns toward Allison for a moment, then to Scott*)

The members of our family—you, me, Allison, Kathy, Jerry, and others, like Grandma and Grandpa, who were saints, for you in particular, honey. All of us have been chosen by God for important missions, important incarnations, throughout the ages.

SCOTT: Okay. Can you give me an example? One of Jerry's better-known incarnations, for instance?

LOUISE: Yes, Scott, as a matter of fact, I can. One of Jerry's more interesting incarnations, according to him, was Abraham Lincoln.

(*Kathy looks at Scott.*)

SCOTT (*Ignores Kathy*): Anyone else of note?

LOUISE: Well, Scott, since you're so keen for a play on words, I'd say Jerry's incarnation as (*Pronounces the name phonetically*) "Richard Wagner" was someone of note.

SCOTT (*Considers Louise's pronunciation for a moment*): Do you mean (*Pronounces the name properly*) "Ricard Vagner," the German composer?

LOUISE: Yes, I suppose. I only read the name in a message from Jerry when we were discussing past lives. This one I do know how to pronounce though—Frédéric Chopin.

SCOTT (*Grimaces for Kathy's benefit*): Dad was Chopin as well?

LOUISE: No, sweetheart.

(*Laughs lightly*)

I was Chopin.

SCOTT: Oh. Well. Right. That makes more sense.

(*Kathy snorts.*)

ALLISON: All right. (*Looking at Kathy*) We'll have none of that.

LOUISE: It's okay, darling. (*Pats Allison's thigh*) This is going to take some getting used to for everyone concerned. Truth be told, Kathy's reaction is better than I expected. Now, let's get back to the question of reincarnation.

SCOTT: Jerry told you about these past lives?

LOUISE: Yes, Scott. (*Adopts a serious tone*) Previous incarnations are the topics of discussion among the sentient beings in heaven, much like classroom studies are discussed by students on a campus. Each individual, for want of a better description, carries the imprint of their past lives, which can be accessed by any other individual, but only occurs when all the parties involved, whether two or twenty-two, will benefit from the exchange.

SCOTT: Holy cow, Mom. You're beginning to sound like a lecture on comparative religion.

LOUISE: I've been reading my notes, which is the whole point of this, as you say, "joint venture." I mean, if I don't understand what I'm putting on paper, how can anyone else be expected to?

SCOTT: Fair enough. But don't you think it's time to acknowledge the elephant in the master bedroom?

LOUISE: (*Tilts her head*) I'm not sure I follow your meaning, honey.

SCOTT: You've told us this fantastic story about the circumstances that have presented you with a new career opportunity. But you haven't shown us how you communicate with our father who art in heaven.

LOUISE: Oh. (*Picks up the pad of paper and pen from her bedside table*) Is there something in particular you'd like to ask?

SCOTT: Uh . . . I'm not sure what I think about everything so far, but I have to admit, I keep having this feeling that Jerry's standing behind me. Is Jerry standing behind me?

LOUISE: Well, Scott, I already know that Jerry's here. He was very excited to see you—both of you, Kathy Sue. Okay, I'll go ahead and ask what he's doing right now.

(*Louise places the pad of paper in her lap. She exhales; her head falls forward, and she begins to write. Her hand tracks across the paper at an incredible speed, left to right, left to right, left to right. The episode stops as abruptly as it had begun. After her hand stops moving, her head returns to its upright position. Louise reads what she's written, looks up, and smiles at Scott.*)

LOUISE: It just so happens, Scott, that your father's been standing behind the rocking chair since you first came into the bedroom. He wants you to know how happy he is to see you, how proud he is of you—and you, too, Kathy Sue. Although, since he's been spending time with me, he's enjoyed the side-benefit of seeing Kathy as well. (*Smiles at Kathy*) More than once, sweetheart, your father's mentioned how pleased he is to see what a fine young woman you've become.

(*Louise continues looking at Kathy with expectation.*)

KATHY (*A beat, then*): That's nice.
LOUISE: Kathy Sue. (*Affecting surprise*) Is that all you have to say to your father after all these years?

(*Kathy glares at Scott.*)

SCOTT: This may sound strange, but I'm feeling claustrophobic. Would it be all right if I open the door?

ALLISON (*Laughs*): Yes, Scott, that would be fine. I'm laughing because, as your mother's about to tell you, this room is packed to the rafters with visitors from heaven.

(*Kathy pushes herself up to sit cross-legged. She looks from Allison to Louise. Louise watches Scott as he opens the bedroom door, then returns to the rocking chair.*)

KATHY: Mom . . . ?

LOUISE (*Looks at Kathy*): Yes, dear?

KATHY: Does that mean this room's full of angels?

LOUISE (*Thinks for a moment, then*): Well, yes and no, sweetheart, which is to say, "*angels*," as we commonly refer to God's heavenly creatures, are actually the lowest order of divine beings. I've received quite a bit of information on this subject, but I'm not conversant with the particulars yet. I can tell you there are three "spheres of angels," and each "sphere" contains three "orders" or "choirs." Isn't that pretty, Kathy Sue, "choirs of angels"?

KATHY (*A beat, then*): Yes.

LOUISE: I *have* memorized the three orders in the First Sphere, though. Now, let me see—

KATHY: Mom, sorry to interrupt, but I have to go to the bathroom.

LOUISE: All right, sweetheart.

SCOTT: So do I.

LOUISE: Okay, then. This seems like a good time for a short break. Kathy, you can use our bathroom, honey. Scott, you can use the bathroom in the hallway.

SCOTT: Right-o.

(*As Scott stands up from the rocking chair and Kathy stands up from the bed, a scrim begins to descend, and the lights start to fade. Kathy crosses the room as Scott steps into the hallway. Kathy enters the master bathroom and closes the door. Scott enters the hallway bathroom and closes the door. By this time, the scrim has fully descended, and the lights have faded to black.)*

ACT TWO

The scrim ascends, and the lights come up as Scott and Kathy step out of different bathrooms and close the doors behind them. Scott enters the master bedroom as Kathy crosses the room to the bed. By the time Scott sits in the rocking chair and Kathy gets situated on the foot of the bed, the scrim has disappeared, and the stage is fully lit. Louise and Allison are sitting in the same positions as they were at the end of Act One.

LOUISE: Okay. Are you kids comfortable?

SCOTT: Bug in a rug.

LOUISE: Kathy Sue?

KATHY: I'm fine.

LOUISE: All right.

(*To Scott*) Where were we, honey?

SCOTT: You were telling us about the angels.

LOUISE: Oh yes, the choirs of angels. Like I said, there are three choirs in the First Sphere. Now, let me see if I can remember.

(*Looking up and to the right*)

The First Choir are the Seraphim, the "burning ones" who continuously chant, "Holy, holy, holy is the Lord of hosts. The whole earth is full of His glory." Next are the Cherubim, the Second Choir, who guard the tree of life in the Garden of Eden as well as the throne of God. And then, of course, the Thrones, who present the prayers of men and listen to the will of God.

SCOTT: Of course. (*Glances at Kathy, then to Louise*) A-plus, Mom. I can't wait to hear the next installment.

(*Louise exhales; her head falls forward, and she begins to write. She fills one sheet of paper, tears it from the pad, and continues writing as the first sheet of paper floats to the bed. Her hand is halfway down the second sheet of paper when it comes to an abrupt stop. Her head returns to its upright position. She picks up the first sheet of paper and spends a moment reading what she'd written. Louise looks from the paper to Scott.*)

LOUISE: Well, Scott, (*A self-satisfied smile*) ask, and it shall be given you.

SCOTT: Okay . . .

LOUISE (*Reads aloud from the first sheet of paper*): The Second Sphere of Angels includes the Dominions who oversee the duties of lower angels, the Virtues who manifest signs and miracles in the world, and the Powers who supervise the movements of all the heavenly bodies—stars, planets, and moons—to maintain order in the cosmos.

(*Louise looks at Scott.*)

SCOTT (*Nodding slowly*): Ah, so.

LOUISE (*Looks back to the sheet of paper and continues reading aloud*): The Third Sphere is made up of the Principalities who guide and protect nations or large groups of people, such as major religious organizations. The next choir is composed of the seven Archangels who are known by name and associated with days of the week—Michael for Sunday, Gabriel for Monday, Raphael for Tuesday, Uriel for Wednesday, Raguel for Thursday, Remiel for Friday, and Sariel for Saturday. (*Picks up the second sheet of paper and continues reading aloud*) Last but not least—

SCOTT: Is that what it says? On the paper?

LOUISE: Well, no, Scott. I'm ad-libbing a bit to lighten things up.

SCOTT: Speaking of the devil, where does Lucifer fit into all of this?

LOUISE (*Frowns*): Let's not get ahead of ourselves. (*Brightens her expression*) Like I was saying—last but not least, the third order of the Third Sphere is the Choir of Angels. These are the angels we're most familiar with because they're involved with all living things. Also, Kathy Sue, the Choir of Angels includes all of the guardian angels.

SCOTT: Wow, Mom. Where were you when I needed research information for my school assignments?

LOUISE: All right, Scott, I'd appreciate it if you'd stop making wisecracks.

SCOTT: No, no, no. (*Holds out both hands*) I think this is fantastic. All of it—really phenomenal. But what are you going to do with it?

LOUISE: Well, Scott, that's what we wanted to share with you and Kathy, why we called you into the bedroom tonight.

SCOTT: Okay, then. I'm all ears. (*To Kathy*) How about you, Sue?

KATHY: I think I should go to bed.

LOUISE: Oh no, sweetheart. This concerns you as much as anyone else, honey.

KATHY (*Glaring at Scott*): It does?

ALLISON: Yes, Kathy. Your mother needs you to hear the rest of her story tonight.

KATHY: Why tonight?

LOUISE: Oh, Kathy Sue. You can stay awake for another half hour or so. Can't you, sweetheart?

KATHY: I guess so. (*Narrows her eyes*)

LOUISE: Thank you, dear.

(*Composes herself*)

Now, where was I?

(*Turns to Allison*)

Do you remember where I left off, darling?

ALLISON: I believe you were telling the children about Jerry's previous incarnations.

LOUISE: Oh, yes, that's right. (*To Scott*) Another one of Jerry's more important incarnations—this one especially difficult for obvious reasons—was Pontius Pilate.

KATHY: Who was Pontius Pilate?

SCOTT: Pontius Pilate in the Bible, Pontius Pilate?

LOUISE: Yes, Scott. (*To Kathy*) Pontius Pilate, honey, was the governor of Judaea, who presided over Jesus Christ's trial and gave the order for his crucifixion.

KATHY: Ugh.

SCOTT: Nail on the head, sis, if any of that were true. I think *crucifixion* should be spelled with *ct* in place of the *x*.

ALLISON (*With a stern look*): All right, Scott. (*To Louise*) Perhaps it's time to tell the children about some of their past lives, darlin'.

LOUISE: Yes, dear, I believe this would be the perfect time.

(*Louise exhales; her head falls forward, and she begins to write. A minute later, she tears a sheet of paper from the pad but does not continue writing. There's a moment of indecision as her hand remains poised at the top of the pad, but then her head returns to its upright position. Louise picks up the sheet of paper from the bed and reads what she's written.*)

LOUISE (*Looks from the paper to Kathy*): Oh my gosh, Kathy Sue, you were Elizabeth, the mother of John the Baptist.

KATHY: I was?

LOUISE: And, Scott, you were John the Baptist.

KATHY: *Eww.*

LOUISE (*To Kathy*): Like I said, sweetheart, the four of us have been chosen throughout history for very important life assignments.

SCOTT: Anyone other than characters from the New Testament?

LOUISE (*Reads for a moment, then to Kathy*): Kathy Sue, you were Ponce de León, the Spanish explorer who named Florida and became the first governor of Puerto Rico. He was also famous for believing there was a "fountain of youth," but that was a myth associated with his name after his death.

SCOTT: Who are you, and what have you done with my mother?

LOUISE (*Giggles*): I'm just a messenger.

SCOTT: So said Gabriel. (*Takes a deep breath*)

LOUISE: As a matter of fact, Scott, I didn't want to tell you this until later, but now that you've brought it up. When I asked if Jerry was in the room, I was told that he *and Gabriel* were standing right behind you.

SCOTT: What are the odds? But then, it's a small world, as they say in Anaheim.

LOUISE (*Reads for a moment, then to Kathy*): Kathy Sue, you were also Marie Antoinette.

SCOTT: *Marie Antoinette.* That's a dubious distinction.

LOUISE: Well, Scott, she *was* the Queen of France.

SCOTT (*Nodding*): Yes, and as such, Her Most Christian Majesty was responsible for inciting the French Revolution, which was the first domino to fall in the collapse of European aristocracy. So, okay, not bad, Sue.

(*Scott gives Kathy a thumbs up.*)

LOUISE: All right, Scott. Maybe you'll be a little less sarcastic when you hear about some of your previous incarnations, such as Frederick the Great.

SCOTT: I was Frederick the Great? (*Makes a face*) Are you sure it's "Frederick," not "Alexander"?

LOUISE: This isn't like ordering off the menu, Scott.

(*Louise exhales; her head falls forward, and she begins to write. Her hand speeds from margin to margin several times, then stops as abruptly as it had begun. When her head returns to its upright position, she reads for a moment, then smiles.*)

LOUISE: Well, Scott, I don't think you'll have a problem with the fact that you were Ludwig von Beethoven.

SCOTT: That would explain why I can play the first movement of the *Moonlight Sonata* with my eyes closed. (*Inhales, then*) The trouble I have with the third movement doesn't jibe so well with this revelation.

ALLISON: All right, Mother, we should get back to the matter at hand.

LOUISE: Yes, of course, darling. Let's see, where was I?

ALLISON: Jerry told you he was going to be away for a couple of days.

LOUISE: Yes, but he also told me to continue checking in while he was away.

KATHY: Where'd he go?

LOUISE: Well, Kathy Sue, at the time, I wasn't sure where Jerry had gone. But he wanted me to keep up with the automatic writing. You know, to improve my ability before I started receiving the information for my book. The funny thing is, I expected the next person I'd hear from would be Grandma Taylor. But when I received the first message from Jerry's stand-in, I could tell it wasn't someone I knew. I mean, they knew me, knew things about me and my life. They mentioned Allison by name, but, like I said, I didn't know who they were—

ALLISON: Which probably has to do with why this was when I discovered Louise asleep on the bathroom floor, surrounded by sheets of paper covered in her handwriting. You can't imagine how bizarre that seemed to me. I'd woken up at two in the morning because I needed to use the bathroom. At first, I thought your mother must be in the bathroom for the same reason, but after five minutes or so, I realized I should get up and see what was going on. I knocked at the door and called her name, but there was no answer. I turned the knob, then opened the door wide enough to see Louise lying on the floor. When I stepped into the room and saw all that paper scattered on the floor, my mind went blank. Truly, this was one of those rare moments in life when you have no idea of what you're looking at.

LOUISE: It was quite a sight. It had been one of my more . . .

(*Turns to Allison*)

Would you say *productive* nights?

ALLISON: For want of a better word. You can't imagine the scene. I counted the pieces of paper as I picked them up—thirty-eight letter-size sheets of unlined paper completely covered with Louise's handwriting—

LOUISE: *And*, if that wasn't enough to give a person pause, some of the sheets had notes in the margins and writing on the back. (*Grimaces playfully*) Not to mention, I'd already hidden a batch of papers from earlier that evening.

ALLISON: When I heard that . . . well, what can I say, I was already speechless?

LOUISE: Allison, "speechless," as we know, is a rare thing. So, I took advantage of the situation to tell as much of my story as possible without interruption.

(*Louise telegraphs a look of triumph, while Allison maintains his characteristic reserve.*)

LOUISE: I started at the beginning, back at Oakcrest with the Ouija board, and I have to say, even with the doubtful look on Daddy's face, he didn't say a word until I got to the part of Jerry leaving for a couple of days and my communicating with someone new. I haven't told you kids yet, but when I asked the new person who he was, he told me he was Allison's uncle.
(*Looks from Scott to Kathy, then back to Scott*)
Now, this is someone I'd never met. I'd heard his name once or twice, but really, nothing more than that. When I described him to Allison, read some of the things he'd told me about his past, Allison said there was no doubt about it. This was his Uncle Frank, who died of a heart attack. (*Looks at Allison*) How long ago, sweetheart?

ALLISON: Nineteen years.

LOUISE: That's right. Uncle Frank died nineteen years ago before I even knew who Allison was. But there we were, having a conversation in the bathroom like we'd just met at a family picnic. Isn't that something?

SCOTT (*Shaking his head almost imperceptibly*): Yes, Louise, that is something.

LOUISE: Well, *Scott*, Allison certainly thought it was. I mean, how could I know all the things Uncle Frank was telling me, things about his wife, Eileen, and their children, Sam and Janey?

SCOTT: You'd never heard their names?

LOUISE: Well, no, honey. Uncle Frank died before Allison and I knew each other.

SCOTT: That doesn't mean you never heard the names of his wife and children.

LOUISE (*Standing her ground*): If I had, I certainly don't remember it. Anyway, Scott, it wasn't only the names he mentioned, he also told me about a fishing trip he'd taken with Sam and Allison and Allison's brother Albert—and their father John, of course, Frank's younger brother. And I'm pretty darn sure I never heard anything about that.

ALLISON: The fishing trip she's talking about was more than forty years ago. I didn't remember it myself until Louise told me Frank had mentioned it.

LOUISE: So, you see, this was when Allison started considering the *veracity* of what I was telling him.

ALLISON: Yes, to some degree.

(*Allison inhales. Louise puts her hand in Allison's. Allison smiles in response.*)

ALLISON: I couldn't deny Louise's knowledge of events that even I'd forgotten. I still don't have a reasonable explanation for that—other than what she was telling me was God's honest truth.

(*Allison grins self-consciously. Louise claps her hands together and giggles. Kathy and Scott exchange glances.*)

LOUISE: Yes, that's right. When I told you about Uncle Frank, you started to think I was really on to something.

ALLISON (*Tilts his head*): Yes, darlin', to some degree.

LOUISE: Oh well. (*Slaps Allison's thigh*) I didn't mean hook, line, and sinker, sweetheart, although it was me telling you about your fishing trip that reeled you in.

SCOTT: Mom, enough with the fishing metaphors.

LOUISE: Really, sweetheart? I thought those were keepers.

SCOTT: Ugh.

(*Shivers theatrically*)

That's sufficient comic relief, Louise. Let's get back to the "matter at hand," as Allison put it, your hotline to heaven.

(*Kathy suppresses a laugh.*)

ALLISON: I agree.

LOUISE: All right, sweetheart.

(*Looks from Scott to Allison*)

Like I said, I'd explained everything to Daddy, from the first weekend at Oakcrest to Uncle Frank's arrival six weeks later.

ALLISON: At this point, I convinced your mother to discontinue her practice of sitting on the bathroom floor until all hours. I told Louise she could sit in the living room if she needed to be alone, or she could sit in bed as long as she turned her light off by midnight. Either way, she had to start getting at least six hours of sleep every night, or she'd start to come apart at the seams, which, by all appearances, was already happening.

LOUISE: As much as I appreciated Allison's offer to sit in the bedroom, I wasn't quite ready to communicate with the spirit world in front of an audience.

(*Pats Allison's thigh*)

So, I set up shop in the living room and agreed to come to bed no later than midnight. That first night, sitting on the sofa with my pad in my lap, I had a list of questions for Uncle Frank from Allison about his family. But wouldn't you know it? (*Shakes her head*) That's when Jerry returned with some pretty big news.

SCOTT: How convenient, as for not having to prove Uncle Frank's credibility.

LOUISE (*Purses her lips, then relaxes her expression*): Like I said, that's when Jerry returned with some pretty big news. I knew he'd left because God had requested his presence. Jerry told me that before he went away. I didn't tell Allison this part when I was explaining what was going on because I wasn't sure myself of what God had in mind. That's what Jerry had gone to discuss, the particulars of our upcoming project. The first thing Jerry told me came as a bit of a surprise, (*Tilts her head from side to side*) that the process of receiving new information would continue for at least *five years*.

Well, I didn't know what to say to that. I mean, Lord knows I wanted to participate, but I'd never considered being involved *for five years*. Then again, it dawned on me, what's the difference—five days, five weeks, five years? I shared this thought with Jerry, and he replied, "That's the spirit! And, by the way, that's exactly how it feels over here—five days, five weeks, five years—what's the difference?"

(*Louise sets the pad and pen on her bedside table.*)

SCOTT: Does this mean you'll be taking dictation from nine till midnight for the next five years?

LOUISE: Not exactly, Scott, which brings me to the next bit of unexpected news from Jerry's meeting with God. They think the transmission of this much information will require more of my time than a couple of hours a day.

KATHY: What does that mean?

(*Kathy pushes herself up to sit cross-legged.*)

LOUISE: Well, sweetheart, it means I'll be devoting more time to the project. Actually, (*Leans slightly forward*) it means I'll be devoting *most* of my time to the project.

KATHY (*Voice wavering*): I still don't understand what that means.

LOUISE: What that means, Kathy Sue, (*Leans closer still*) is that this undertaking is so important—not just for me, sweetheart, but for . . . well, *everyone*. It's so important that it will require as much time as I have to give.

KATHY: Does that mean you're going to stop working at the office?

LOUISE: Yes, sweetheart.

(*Kathy looks at Allison, then back to Louise.*)

KATHY: Are you going to stay home all day while you're working on this?

LOUISE: Not necessarily. (*Leans toward Kathy*) Which is why we wanted to celebrate tonight with the whole family, why we wanted to share what was going on while Scott was here with us.

ALLISON: Yes. But, darlin', I think you may be getting ahead of yourself—that is, if you want to share the whole story with the children.

LOUISE: Well, of course, I do. (*Shakes her head slowly*) All right, then. Uh,

(*Turns toward Allison*)

Do you remember where I was, sweetheart?

ALLISON: I believe you were in the living room for the first time when you realized Jerry had returned from his meeting.

LOUISE: Oh yes, that's right.

(*Arranges herself and the bedclothes*)

Like Daddy said, I was in the living room. Let's see, now . . . it was Sunday night. I remember it was the first of September because Kathy had returned from Long Beach, and I had to wait until she went to bed before I set myself up in the living room. After I saw the light go out in Kathy's room, I sat down on the sofa with my pad and pen and the list for Uncle Frank—well, you knew that already. Okay, like I said, you can imagine I was more than a little surprised when I realized Jerry was back. And also, right away, I could tell he was excited.

KATHY: How could you tell he was excited?

LOUISE: Oh well, Kathy Sue, you can just tell by someone's words, even if you can't hear their voice. It's like reading a letter from someone you know really well. You know what I mean, don't you, sweetheart?

KATHY (*An edge in her voice*): No.

SCOTT: Okay, you could tell that Jerry was excited.

LOUISE: Yes, honey—you know, by the words he was using.

ALLISON: All right, Mother. I think we can agree that Jerry was excited. Why don't you tell the children why?

LOUISE: I'd be happy to.

(*Tucks a wisp of hair behind her ear*)

You remember that Jerry had to leave because he had an audience with God.

SCOTT: Sounds like something from the Brothers Grimm—an audience with the almighty king.

LOUISE: It wasn't an audience with the almighty king, Scott. It was an audience with the Almighty. (*Raises her brow for*

263

emphasis) The first thing Jerry told me was that I needed to do as much automatic writing as possible to improve my speed. He said I was already doing really well. In fact, he said his only complaint since we started communicating this way was hearing from everyone how fantastic my writing was coming along.

SCOTT: They must have thought it heavenly.

LOUISE (*Smiles at Scott, then narrows her eyes*): Anyway, (*To Kathy*) the next thing your father told me *really* took me by surprise, and I'm still trying to come to grips with it. He said I needed to gain some weight, at least ten pounds. "Why ever for," I blurted out.

(*Shakes her head*)

But Jerry didn't answer. At least for longer than usual, he didn't answer. Finally, Jerry communicated, "Sorry. I was laughing."

Right away, I whispered, "Well, I'm glad one of us finds this amusing because I certainly don't."

KATHY: Why did Jerry want you to gain weight?

LOUISE: Jerry didn't want me to gain weight, sweetheart. God did.

SCOTT: Okay. I'll bite—whoops, sorry, sounds like we're back to fishing metaphors. Anyway, why did God want you to gain weight?

LOUISE: Evidently, people in the past who've communicated through automatic writing for extended periods start to have physical problems, especially if they drink alcohol or smoke cigarettes.

SCOTT: Lord knows you don't drink alcohol more than once or twice a year.

LOUISE: Yes, Scott, he does.

SCOTT: But you smoked a cigarette with me at Oakcrest yesterday. How does that figure in the scheme of things?

LOUISE: Well, Scott, (*Looks at Allison*) Allison will confirm that I decided to have my last cigarette with you when you were here visiting. I thought it was something that we could share—not that I support your smoking habit, because, of course, I don't. But I knew I had to stop smoking altogether, so I chose to have my last cigarette with you on the deck at Oakcrest. That in mind, sweetheart, maybe you'd consider stopping with me.

SCOTT: Sorry to disappoint, but no can do. As a matter of fact, this seems like a perfect time for a cigarette break.

LOUISE: Oh no, honey. You can wait a little longer, can't you, Scott? It's just that it's getting so late, and I'd like to go on with my story. (*Changes tone*) If that's okay with you.

SCOTT (*Narrows his eyes for a moment, then*): All right. But I'd like to step outside sooner than later. Please keep that in mind when you arrive at a convenient place for a break.

LOUISE: Yes, dear, I will. Now . . . oh gosh, I'm having such a time keeping track of what I've already said.

SCOTT: You were telling us why God wanted you to gain weight.

LOUISE: Yes, that's right. God was looking out for my best interests, which wasn't much different than a businessman protecting an asset, when you think about it. (*Adjusts the neck of her nightgown*) Anyway, I've been eating more than usual, as well as more often—snacks in the afternoon and whatnot—in hopes of satisfying *our Heavenly Father's* unusual request.

SCOTT: How does *our Heavenly Father* feel about you making light of his name? Isn't there something or other about eternal damnation and hellfire?

LOUISE: Actually, Scott, (*Smiling softly*) that would be "eternal hellfire and damnation," neither of which will be visited upon me because God likes my sense of humor.

SCOTT: God told you this?

LOUISE: Yes, Scott, more than once, as a matter of fact.

SCOTT: I don't think you understand what those words mean.

LOUISE: Which words, honey?

SCOTT: "A matter of fact." A matter of fact is something that's indisputably true, which, it seems to me, is the polar opposite of a faith-based experience, such as a thumbs up from God—twice, as if once weren't enough. If God had given me a pat on the back, I'd be walking on air for the rest of my life, however long or short that might be. Isn't that how it works? Like with Moses, for example, or Joan of Arc?

LOUISE: I doubt this will support the point you're trying to make, Scott, but I can't help mentioning, since you brought it up, that I was Joan of Arc in one of my past lives.

SCOTT: Of course you were. Man, oh, man, this gives "preaching to the choir" a whole new meaning. Okay, well, never mind. What else did Jerry have to say when he got back from his meeting with I Am That I Am, or does that moniker only apply to his stint with the Children of Israel?

LOUISE: All right, Scott. I don't think this is the time and place for you to exercise your intellect. You'll be back at school tomorrow, honey. Why don't you save your clever remarks for the teachers who are getting paid for the privilege of listening to them? Okay, sweetheart?

SCOTT: You bet. (*Pulls an imaginary zipper across his lips*)

LOUISE (*Shaking her head*): Now I understand why Jerry wanted me to enroll in a public speaking class.

KATHY: Excuse me. Did you say Jerry wants you to take a public speaking class?

LOUISE: Yes, sweetheart.

KATHY: Why?

LOUISE: Well—

(*Looks from Kathy to Scott*)

I think part of the reason has to do with discussions like this being hijacked by smart alecks like your brother.

SCOTT: Humph.

LOUISE: Jerry told me that not only will I be receiving revelations from God, I will also be lecturing and conducting discussion groups as the information becomes known to me. The public speaking classes are meant to bolster my confidence when I'm speaking to, well, (*Shaking her head*) the public.

SCOTT: I, for one, would pay to see a lecture demonstration. The automatic writing alone would be worth the price of admission.

LOUISE: Now, Scott . . .

(*Sits up straight*)

I thought you were taking a time out. If not, I'll thank you in advance for keeping your comments to yourself unless I ask for them.

SCOTT: Holy cow, Mom, you don't need a public speaking class to gain confidence. Keep doing like that just now, and you'll be fine.

LOUISE: Thank you, dear. But standing in front of an auditorium full of strangers is a tad different than sitting in bed talking to my family, wouldn't you say?

SCOTT: Absolutely.

(*Leans forward*)

Then again, what can higher education teach you that a higher power can't?

LOUISE: Well, sweetheart, I guess I'll find out soon enough. As for whether or not a class will help, I've already signed up for one at Santa Rosa Junior College.

KATHY: You have? When? What class?

SCOTT (*To Kathy*): Aren't they teaching you to speak in complete sentences at that school of yours?

KATHY (*To Scott*): Shut up.

SCOTT: Case in point.

LOUISE (*Looking from Kathy to Scott*): All right, you two, try to behave like adults.

(*To Kathy*) In answer to your first question, Kathy Sue, I went to the campus on Friday afternoon. Even though classes had started three weeks earlier, after I told my story, the woman in the enrollment office said she'd put the paperwork through if the instructor agreed to a late admission. So, I sought out the teacher, a really nice older gentleman named Harvey Thomas, and we really hit it off. He said he'd be pleased to include me in his Mastering Public Speaking class, and if our chat was any indication, he reckoned he might learn a thing or two from me.

SCOTT: Wow, Mom. You, a college coed. Who'd a thunk it?

LOUISE: It's only one class, Scott, but it is exciting.

(*Rests her hand on Allison's thigh*)

And a little daunting, what with everything else I'm supposed to be doing.

KATHY: What else are you supposed to be doing?

LOUISE: My gosh, Kathy Sue. (*Furrows her brow*) Aren't I doing enough already? Watching what I eat, abstaining from alcohol and tobacco, getting more exercise, improving the speed of my writing.

SCOTT: Now that you're listing your dos and don'ts, I don't remember God telling you to get more exercise, number one. And, number two, it occurs to me, if you add caffeine to your list of don'ts, it would be eerily close to the religious persuasion of your childhood.

LOUISE: Maybe I forgot to mention it, Scott—after all, this story has a lot of moving parts—

SCOTT: You can say that again.

LOUISE: Yes, dear, but I won't. (*Smiles briefly*) Anyway, when Jerry advised me to gain some weight, he also told me to start walking for at least forty-five minutes every day, preferably in the morning, which I've been doing for the last three weeks. As for the caffeine remark and how it relates to The Church of Jesus Christ of Latter-day Saints. Throughout history, religious factions have tried to control their follower's conduct, from dietary restrictions to sexual abstinence, but that is nothing more than small-minded men exercising control for the sake of lining their coffers. God isn't concerned with what people eat or drink or how they express their love as long as they don't harm themselves or anyone else.

SCOTT: I've already said this, but I have to say it again. Who are you, and what have you done with my mother?

LOUISE: I think you may have to get used to the idea, Scott, that I'm no longer speaking as your mother. I'm speaking as the messenger of God.

SCOTT: So far, your God seems like a nicer fellow than everyone else's, especially when it comes to sexual abstinence. I can't wait to hear what the Catholic Church has to say about that after two thousand years of cruel and unusual punishment.

LOUISE: Shedding new light on these issues is precisely why God has decided to reveal himself, here and now, without confusion or interpretation. His word, transmitted through me, will be clear and concise. Finally, after millenniums of conflict and discord, mankind will know the mind of God.

SCOTT: As well they should. Do we get to meet him? Is he here tonight, with his heavenly host?

LOUISE: Before I answer that question—

(*Looks from Scott to Allison*)

Let me get back to Jerry's checklist of what God was expecting from me. Last on the list, and the most difficult to understand, was the need for me to be in different locations—different cities and different countries—when I receive the transmissions from heaven.

(*Kathy looks at Scott, then at Louise.*)

LOUISE: Well, I didn't know what to think when I heard that. Aside from the time I was already expected to put in, the thought of gallivanting around the country, not to mention different countries, all I could say was I didn't know what to say. And, of course, how would I pay for travel and lodging?

KATHY: And . . . ?

LOUISE (*Laughs softly*): This is where it gets very interesting and very confusing at the same time.

SCOTT: I know the feeling.

LOUISE: I'm sure everyone's experienced something to that effect. But getting mixed signals from God has to qualify as above and beyond your everyday dilemma.

SCOTT: I don't know about that. Getting mixed signals from God sounds very much like an everyday dilemma.

(*Raises his hands, palms up*)

I'm just saying.

LOUISE (*Shaking her head*): Anyway, Jerry told me not to worry about where the money would come from. He assured me it would appear, in the right amount, at the right time. He then told me I should communicate with my father and left it at that.

After a few seconds of silence—when I'm not writing, you know, it seems like there's silence on the other end. Anyway, after a few seconds of silence, I asked, "Why should I communicate with my father? Is that where you think the money will come from? If it is, if that's who you think will provide financial support for me taking my show on the road, you've got another think coming."

SCOTT: Does that mean you did *not* talk to Grandpa?

LOUISE: Not right away. (*Purses her lips*) I mean, I knew that Grandma and Grandpa were financially secure, not wanting for anything anyway. All the same, there was never any indication of more money than necessary to live as simply as they do.

(*Looks from Scott to Kathy*)

To tell the truth, I think Uncle Donald helps out from time to time—not that he'd feel the pinch in between buying motorboats and airplanes.

ALLISON: All right, Louise. Let's not dredge up family issues.

LOUISE: Yes, you're right, *of course*. (*Smiles at Allison*) We need to be looking ahead—

SCOTT: Hold on a minute. You said "not right away," which means you did talk to Grandpa. Now that would have been an interesting conversation. There's no way you could have explained all of this to Gus. He would have sputtered something or other after hearing you were communicating with your dead ex-husband, not to mention—(*Jerks his thumb toward the ceiling*).

LOUISE: No, Scott, you're right. I knew better than to tell Grandpa everything I've told you—well, you and Kathy and Allison. I told Mother more than I told Daddy, but they're pretty much set in their ways when it comes to discussing God and religion.

SCOTT: I know you don't get out much, social gatherings and such, but you should know by now that everyone on this planet is pretty much set in their ways when it comes to discussing God and religion.

LOUISE: For crying out loud, Scott. We're not shut-ins.

SCOTT: No, you just prefer to stay in. But that's not my point.

LOUISE: What is your point?

(*Louise folds her hands in her lap.*)

SCOTT: You've enrolled in a public speaking class with the intention of lecturing to large groups of people about the word of God. That's all well and good in that those people will come to hear you because they will be, for the most part, like-minded individuals. It's everyone else I'm worried about. History has proven, time and again, that religion is the powder keg with the shortest fuse. What I mean to say is . . . you sound like you expect to be welcomed into the fold, but I think you need to allow for the possibility of being left out in the cold—sorry, I wasn't aiming for a rhyme. In other words, you're touting yourself as a messenger of God, but that may be nothing more than a fool's errand.

(*Louise takes a slow breath.*)

LOUISE: You make it sound like this is my plan, Scott. But this is not my plan, none of it's my plan. This is God's plan, and I have to believe that I will be directed to what is right and good, that I will be welcomed by, as you say, like-minded individuals, that God has chosen me because I'm up to the task. This is God's plan, Scott, and he's doing it for the betterment of mankind.

SCOTT: Exactly. That's *exactly* what I'm saying. God gave his only begotten Son for the betterment of mankind, in response to which mankind nailed him to a cross.

ALLISON: All right, Scott, that's enough. (*Looks at Louise*) Please get back to telling your story, darlin', after you'd spoken to Gus and Marguerite.

LOUISE: Yes, sweetheart. (*Looks from Allison to Scott*) Mother and Daddy were confused by what little I told them, and they made it clear they would do whatever they could if I were in trouble, but they were in no position to, as Daddy put it, "send me on a trip around the world." (*Makes a* face) I'm sure he said more than that after he hung up.

SCOTT: Oh yeah, you can take that to the bank. But God love him— whoops, sorry—anyway, he'd give you the shirt off his back if you were in trouble.

LOUISE: Yes, dear, your grandfather's been very good to you.

SCOTT: In the sense that he's *been* a grandfather to me.

KATHY: I don't know how much longer I can stay awake.

SCOTT: What time is it?

ALLISON (*Glances at the clock on his bedside table*): A few minutes before midnight.

LOUISE: Oh my gosh, I had no idea it was that late. Maybe we should call it a night.

SCOTT: What? No way. I have to catch a bus in eight hours, and a plane three hours after that. I'm not going to bed until I've heard the whole story. However, (*Standing up*) I'm going to start biting my nails if I don't go outside and have a cigarette.

KATHY (*Lowering her feet to the floor*): I'm going with him.

LOUISE (*Turning toward Allison*): I don't know.

KATHY: I'll be fine. We're only going out to the sidewalk in front of the building, right?

SCOTT: Right. If we're attacked, Kathy will protect me.

LOUISE: All right, Scott . . .

(*Kathy follows Scott out of the master bedroom.*)

SCOTT (*Over his shoulder*): Not to worry, we'll be back before you know it. Ha! Remember what Jerry said about time? Not really a thing.

(*The scrim begins to descend, and the lights start to fade.*)

LOUISE (*Calls out*): Kathy Sue, put on your wool coat, sweetheart.

KATHY (*Offstage*): I am.

(*Scott steps into the hallway wearing a flannel shirt, followed by Kathy wearing a plaid coat and red Mary Janes over white socks. They proceed downstage toward the stage-right wings.*)

SCOTT: Love the shoes.

KATHY: Me too.

SCOTT: I'm serious.

KATHY: So am I.

(*The scrim has fully descended, and the lights have faded to black.*)

ACT THREE

Scene I

The scrim ascends, and the lights come up as Scott and Kathy walk from the stage-right wings into Kathy's bedroom. Louise and Allison are sitting in the same positions as they were at the end of Act Two.

LOUISE (*Calls out*): All right, you two. It's already past midnight, and everybody's got a big day tomorrow.

KATHY (*Offstage*): Yes, Mother, we know.

> *(Scott steps into the hallway without his flannel shirt, followed by Kathy in her pajamas and slippers. They return to the master bedroom. Scott sits in the rocking chair with his feet on the floor and his arms on the arms of the chair. Kathy stretches out on the bed.)*

LOUISE: Is everybody comfortable?
> *(Pats Allison's thigh)*
> Daddy?

ALLISON: Yes, darlin', I'm fine.

LOUISE: Kathy Sue, wouldn't you'd be more comfortable with a pillow, sweetheart?

KATHY: No.

> *(Louise looks at Scott for a moment. She exhales; her head falls forward, and her hand starts to move from side to side on the pad of paper in her lap. After a few seconds,*

the episode stops as abruptly as it had begun. Louise reads what she's written. She smiles, then looks at Scott.)

LOUISE: Your father wanted you to know that the way you're sitting right now reminds him of his memorial in Washington, DC.

SCOTT (*Tilts his head, then chuckles*): The Lincoln Memorial, right?

LOUISE (*Nods*): Yes, honey.

SCOTT (*Crosses his legs at the knees*): All right, Mom. What happened next?

LOUISE (*Closes her eyes for a moment, then*): Like I said, honey, Jerry told me I should communicate with my father, which I did, but that didn't work out the way I'd hoped. Actually, it worked out exactly as I knew it would, but you know what I mean. Anyway, I have to say I was starting to lose faith in the idea of making myself available for this project. Jerry kept assuring me the financial support would manifest itself when the time was right, but I couldn't put everything else on hold until who knows when.

(*Adjusts the neck of her nightgown*)

I discussed my concerns with Allison and came to the conclusion that I'd tell Jerry I would need something more concrete than his assurance before I started making preparations to embark on this journey with him.

(*Kathy yawns, then rolls onto her back.*)

LOUISE: That night, when I sat down with my pad and pen, even before I began to write, I could tell something was different. Usually, I wait for a greeting from the other side before I ask whatever questions I want to bring up. But this was different, right from the start, (*Looks at Scott*) right from the first word.

SCOTT (*A beat, then*): What *was* the first word?

LOUISE (*With a beatific smile*): Well, Scott, the first word was "holy."

(*Pause.*)

SCOTT: And . . . ?

LOUISE (*Leans slightly forward, places her hands in her lap, and appears to be surrounded by an aura of white light*): The first words were "Holy Mary, Mother of God."

(*Pause.*)

SCOTT: So, that was not Jerry, right?

LOUISE: Yes, Scott. that was not Jerry. (*Looking radiant*) Those were the first words directly from God.

(*Louise leans back, and we see her halo-effect was lamp-light reflecting off the pillowcases behind her.*)

SCOTT (*Clears his throat*): God's communicating directly with you now?

LOUISE: Yes.

SCOTT: And, if I may be so bold, why were those his first words?

LOUISE: It was his way of greeting me.

SCOTT: By name?

LOUISE: Yes, Scott. It was God's way of greeting me by name.

SCOTT (*In a low voice to himself*): Greeting you by name. (*Then to Louise*) You were Mary, as in "away in a manger?"

LOUISE (*Nods slowly*): Like I told you, honey, God has chosen the four of us for special incarnations throughout history. Not only people of religious importance but also artists and politicians, such as Beethoven and Abraham Lincoln, as I've already mentioned.

SCOTT: Right. Jerry was Abraham Lincoln, and I was Beethoven.

LOUISE: Yes, dear. (*Squeezes Allison's hand*) Among others.

SCOTT: Does that mean Jerry's one of "the four of us" you keep referring to?

LOUISE: No, honey. When I say "the four of us," I'm referring to the four of us in this room. But also, as I told you, Jerry and Grandma and Grandpa and other members of our family have played important roles in all facets of society throughout history. I know that Uncle Donald was Antonio Vivaldi in a previous incarnation, which explains his virtuosity on the violin at such a tender age. And Uncle Robert was Johann Sebastian Bach, which explains his prodigious musical talent.

SCOTT: *Prodigious.* Have you been reading a dictionary?

LOUISE: I'm not as simple as you might think, Scott.

SCOTT: Certainly not in the eyes of God.

(*Raises his shoulders*)

I mean, you don't get much higher on the ladder of life than the Virgin Mary—as a woman, that is.

(*Louise exhales; her head falls forward, and she begins to write. When her hand stops moving, her head returns to its upright position, and she studies the pad of paper.*)

LOUISE (*Reading aloud in a solemn voice*): "Greetings, Jerrold Scott Henry, prodigal son of the Blessed Mother, elder brother of Kathy Sue Henry and Jerrold Henry Giuliano.

Honor thy mother, as I, thy God, hath commanded thee, that thy days may be prolonged, and that it may go well with thee, in the land which I, your God, giveth thee."

SCOTT (*Leans slightly forward*): Wow. How do you do, . . . sir?

(*Louise exhales; her head falls forward, and she begins to write. After a moment, her head returns to its upright position.*)

LOUISE (*Reading aloud*): "I do good works, as one well knows. Rather than inquire the same of you, since I know the answer, I'll ask you to keep your comments to yourself and to show your mother the love and respect she so richly deserves."

SCOTT: Really? We're going from biblical prose to trite admonitions?

(*Before Scott finishes his remark, Louise exhales; her head falls forward, and she begins to write. She continues writing on a second sheet of paper as the first sheet flutters to the bed. Her head returns to its upright position, and she picks up the first sheet of paper.*)

LOUISE (*Reading aloud*): "Whether lyrical or . . . *hackneyed*—"
　　　　　(*Looks at Scott*)
　　　　　Do you know what that means, honey?

(Sc*ott lowers his eyelids and nods.*)

LOUISE: All right. (*Looks at the paper and reads aloud*) "Whether lyrical or *hackneyed*, prose or poem, whether taken at face value or with a grain of salt, the word of God illuminates the language of man, as the sun casts its light upon the earth entire. For nothing is secret, that shall not be made manifest, neither anything hid, that shall not be known and come abroad."

SCOTT: Right on.

(*Kathy stifles a nervous laugh. Louise affects a Sphinx-like smile.*)

SCOTT: I'm wondering if your connecting with God was the reason for our big time in the little city, you know, sparkling wine and steaks all around?

LOUISE: Well, Scott, not exactly, although God's arrival would have been cause for celebration.

SCOTT: No kidding. Just ask the Seventh-day Adventists.

LOUISE (*Adjusts the collar of her nightgown*): Like I said, Jerry assured me on more than one occasion the money necessary for our undertaking would manifest itself in the right amount, at the right time. And also, with regard to this, he told me to communicate with Daddy. Well, naturally, when Jerry told me to communicate with "Daddy," I thought he was referring to my father, to Grandpa. But yesterday, (*Shakes her head*) well, *Saturday*, the day before yesterday, after everyone had gone to bed, I received a message from God that really threw me for a loop. When I asked for clarification about the money, God's reply was short and to the point. The financial support for our project would be provided by Allison.

(*Scott makes a face and cocks his head.*)

LOUISE: I know. Isn't that *unbelievable*?

SCOTT: In a word.

LOUISE (*Lowers her voice as if revealing a secret*): Jerry had misinterpreted one of God's instructions. When God told him I should communicate with "Daddy," Jerry thought that meant Gus. That's why he told me to communicate with my father, but God wanted me to communicate with Allison.

SCOTT: *Okay*, I get it—I guess. Seems to me the angels in charge of public relations would come up with a better method of conveying God's instructions than a heavenly version of the Telephone Game. When it comes down to it, 1968 AD doesn't seem all that different from 1968 BC. Although considering time and place, Jerry's a better bet than a burning bush.

LOUISE: Well, Scott, I think that's where I fit in.

SCOTT: Good point. So, when are you taking your show on the road?

LOUISE: As much as the whole idea overwhelms me, it seems that there's no time like the present.

SCOTT: Which means what exactly?

LOUISE: The first thing I need to do is get Kathy situated.

KATHY: What does that mean?

LOUISE: Well, sweetheart, it won't be possible for you to stay here alone.

KATHY: What do you mean, "stay here alone?"
    (*Looks from Louise to Allison*)
    Where's Daddy going to be?

LOUISE: That hasn't been decided yet, sweetheart.
    (*Rests her hand on Allison's thigh*)
    But we know a girl your age needs to have a sense of security about school and friends. Everything considered, honey, we think a move now is the best option before you

get accustomed to this school and start making friends in Santa Rosa.

KATHY (*In a plaintive voice*): What are you saying? You're going to send me away?

LOUISE (*Shakes her head*): No, sweetheart.

We're not sending you away. I mean, not really. We're making arrangements for you to live with Auntie Marguerite while you're still in high school, honey. That's only three years.

KATHY (*Wails*): *Three years.*

LOUISE: Now, Kathy . . . sweetheart.

(*Leans forward and takes Kathy's hand in hers*)

Auntie Marguerite and Uncle Don have a beautiful home and a loving family. Not only that, who wouldn't want to spend three years in Laguna Beach?

KATHY: Me.

(*Withdraws her hand and pushes herself up to sit cross-legged*)

If you send me to Auntie Marguerite's, I'll be cleaning the house and babysitting for three years. I don't want to live with them. Maybe I can go back to Long Beach and live with Karen Diotte's family.

LOUISE: That's not a good idea, sweetheart. Like I said, Daddy and I aren't exactly sure of where we'll be or what we'll be doing from one week to the next. We want to have a sense of security about you and your living arrangement. That's why we think it's important for you to be with members of our family, not the family of a childhood friend. You understand, don't you, sweetheart?

KATHY (*More an accusation than a question*): Daddy's going with you?

LOUISE: Not right away, sweetheart.

(*Louise places her hand in Allison's.*)

SCOTT: Does that mean Allison's been invited to participate in the project? Or does he have visiting rights because he's paying the bills?

LOUISE (*Looking less serene*): Like I said, Scott. We're not exactly sure of who will be doing what until everything's underway.

SCOTT: But you'll be taking dictation, so to speak, and God will be handing down the word, right?

LOUISE: Yes.

SCOTT: What about Jerry? (*Glances over his shoulder*) Is he still in the mix, or has he been relegated to the sidelines?

LOUISE: I'm not exactly sure what God has in mind for Jerry.

(*Arranges the pad of paper in her lap*)

I thought he was going to be the middleman, you know, the go-between. But now that God's communicating with me directly, I don't know who else will be involved.

SCOTT: Except for Allison.

LOUISE: Yes, Scott. (*Removes the tissue from her sleeve*) I believe Allison will be involved. I'm just not sure in what capacity.

(*Louise wipes her nose, then returns the tissue to her sleeve.*)

SCOTT: And you plan to move from city to city, country to country, pillar to post, something like a born-again nomad?

LOUISE: I wouldn't say "born-again," Scott.

SCOTT: You were raised as a true believer in the Church of Jesus Christ of Latter-day Saints, from which you strayed when you married my father. You and Allison were married by a chiropractor in a movie theater, surrounded by members of the Long Beach chapter of the Church of Religious Science. If you'd spent time in the company of L. Ron Hubbard, you would've hit a splinter-group trifecta.

LOUISE (*Takes a slow breath, then*): I've always believed in a higher power, Scott, by whatever name you choose to call it. It's just that now I have a personal relationship with the higher power, and I know his name is God.

SCOTT: Is it really? I don't mean to quibble, but is his name "God," or is that just his title? The same as Queen Elizabeth's name is "Elizabeth," not "Queen," and the Virgin Mary's name is "Mary," not "Virgin"—no disrespect intended.

LOUISE: None taken.

(*Louise exhales; her head falls forward, and she begins to write. When her head returns to its upright position, she focuses on the sheet of paper.*)

LOUISE (*Reading aloud in a pensive voice*): "What's in a name? That which we call a rose—"

SCOTT: Ha! "By any other name would smell as sweet."
    (*Leans forward*)
    Are you serious?
    (*Tilts his head*)
    Is that the message?

LOUISE (*Matches Scott's intensity*): If you'd be quiet, Scott, I'd finish reading what I wrote, all right?

(*Scott nods.*)

LOUISE: "What's in a name? That which we call a rose, by any other name would smell as sweet."

(*Looks at Scott for a moment, then continues*)

"Wise words written in a different place at a different time by the one who in this place and at this time goes by the name of Allison Merlin Eddy."

SCOTT: Oh boy.

(*Scott leans back and looks away.*)

KATHY (*Looks from Scott to Louise*): What does that mean?

LOUISE: Well, Kathy Sue, that means Daddy was William Shakespeare, honey, in one of his previous incarnations.

KATHY (*Little pause*): Oh.

SCOTT (*Bursts into laughter, collects himself, then whispers*): Sorry.

(*Louise raises her brow as an invitation for Scott to share his thoughts.*)

SCOTT: It's just that (*Laughs to himself*) you know how I like to come up with oblique interpretations of famous quotes?

(*Scott waits for a response.*)

LOUISE: Yes, Scott. You're the poster child for abstract reasoning, as you've told us on so many occasions.

SCOTT: Uh, right, well, "abstract reasoning" is what the experts call it. As far as I'm concerned, it's just the voice in my head. (*Taps his head with the heel of his hand*) Anyway, sort of like God using a quote from Shakespeare in reference to his name, it just occurred to me, with so many VIPs represented by the four of us in this room, you could apply one of Churchill's famous quotes to our little group. "Never in the history of mankind has so much been owed by so many to so few."

(*No one responds. But then Louise exhales; her head falls forward, and she begins to write. When her hand stops, she raises her head.*)

LOUISE (*Reading aloud in a serious voice*): "Not delivered in Parliament as cited by Jerrold Scott Henry for the presumption of primacy over my son and his disciples. It therefore became 'Never in the field of human conflict has so much been owed by so many to so few.' Winston Leonard Spenser-Churchill's transition occurred after these four began. He is not represented by any in this room. I offer this to Jerrold Scott Henry—every famous person does not have vestigial lineage to a member of his family."

SCOTT: "Vestigial lineage." (*Furrows his brow*) Is that a thing?

LOUISE (*As if discussing the weather*): That's a reference to the effect of previous incarnations, honey. The earlier experience is not a part of conscious memory, but the lessons learned are still in play, such as musical talent or political prowess. Somewhat the same as genetic inheritance, by which physical attributes are passed from one generation to the next, vestigial lineage allows personality traits to be passed from one lifetime to another.

SCOTT (*Shakes his head*): Whatever's going on here, Mom, you've definitely plugged into something. A cosmic encyclopedia, if not the mind of God.

LOUISE: Or both. In that one is the other.

SCOTT: (*Shifts his torso from side to side*) Meanwhile, back at 1530 Boston Court. What's next?

LOUISE: What's next is getting down to nuts and bolts, so to speak.

SCOTT: Care to elaborate?

LOUISE (*Squares her shoulders*): Since I'll be spending so much time on the road, Allison's giving me the Volkswagen Bus. (*Beams a smile at Allison*) So, priority number one is getting the bus in shape for extended travel, setting up a rod for hanging clothes, getting some containers for towels and blankets and pillows. You know I prefer to travel with my own bedding. And writing supplies, of course. And some nonperishable food. Tea that I like, dried fruits and nuts, crackers and peanut butter, things for snacks along the way.

SCOTT: If you add all of God's creatures, two of each kind, this would be Louise's Ark. You could start with a couple of cats to keep you company.

LOUISE: Good Lord, Scott.

(*Puts a hand to her throat*)

The last thing I need is a couple of cats. Speaking of which, maybe I should invest in a small vacuum cleaner in case I need to touch up my motel room or if I spill something in the car.

SCOTT: You know, Mom, that's why God created housekeeping staff and car washes.

LOUISE: That may be so. (*Tilts her head from side to side*) But I'll be on a tight budget, honey, and anything I can do to keep expenses down will be much appreciated by my sponsor here.

(*Louise pats Allison on the thigh.*)

KATHY (*In a flat voice*): When are you leaving?

LOUISE: I'm not exactly sure, sweetheart.

(*Louise leans forward. She moves her hand from Allison's thigh to Kathy's knee, lowers her head, and looks into Kathy's eyes.*)

LOUISE: Not until we get everything squared away with you and your new living arrangement, sweetheart. I'll spend some time with you at Auntie Marguerite's, helping you get your room in order and taking care of everything at your new school.

KATHY (*More alarmed than surprised*): You've already discussed this with them?

LOUISE: No, sweetheart.
   (*Leans closer and caresses Kathy's arm*)
   But I'm sure everything will be fine.

KATHY (*Shifts position without breaking contact*): I wouldn't be so sure of that if I were you, starting with Janet having to share her bedroom.

LOUISE: Well, we'll cross that bridge when we come to it. All right, sweetheart?

(*Kathy wipes away a tear.*)

SCOTT: Mom, how long have you been in direct contact with God? When did he come a-knockin', as it were?

LOUISE: Tuesday night of last week. That's when we had our first conversation.

SCOTT: That's when you found out you were Mary? That's when God greeted you as "Holy Mary, Mother of God"?

LOUISE (*Nods serenely*): Yes, Scott.

SCOTT: And . . .
   (*Furrows his brow*)
   Allison was Joseph?

LOUISE: No, Scott.

> (*Places her hand in Allison's*)
>
> Allison was not Joseph, honey. . . . Allison was Jesus.

SCOTT: And that would be where you crossed the line.

LOUISE: Which line is that?

SCOTT: The line between divine revelation and manifest lunacy.

> (*Louise removes her hand from Allison's, then picks up her pen.*)

SCOTT: Was this tidbit revealed to Allison before or after he offered to finance the reappearance of God?

> (*Louise exhales; her head falls forward, and she begins to write. When her hand stops, her head returns to its upright position.*)

LOUISE (*Reading aloud in a stern voice*): "Thou shall not scorn The Mother. Thou shall not scorn The Son. Cease thy mockery or lose thy tongue."

SCOTT (*Chortles, then tilts his head forward*): Are you kidding me?

LOUISE: Scott, those words are not mine.

SCOTT: Yes, Louise, those words are yours.

> (*Little pause.*)
>
> This was all very interesting until about three minutes ago. The automatic writing is awesome. Awesome and astonishing. So is the information. Your subconscious mind should be studied by a team of Nobel laureates. Beyond that, and I say this with all due respect, you need to get a grip.

> (*Louise exhales; her head falls forward, and she begins to*

write. The episode is brief, no more than a few seconds. When her hand stops, her head returns to its upright position.)

LOUISE (*Reading aloud in a stentorian voice*): "Jerrold Scott Henry, heed me now, for this I promise. Speak of this to anyone who listens, and you shall lose the gift of speech as they shall lose the gift of hearing."

SCOTT (*Rises to his feet*): Okay, that concludes the show-and-tell part of this evening's entertainment. I have to catch a bus in a few hours, and Kathy has to go to school. (*To Louise*) Seems to me, a good night's sleep will do all of us a world of good. (*To Kathy*) Okay, Sue, let's go, let's go, *let's* really go.

(*Kathy stands up from the bed and follows Scott out of the room. Neither says a word until Scott closes the door behind them. The lights for the master bedroom fade to black. The hallway fixture remains lit.*)

KATHY (*Whispers*): *Jeez.*

SCOTT (*In a low voice*): Don't get me started. And don't take Allison's name in vain.

(*Kathy punches Scott in the arm.*)

SCOTT: Who's your daddy?

KATHY: He's not my daddy!

SCOTT (*Pauses halfway through Kathy's bedroom door*): You mentioned his name.

KATHY: Cut it out, and I mean it.

SCOTT: Yes, ma'am.

(*Kathy steps toward the stage-right wings, then turns around.*)

KATHY: What's going to happen now?
SCOTT: God only knows.

(*Scott makes the sound of a rimshot.*)

KATHY (*Shakes her head*): I'm going to bed.

(*Kathy turns around and walks toward the stage-right wings.*)

SCOTT: Okey-dokey, Sue. I'll see you mañana morning—actually, later on today.
KATHY (*Over her shoulder*): Whatever.

(*Scott steps into Kathy's bedroom and closes the door. Kathy walks into the stage-right wings.*)

Scene 2

Lights behind the bedroom windows fade in as exterior daylight. The bed is empty with both sides of the bedclothes thrown back. Allison closes a bureau drawer, then crosses the room, wearing a white short-sleeve doctor's shirt, dark trousers, dark shoes, and socks. He lifts a lightweight jacket from the back of the rocking chair, opens the bedroom door, steps into the hallway, and closes the door behind him. Allison steps to Kathy's bedroom door and knocks.

SCOTT (*Offstage*): Yes?

ALLISON: We need to leave in five minutes.

SCOTT (*Offstage*): Okay.

ALLISON: I'll be in the living room.

SCOTT (*Offstage*): Okay.

(*Allison walks toward the stage-right wings as Kathy emerges from the stage-right wings, walking toward the hallway. They exchange words as they pass one another.*)

ALLISON (*Perfunctory*): Good morning, Kathy.

KATHY (*Subdued*): Good morning.

(*Allison proceeds into the stage-right wings. Scott walks out of Kathy's bedroom, wearing a stylish jacket over a penny-collar shirt, bell-bottom pants, and brown suede stacked-heel loafers. He's carrying a small faux-leather duffle bag in his left hand. Kathy and Scott come to a stop, a few feet apart.*)

KATHY: You look very mod.

SCOTT: I am very mod.

KATHY: Now that that's settled . . .

SCOTT: Okay, enough small talk.

>(*Lowers his voice and tilts his head toward the stage-right wings*)

>God's only begotten son of a bitch is waiting for me right here in your living room. Can you believe it?

(*Kathy stifles a laugh.*)

SCOTT: You know I'm not big on goodbyes.

KATHY: Okay, well. See ya later.

SCOTT: See ya later, sis. Don't let 'em get you down.

(*Kathy walks toward her bedroom as Scott walks toward the wings. The scrim begins to descend, and the lights behind the scrim start to fade. The apron remains well lit.*)

KATHY (*Over her shoulder*): Easy for you to say.

(*Scott walks into the wings. Kathy proceeds into her bedroom and closes the door.*
   Scott and Allison walk onstage from the stage-right wings and proceed toward the stage-left wings.)

SCOTT: How are things with Mom this morning?

ALLISON: That remains to be seen. She was in the bathroom when I came back from the kitchen.

SCOTT: Is she coming to the office today?

ALLISON: I'm not sure, Scott. After last night, anything's possible.

SCOTT: Right. *So*, I'll call you at the office when I get home from school.

ALLISON: I have a full day, Scott. I'm not sure that I'll have time for a conversation.

SCOTT: That's okay, we don't need to have a conversation, but I'd like to know what's going on. I have a class from four to five. I'll give you a call around five thirty.

(*When Scott and Allison are offstage, the lights on the apron slowly become brighter, then slowly return to their previous setting.*)

Scene 3

As the lights on the apron become less bright, two platforms, six feet wide by four feet deep, roll into view from opposite wings as far downstage as possible. The stage-left platform has a floor of brown-flecked linoleum. Allison is seated at a desk, writing notes in a patient's file. There's an unattractive metal lamp and a black rotary telephone on the desk. The stage-right platform has a checkerboard floor of one-foot-square black and white tiles. A potted palm stands behind a Swedish modern chair, horizontal rolls of orange velvet on sled legs. A black rotary telephone and black leather address book sit on a small table beside the chair. As soon as the platforms are in place, Scott enters from the wings, directly upstage of the stage-right platform. He shrugs off his jacket and drapes it across the corner of the chair. He steps onto the platform and sits down, looking very much at home. Scott places the telephone in his lap, opens the address book, flips through a couple of pages, then dials a number. A moment later, the telephone on Allison's desk rings.

ALLISON (*Disturbingly saccharine*): Doctor Eddy's office, this is Doctor Eddy. How may I help you?

SCOTT (*Vibrates with revulsion, then steadies himself*): Hello, Allison. This is Scott.

ALLISON (*Now curt*): Yes, Scott?

SCOTT (*Raises a clenched fist*): I'm calling to find out what happened this morning after I left.

ALLISON: With your mother?

SCOTT (*Raises both fists, one clenched, the other holding the handset. He returns the handset to his ear*): Yes, with my mother.

ALLISON (*Preoccupied*): When I returned from dropping you at the bus stop, Louise was standing at the curb, dressed in her uniform like any other workday morning.

SCOTT: Did she say anything about last night?

ALLISON: She said she was putting the whole thing behind her, and she didn't want to discuss it any further.

SCOTT (*Shakes his head slowly*): And . . . that's it?

ALLISON: Yes, Scott. That's it. Was there anything else?

SCOTT: No.

ALLISON: All right. I have quite a bit of paperwork in front of me.

SCOTT: Right. Okay. Uh, good luck, then—with, you know, *the situation*. I hope it really is over and done.

ALLISON: Yes, Scott. All right, then. Goodbye.

(*Allison hangs up.*)

SCOTT *(Holds his handset at arm's length)*: Goodbye, asshole. And, by the way, you're welcome.

(*Blackout.*)

END OF PLAY

EPILOGUE

Louise never spoke again of her brush with divinity.

AUTHOR'S NOTE AND ACKNOWLEDGMENTS

Of the book's main characters, Louise Eddy and Allison Eddy are no longer living; Kathy Henry and Scott Henry are alive and well.

References to music and films and included poetry are as follows: "I Heard It Through the Grapevine," written by Norman Whitfield and Barrett Strong; "The Sound of Silence (Remix)," written by Paul Simon; "The Windmills of Your Mind," written by Michel Legrand with English lyrics by Alan and Marilyn Bergman; *Funny Girl*, written by Isobel Lennart; *The Graduate*, written by Calder Willingham and Buck Henry, based on the novella by Charles Webb; *How Sweet It Is!*, written by Jay Black and Brian Herzlinger; *The Thomas Crown Affair*, written by Alan Trustman; "On Love," from *The Prophet* by Kahlil Gibran.

I am eternally grateful to my sister, Kathy Henry, who shouldered the weight of our mother's final year. For a summer season of morning walks, Doreen Rallo not only listened but also paid attention. Richard Schack's careful eye caught several problems I had missed. Throughout the process, Kim Lorber's love and support spurred me on.

www.ingramcontent.com/pod-product-compliance
Lightning Source LLC
Chambersburg PA
CBHW022136170626
46807CB00005B/1959